THE HARDEST WORD

DREW HUBBARD

THE HARDEST WORD

Copyright (c) Drew Hubbard 2025

This is a work of fiction. Names, characters, places, dialogue and incidents are either products of the author's imagination or used fictitiously. Any resemblance to actual persons, living or dead, events or locations is purely coincidental.

All rights reserved.

No part of this publication may be reproduced, stored in a retrieval system, or transmitted in any form or by any means, electronic, mechanical, photocopying, recording or otherwise, without the prior written permission of the copyright owner, nor be otherwise circulated in any form of binding or cover other than that in which it is published and without a similar condition including this condition being imposed on the subsequent purchaser.

Published by Drew Hubbard
Cover by Darren Adams

Printed in the United Kingdom

ISBN: 9798284091555
Imprint: Independently published

CONTENT NOTE

This novel contains themes of transphobia, internalised homophobia, manipulation, online harassment, emotional abuse, substance abuse, anxiety and death. Whilst these themes are handled with care, they may be distressing for some readers.

For Elphie.
The goodest girl, whose unconditional love will be remembered forever. I miss you every day.

Chapter 1

Goodbye, bungalow I've spent my whole life in. See ya, precinct with your boarded-up shops. Fuck all you small-minded people I hope I never see again.

So long, Carmingham, a concrete hell-hole so repulsive, most people shorten it to Ming.

I barely glance at the graffiti on the wall near the chippy. I can't see what name is up there, but the *is a faggot* can't affect me.

Today is the best day of my entire life.

The further away we get, the more the rocks I've carried inside me crumble away. I'm light as air by the time we get to the train station. The only things keeping me from floating away are two suitcases and a giant rucksack.

Standing on the platform, I wonder if people think I'm going on holiday. Better. I'm leaving for somewhere I can be myself at last. I've wanted to get out of this place for twenty-five years. It didn't happen for uni, then events conspired against me to keep me caged.

"Right, Benny love." Here comes Mum's weepy speech.

She already cried when she saw my empty room, and when the taxi pulled up. "It's not much, but I've been saving."

She hands me £100 cash, a £100 Asda gift card, and £50 Just Eat gift card. How did she save for this? OK, this little station must be super dusty.

My train pulls up. Mum hugs me until the guard whistles. I'm glad I told her I didn't want Shaun and Jeremy seeing me off. This is enough.

"Mum! Let me go." I can't be late. Maya will be waiting. I wouldn't even be going if it wasn't for them.

I heave everything on.

"I'm so proud of you presh-pots. Phone me when you arrive. I love you."

This is it.

My stomach flips as the train pulls away, but keeps on flipping. This train is boiling.

I pull off my hoody, put my right hand over my heart and tap my little finger. Taptaptap. Taptaptap. It helps. Always does.

Mum waves like mad, smiling and crying as she runs, but she can't keep up. She starts coughing. Again. It's driven me mad the past month, I won't miss it.

My final view of Ming, is Mum putting her right hand over her heart and tapping her little finger three times. Oh, she thinks I was doing it to her, it was just calming me down. She'll no doubt write about that in her diary.

I store my things and relax in my getaway train seat. Why am I still so hot?

I take a few selfies, choose the one I look least sweaty in, and put it up on Facebook with the word *BYEEEEE*.

That will keep Mum happy. Within seconds she's liked it. Within minutes, Shaun has commented: *Hope it's everything you want it to be. Love Shaun & Jeremy xxx.*

I keep my eye on it for the next twenty minutes, to see if Rahul comments. He doesn't. Oh yeah, I deleted him when we split up.

There really isn't anything holding me back. It makes me want to dance up and down the aisle. I won't.

I pass the time on TikTok, and today gets even better. I've done it. I've finally hit 10 thousand followers. People do like my silly little queer videos.

I edit the content I filmed last night of different queers packing for a holiday. For the gays I had loads of little booty shorts and cute tops all rolled neatly. For the lesbians it was mainly boots and jeans lobbed in. For the bisexuals it was full of checked shirts, which takes me a while to edit, as I only own a couple of checked shirts. Photoshop FTW!

Filming took ages last night as Mum kept knocking on my door asking stupid questions she knew the answer to. It probably would have been easier if I had told her about the TikToks from the start, instead of doing them in secret all this time, behind my mask.

Still, *@the.enigaymatic.mystery* being my own thing nobody knows about, nor knows it's me, has got me through the last eight months. 10 thousand people also think I'm amazing, so it was absolutely worth losing my job over. Besides, I would not be on this train right now if I hadn't.

I already have a few super-fans who always like and comment. There's one in particular, who goes by the random name of *@gnotq876941* and keeps asking when I'll do the rest of the acronym.

Does this person realise how much time it takes to do the Gs, Ls and Bs?

I always reply to comments, especially the good ones. Gotta keep interaction up. The negative ones, I enjoy calling their queerphobia out.

I finish editing and I'm almost there. Almost here. Almost home? That feels weird to say. I'll upload at the house when there's decent Wi-Fi, this train one sucks.

I'm already waiting by the doors before the tannoy says, "We are now arriving at Manchester Piccadilly. Please make sure you take all your belongings with you."

This station is massive. Heaving. The one I got on at was just a ticket machine and a broken waiting shelter.

I head to the exit. Burger King tempts me but I need to hurry and meet Maya, they said they'd meet me at the far end of Canal Street. The map on my phone gets me over the bridge, past a hotel across the... BEEEEEP. Oops, almost got hit by a tram. Maya warned me about them.

Oh.

Wow.

I have to get a photo.

Manchester's Gay Village.

I have never seen anything as blatantly queer as this in my life. The nearest I've come was last year when me and Ra went to a Pride parade a few towns away. It was a glorified market with music, at best. This is a whole series of streets. It's here all the time. Everyone is out and proud. Ming would homophobically-implode if it saw this.

I'm meeting Maya at the other side, so slalom my cases

through the busy street. There's queers everywhere. I love it. I pass a group of six gay lads, in their best crop tops and skinny jeans, doing shots. I almost run into a lesbian couple sharing a chicken burger. Arms around each other. The butch one takes a bite, passes it to her slightly-less-butch girlfriend.

Outside a quiet bar, a tall drag queen winks at me. She takes in my baggage... wait, is it he? No it's she in drag isn't it? She totters over, puts a leaflet in my hoody pocket. "Welcome to Manchester," she says in the most northern accent I've ever heard.

There is more racial and ethnic diversity on this street than the whole of Ming.

Two men dressed in leather walk by, hand in hand. I spot a guy with a hand down another guy's jeans. Bloody hell.

The end of Canal Street is in sight. I stop to adjust my rucksack and notice the rainbow bunting over my head. I look back, they're all down the street. Is it like this all the time, or have they forgotten to take it down? Manchester Pride was at the end of August, barely a month ago.

I've seen stuff on TikTok where people take the piss out of companies who put up rainbow stuff in their shops over Pride Month but it's down come July. It must be Pride Month all the time around here. I've never once seen a pride flag up in Ming. I did ask my ex boss once if he was going to do it, he gave some excuse about not having the window advertising space.

I finally make it to the end of Canal Street. How big is this place? I can't wait to find out. My new boyfriend might be around here somewhere.

I turn left towards the crossroads. It's 7.15pm. Maya said they'd meet me at 7.10pm, but I can't see them anywhere. Actually I'm relieved to have a moment to catch my breath.

I message Maya to see what's going on.

Ten minutes later, still no answer. Where are they?

"Ee-ah mate, ya want any drugs? I got weed, coke, molly." Some random woman in dirty trackie bottoms and a huge green puffer jacket has come right up to me. She's not even whispering. People are walking past but she doesn't care.

She unzips her jacket, revealing a bumbag. Opens it to show me the stuff.

"No thanks." I walk away but she follows. Why is this happening, and where is Maya? She said she'd be here and still no message.

"Mate, mate, it's fine. Listen, can ya do me a favour?" She's right by my side. I don't like this. I shake my head. "Please mate. I've got to go Union to see someone, but they'll check me. Can you watch my gear?"

I am not getting involved with this. I tell her to please leave me alone.

"Ah mate, it's not dodgy or nuffink. I'll be dead quick. I'll give you some weed for free if you do it for us."

She's not going to leave me alone, is she? Then again, I didn't bring any weed with me because I was worried I'd get searched on the train. I didn't know if they do that sort of thing. I'm tempted. I have to wait for Maya anyway.

"Ok."

She takes off her bumbag and tells me to put it in my rucksack so nobody can see it. Have I enough space? She glances inside as I open it. I quickly put the bumbag in before she sees my laptop in there.

"In a bit yeah?" And she's gone. Phew.

I sit on one of my suitcases. I worry I look dodgy right now, but nobody knows I've got a load of drugs in my bag. Hopefully she won't be long. OK, breathe.

Still nothing from Maya. I call them but it rings out. I open maps to see how far it is to my new house. It looks complicated. Maya said I can get a tram but I don't know how they work.

As I wait, I catch two police officers watching me.

Act casual. I'm trying, but I'm sure my racing heart is vibrating my whole body.

Fucking hell, Maya, where are you?

The police are coming over. Please walk past. Please walk past.

"Y'alright, my friend?" The policeman says to me with an Asian accent.

"Waiting for someone." I try to hide the nerves in my voice.

"You been asked to hold anything for anyone?" The policewoman asks. She's well-spoken but looks like she could kick the shit out of me.

That's a weird thing to ask a random stranger. In my pause, they glance at each other.

"Right sir, we're going to have to do a stop and search." The woman steps closer.

Can they do this? I've never dealt with police before. What do I do? Should I record it like I've seen on TikTok? No, that's in America when racist cops are involved.

I open up my suitcases. I ask if I need to move anything, like they do at airport security, but they're not interested.

"What's in this?" The woman points to my rucksack. I can't seem to form words. "Well?"

"N... N... Nothing. Stuff. Books. Laptop."

"Show us!" the man says.

Oh god why me? I've just got here.

With shaking hands I carefully open it, quickly grab the T-shirt in there and wrap it around the bumbag. I hold it in one hand as I move stuff inside the rucksack with the other.

They give each other a look. Are they satisfied? Maya why the fuck aren't you here?

The man nods. I'm OK. I've done it. I put the T-shirt back in, but he grabs it.

The bumbag falls out.

Hits the ground.

Powder, pills and weed scatter.

They both stare.

My stomach turns to stone.

Chapter 2

"Don't run off."

"Sarge, we've got one."

"Who you dealing to?"

"He's looking at ten years, do you think?"

I'm turned around, pushed up against a wall, hands forced behind my back, "where we can see 'em."

Where's Maya when I need her?

How am I going to get out of this?

The man spins me around, grabs the front of my hoody, says, "We're taking you down the station."

"It's not mine." I try to force tears back into my eyes.

"We believe you, mate but you'll have to find a solicitor."

"Alright if I do a body search?"

I nod. I want to wipe my eyes, but I'm too scared to move my hands. I should stop watching American cop shows. They're not like that here, are they? He rocks me as he pats me down, or maybe I'm the one rocking? He takes out my wallet.

The woman looks at me with pity. "We don't want to do this any more than you."

I doubt that's true by the smile at the corner of her mouth.

"There's a lot of paperwork to fill out. You'll be there all night." The man flicks through the cards in my wallet, pulls out the money, the gift cards from Mum, and my debit card. "Unless..."

That sounds hopeful.

"We might be able to let this drop. Busy night and all. What do ya reck?"

I nod. He pockets them.

"Phone?" the woman says, as she looks through my rucksack. I show her. She pulls a face, shakes her head. I guess it's too cracked and too old to be worth anything.

She digs deeper into my rucksack, finds my laptop and graphics tablet.

"Please, not them. I need them for my job."

"You'd prefer a trip to Strangeways, would ya?"

This doesn't feel right, but I've got no choice.

I've made a stupid mistake thinking I could do all this.

Maybe I should get on the train back to Ming. I'd have to deal with Mum saying, *I told you, you couldn't do it*, but that's better than this.

"Clear off!" someone shouts.

The police pause. I glance over to see a guy in a suit, running up to us. I can't take anything in as he's shouting in the police officers' faces. The woman grabs my laptop.

"Get lost, thieving bastards!" he screams.

Is this how people talk to police in Manchester?

The guy gives me a concerned look and chases after the police, but they're too fast. They're both gone in seconds.

"They weren't genuine police. I've seen this happen before. You've been scammed."

I turn and vomit. How did I not see it? The way they talked, the way they behaved. I'm an idiot.

"It's over now. Are you alright? I'm William. You are?"

I whisper, "Benny," and burst into tears.

William pats my shoulder. The fake police had seen inside both my suitcases, but I guess none of my clothes were worth anything, nor my graphics tablet Mum got me last Christmas apparently. William carefully folds a couple of T-shirts.

"Let's get your suitcases fastened back up and you can be on your way."

He pauses as he moves a jumper, revealing my TikTok mask and cheap ring light. Is he trying to work out what it's for? He looks like he's in his 40s, he's not going to know. He puts the jumper on top. Closes everything up. Picks up the bumbag from the floor.

"Thats..." I've still got the drugs. Maybe I could sell them to make my money back? No. Bad idea, although I could smoke some weed, I need it.

I collect what's on the ground. "They left all this."

"It's all fake. Flour and..." he opens a bag of weed. Sniffs. "Oregano. Part of the scam."

I don't know what to do. I don't know what to say.

"Where you heading?" William says to me, as he bins the bumbag of lies.

How pathetic do I look bringing out my phone to get the

address?

"Don't worry. Our community sticks together. I've got you."

Within minutes he's flagged down a cab, helped me in, sits in the back with me.

He's quite good looking. Well-dressed, nice hair cut short. Weirdly he looks familiar.

I've still not heard from Maya.

I've been scammed.

Lost all my money.

My laptop too.

And I'm now in a taxi to who knows where with a stranger.

This could get a whole lot worse.

He advises me to alert my bank. Luckily I can block the card on the app. It's going to be a right faff getting that replaced.

He asks me where I'm from, what I'm doing here, but I'm too exhausted to say much. He tells me he's seen this before. He's seen them prey on young — he whispers "gay men" — in particular. He's sorry it happened to me.

I don't even look that gay today. I try not to in Ming. I guess people are more perceptive in Manchester.

"I'll help you get back on your feet, don't worry."

"You don't have to do that."

"I know, but I'm going to. I remember what it was like to be young," — he mouths *gay* — "and new to a city. I've been there. I wish I had someone to take me under their wing."

How have I got super unlucky, and lucky in the same

moment? What an amazing guy. It bugs me though because I recognise his southern accent and confident voice. Maybe a TikTok?

"Do you always help young queers?" I ask.

For a split second his smile drops. Was that a grimace? Quickly he's smiling again, says he does what he can for his community.

He pulls out a business card.

"Get yourself settled, then get in touch. Don't feel too proud. I'm a man of my word. People like us have to help each other, because nobody else wants to help us."

I look at his card. No way! He's William Gale. Who cares about the scamming now?

He's even more brilliant in real life. Should I tell him I know him? Is it weird to fangirl this hard, this close? I need to play it cool. Unfortunately, I open my mouth.

"You came to my uni a few years ago for a guest lecture about design and marketing, and it was amazing. You were super inspiring and I made up my mind to work for your company one day. I used your talk as reference in my dissertation, which I got a 2-1 for, and all the advice you gave that day I used in my design job. It was a silly little print shop, but what you said about pushing design forward always was my mantra, and will continue to be at Colin Fishburn Design and Marketing which I start on Monday." Yeah, very cool Benny.

At least I didn't tell him that I thought he was hot when he did his lecture.

He seems super chuffed. We talk about our jobs for a bit. I feel like a proper adult talking shop. It's putting me at ease, but I'm distracted by a missed call, and texts from Maya. Finally!

So so so sorry
Still waiting?
I can get someone to meet you?

I watch typing bubbles appear. Hell no. I close Messages instantly, slam my phone face down onto my lap.

I try to focus on the story William is telling me about setting up his company, with his business partners, from nothing.

My phone vibrates on my leg. I don't want to read it.

More vibrations make me look. They distract me enough for William to ask if I'm alright.

"It's the friend I was supposed to meet."

"Is this a friend, or a friend friend?"

"They're not a guy, so..."

"Ah. Female friends are extremely important."

"Oh, they're not quite female. They use she and they pronouns. Emphasis on they. They had an accident."

I'm not quite sure if accident is the right word. I show him the texts.

I'm such a doofus
Been binding this week
Stupidly did it too tight
Collapsed B4 the end of my shift
In hospital. Having X-rays in a bit to
see if any ribs are cracked

Pleasssssssssssse don't be mad

William glances at the name at the top. "Maya?" He goes quiet for a moment. "The things they do to their bodies. This is why..." He softens, looks at me concerned. "Sounds like she's after your forgiveness. I'd keep an eye on her if I were you. I've had so-called friends like her."

"Maya's not like that. They're the reason I came to Manchester."

He pulls a face, like he's smelt something bad. "Be careful is all I'm saying. She could be trouble. I'd get out while you can. Trust me, you'd do better keeping well away."

He asks how much I really know about Maya. When I tell him we've only met in real life once, he says, "You've been scammed once this evening. Don't let it happen again. You'd be wise to end that relationship before it does you further harm."

I go to Maps. We are almost at the pin I dropped. I thank William again for all his help.

"Think nothing of it. You probably don't have any friends in Manchester, let alone any like me and you. I assure you there is nothing weird going on here. I'm a normal"— he mouths *gay*—"guy, and I want to help you because this is a particularly scary moment in time. It would break my heart if I didn't."

It's funny. He's about the same age as Shaun but has a vastly different attitude. Not as preachy. He's amazing.

We pull up outside an end terrace I recognise from the pictures my new housemate Jacinta sent me. He pats my shoulder, tells me I'd better call him this week, once I'm settled, as he's got an old laptop I can have.

He helps me up to the front door of my new home, smiles, gets back in the cab and goes.

The front door opens. A white bob in a flowing black dress pulls me into a massive hug. I've done a few zooms with Jacinta, but this is our first proper meeting. I was hoping the other two housemates would be here, but Jacinta tells me they're hardly ever in.

She invites me into the lounge, where she's got a pot of tea, biscuits, and sandwiches waiting. The lounge feels much smaller in real life. It's an odd shape, and what's with the window?

"It's the first thing everyone notices," she says, following my gaze to the window with a wall in the middle of it. "I assume they wanted to make the room next door bigger. It used to be a dining room. It's Zoe's bedroom now."

She asks about my journey, but my mind is too busy considering what to do about Maya. I bet Jacinta would give good advice, but I don't want her first impression of me to be asking pathetic questions.

"You're going to love it here." Jacinta helps me upstairs. "The bathroom is this one. This room is David's. This is mine."

David's door is shut, but Jacinta's is open. I take a sneaky glance as she tells me about one of the house rules. We must always knock and wait for an answer. If there is none, we can knock once more, but after that we have to do one.

Her room is all black candles, pentagrams and posters of, as she puts it when she notices me looking, sword-lesbians.

"This is yours." I smile at the *welcome* helium balloon on the bed. "Get settled. I'll be downstairs if you need me. Welcome to your new home." She gives me another hug, and it feels good.

It's weird being in a new room. It's smaller than my one at home, but it's decent enough and overlooks the quiet street.

I'm halfway through unpacking my rucksack when Mum phones.

She's all questions and coughs. I only left her a few hours ago and now she wants to know all the details.

"Mum, I'm tired. The journey was... fine, and the room is fine."

"Did something happen?"

How does she always know?

I tell her nothing, but she keeps asking.

"I got approached, they didn't get much."

"Much? Benny Cedar, what did they take?"

If I tell her about the money, she's going to tell me how much of a mistake I've made and make me come home. "Ugh. My laptop, but it's OK. William said he's going to give me one of his old ones."

I knew it was a mistake saying his name the moment it came out of my mouth. She goes on asking questions about him as though I'm a child and he's a stranger enticing me into his car with promises of puppies.

"Mum, he was the guest lecturer I went on about for months. He's one of the co-managers of GFP. The company I'm desperate to work at?"

I knew that would shut her up, mainly because she

knows it's her fault I didn't get a job there when I was applying for Manchester jobs. She didn't tell me they were advertising until it was too late and I missed the deadline. Then she spent weeks telling me she did tell me about the job but I, apparently, wasn't interested because it was low-skilled.

We argued about that constantly until she finally realised she was wrong.

I change the subject before she can start it up again. I tell her what happened with Maya.

"Oh, the poor love. Have you texted them back? You know it's not their fault, and even if it was, they're your friend, Benny."

After Mum hangs up, I finish unpacking and realise I've missed another text from Maya.

You alive? Plsssssssss reply

Mum is right. Maya is my friend. A better one than any I've ever had.

But I can't stop thinking about what William said.

This move is meant to be my new life. I've got to put myself first.

What to text back?

Chapter 3

Why did nobody tell me how exhausting it is to work in a city and live by yourself? My new job has been manic, even if it has been basic AF. I work, come home tired, then I have to cook food for myself. At weekends I have to wash clothes, get them dried, and ironed.

I thought I'd be out every night. Maybe a date once a week.

The reality is, in two months I've not had the energy to go out once.

If it wasn't for Jacinta asking me to join her in the lounge to watch TV, I'd feel like a right loner, but she is always in bed by 9.30pm.

I've got to know her quite well. Apparently she is one of the original housemates when it was first rented out twelve years ago. She moved in after uni.

On my first day at work, she caught the bus with me and walked me to the office.

I finally met Zoe, but it took a month. She's usually a

blur on the landing because she starts her teaching assistant job super early, and works evenings and weekends in one of the theatres.

Zoe had the day off when we finally met in the little kitchen just off the hallway. She and Jacinta were talking politics, which went over my head. Ha. That's funny because she's like five foot, if that. The first thing she said to me was, "You better not be a Tory."

I didn't dare tell her I've never voted, but I did say she looked nice and was she going somewhere special. "Can't I look nice for no reason? I look nice for myself, not the patriarchy."

Luckily, she was "testing to see if you're as much of a melt as the homo whose room you've taken."

I still haven't met David, but I've seen evidence of him: several wigs drying on the landing, eyelashes stuck to the bathroom mirror, and a few weeks ago I'm pretty sure I saw a pair of fake boobs in the dishwasher.

Mum phones three times a week. I did phone her a few times. Once I needed to ask how to use the washing machine because I didn't want to embarrass myself in front of my housemates, and three separate times I asked for a certain recipe I wanted to try.

Only one of those worked out. I'll never make lasagne from scratch again. What. A. Faff.

She's sounded quite down recently. Must miss me. At least she's finally got a doctor's appointment about that cough. She told me she might be allergic to the new wash powder.

That's another thing. How expensive is wash powder?! If

I didn't have to wash all my own clothes I'd maybe have more money to go out.

William has taken me for lunch every Thursday. I phoned to thank him a few days after he rescued me. He asked to meet and gave me a laptop. Wouldn't take no for an answer. It's way better than the one that got nicked too.

He always asks about my job, and what I've been getting up to in my spare time. He must think I'm super boring because I always say I've stayed in and cooked tea, which is true, but he seems disappointed.

I've spent a lot of time filming. My content has been hit and miss. More miss than hit, but I did finally creep over 12 thousand followers so it's not all bad.

My most popular TikTok ever was one I did last week. How gays, lesbians, and bisexuals make a bed, inspired by a nightmare I had last month trying to put a duvet inside a duvet cover. I wouldn't have bothered but Mum asked every time she phoned if I'd changed my bedding. So I finally gave in because I was sick of her asking.

I look again. It's hit 200k likes. I go through the comments and reply to as many as I can, until I see my superfan *@gnotq876941* is back, and says, *You should do trans characters, you'll be hilarious. Please follow me.*

He only has ten followers and zero posts which I wouldn't normally bother with, but I notice he's put his name in his bio. *Mr. W. Gale.*

It can't be.

I follow him. He won't know it's me.

My phone buzzes. Randomly, it's William.

Want to meet up tonight in the Gay village?

Hell yes I do.

***

I don't know the name of this bar but William has bought me a couple of really good cocktails. I'm having the best night ever.

"I like to paint when I'm alone. Do you paint?" he asks. I shake my head. "What is it you like to do?"

He gives me a strange smile. I change the subject. "I was hoping I'd be out on Canal Street every week meeting people, maybe more but I've been busy with work."

"You're not missing much. There's a culture of sleeping around and it's detrimental to the gay community. You'd do well to avoid it."

"I will." I mean, I like sleeping with guys, but I've never been one for sleeping around. "I like to get to know people first anyway."

"Be careful saying that around here or one of the new alphabettigays will add you to the acronym."

I laugh, but... "What?"

"You'll never meet a nice lad if people think you're one of those so-called asexuals."

I'm not sure what he's getting at. Jacinta told me she's ace and it's not stopped her dating. Maybe William doesn't understand. "I think asexual means—"

"I'm joking. Come on."

I follow him as he introduces me to people, between tales of the celebrities he's seen in this bar. I'm soaking it all in. Everything is beautifully queer. It's giving me brilliant content ideas.

I hope he isn't going to quiz me on all the people I've met so far. They all look like clones of William. Suit-wearing, seemingly wealthy, white, cis gay guys. Well, apart from a few lesbians, but they also mostly fitted that description too.

There must be a funny TikTok in this somewhere.

William finds us seats and introduces me to James. "This is Ben. Ben, James."

I should correct him. People have called me Ben or Benjamin, thinking Benny is a nickname. They're often surprised when I tell them that's my full legal name. I did say Benny that first time we met, but it's been two months of this. I'll look stupid if I tell him now.

"The Ben?" he says with a Scouse accent, shaking my hand.

He might be a bit older than William. He's balding, but has a moustache and beard. His suit, shabbier than all the other suits I've seen tonight, is thinning at the seams. The buttons are on their last thread around his stomach. This is why I hate wearing form-fitting stuff. I'd rather go baggier than look like I'm squeezed in like James.

He asks me about my job and how I'm finding Manchester. He laughs at each of my answers for some reason. He tells me he works "a boring day job," which tracks. He looks like one of those people who sell houses. Apparently his job gives him "plenty of time to be part of a few good online communities."

I bet it's some awful Facebook thing. He looks like he enjoys a good Facebook rant.

"Everything OK, William?" I catch him massively side-eyeing a handsome guy standing behind him. The guy's got a beard, but he's wearing make-up and a skirt and I'm getting non-binary vibes. I've been reading up on enbies so I don't say the wrong thing to Maya.

I realised Mum was right. I told Maya what happened and she was super apologetic and blamed themself. I said it wasn't their fault, but they still want to make it up to me by showing me around.

That's not happened yet. The most we've had are quick half-hours between their uni and job, but they promised when they've got time, they're going to take me to their secret places.

I can't wait.

We message every night though. All we do is talk about our day, and what we're having for tea. Super boring, but I go to bed much more relaxed compared to the couple of times she's been on a late and we've missed it. It's our little bedtime ritual now.

Anyway, I think this person is an enby because they look exactly like one of the people I work with, who's also non-binary in a beardy-long-haired-pretty-but-masc way. Except this person is black.

"It's nothing, and please call me Will," he says, and noticeably turns his back to them.

I catch James glance over, before meeting Will's gaze. He grimaces.

I'm well curious now. "Who are they?"

"They? It's one person. I thought I was mentoring a smart young man?"

What? I didn't even realise he was mentoring me. I've admired this man for ages. I nod in an effort to hide this soppy smile I can't seem to get rid of.

"Good lad. He's nobody. I've got a bit of personal stuff going on and that attention-seeker is part of it, not that he knows it's me. Anyway, my friends are in higher places than his."

Will and James clink their ciders.

I can't tell if I've got silly drunk brain, or if he's being cryptic.

The pretty-beardy... guy walks past carrying leaflets that say something like *Mighty* on the top. He stops to talk to some people. I hear him mention protecting baby eggs but Will stands abruptly, downs his pint. "Come on."

James gets straight up, but I can't down my cider. I leave half of it and follow.

This new pub, Will tells me, is the oldest gay pub in The Village, here long before anything else was. The crowd is mixed. Not like the gay club near home, where everyone is young and looking their absolute best. In here are people of all ages, races, body shapes, and sizes. Will introduces me to fewer people in here thank god. I can't even remember the names of the people I've already met.

I feel like I finally belong in the queer community for the first time ever, and not because I've been eyed up three times.

He finds us seats, tells me to wait so he knows where to

find me, and introduces me to an older guy at the next table. Will and James head to the bar. Older guy keeps asking me about myself, but he's touching my leg. He's either Scottish or Irish. I can't make out what he's saying, but with every point, his hand is getting higher.

I try to get Will's attention but him and James are in serious conversation. James says something and Will glances over.

I guess I look terrified because he's rushing over.

"You're old enough to be his great-grandfather. Leave him alone," Will says as he pulls me up.

"Come on, Ben. You're safe with me."

He tells me we're moving on. James is waiting for someone so we leave him.

We head past a super colourful bar. The people inside are closer to my age. The full acronym is in there, I know it.

A sign advertises drag queens. Is one of them David's alter ego? I'm not entirely sure. I should ask Jacinta if *Mancunoir* is David.

"You don't want to go in there. Trust me, I'm doing you a favour." Will walks around the corner. I guess he knows best. I hurry to catch up to him down a side street.

"I'm having such a good night. I've never seen this many queers in one place."

His smile drops and he stands still. He puts a hand on my shoulder. I've never had a dad, but this feels like how I imagine having a dad give you a stern talking to would start.

"I don't want to fall out with you, but I want you to know I dislike that word." He sighs at my confusion. "I grew up under Section 28, a time when it was forbidden to talk about being gay. The only things I heard were negativity and slurs, with that Q word being the main one."

"I didn't realise."

"I was called it by my own parents, by people at school, college, and uni. Including teachers. I don't know why people say it was reclaimed. I never reclaimed it. It's as bad as the F slur. I despise that too. I was physically attacked multiple times by people shouting it. You wouldn't use that one, so I'd appreciate it if you didn't use the Q one in front of me. In fact, if you know what's good for you, as a good gay lad knowing your gay history, you wouldn't use it at all."

I never knew people felt that way. Which is weird because Shaun is the same age as Will, more or less, and he and his husband use it. I should know more about queer—I mean, LGBTQ+—history. Wait, can I say LGBT... Q? Will never uses the acronym either, maybe I shouldn't in front of him.

I nod. "Of course."

He smiles, gestures to follow again, to a place where cheesy music and flashing lights spill out into the street.

Inside he leads me around talking to these people, not those people, these are nice people, don't talk to them. I feel like I have a gay fairy godmother keeping me on the right track. I don't know what's wrong with the people he told me to avoid, but I don't ask.

"Is this him?" a stern-looking woman says to Will.

"Ben, meet my incredibly good friend Michelle."

"Nice to—" is all I get out before Michelle starts talking at me. Within moments, I learn she is a proud lesbian, a local MP, a born-and-bred northerner, loves stout, hates remoaners (whatever that is) and is married to Pauline, who is high up in publishing.

Will talks about work with her. Thank god I can switch off now. They're talking about meetings and feminism for some reason. They've naturally huddled away from me.

I don't mind. I want to appreciate this time and place.

It's busy. There are all sorts of people holding hands. I feel a bit sad I've not got anyone to hold hands with. Maybe I should have held Rahul's hand more, when I had the chance?

Will heads to the bar. People seem to part for him, almost as if they don't want to get too close, or maybe I've imagined that. The crowd reforms behind him. I have to squeeze through people as they dance to Kylie, arms in the air, sweaty hairy pits in my face. I'm not mad.

Will gets us shots and we dance. Will isn't a dancer. Michelle hasn't come anywhere near the dance floor.

The song is a dancey ABBA song, which reminds me... it's Mum's call night. Yep, I've missed three calls from her. Oh well, too late now. I close my eyes, let my body take over, arms in the air. This is everything I wanted Manchester to be.

I open my eyes when I get a tap on my shoulder. Will is looking at me strangely. The kind of look you give someone when they say something stupid.

Or do.

Is it my dancing? I put my arms down and copy his subdued moves.

"Good lad."

I didn't realise my dancing was that bad.

He gestures behind me. I follow his gaze. Someone is dancing exactly like me and knocking into everyone. He looks like he's having a great time, but I guess I can see what Will sees, he does look a bit of a dick. Fair enough.

I dance again, no arms this time. Will goes back to Michelle. From this angle, she looks like one of those women who always wants to speak to the manager. She catches me looking at her, and smiles, but it's a scary smile. Remind me not to get on her bad side.

Someone takes my hand. A boy. Well, a man. He's hot.

"Hey cutie." Was he in the group of people Will told me not to talk to? I'm not sure. He has make-up on, glitter in his goatee and afro, and painted nails. I can't help but notice his legs. He's got a skirt on like that person in the first bar, but this guy's skirt is much shorter. I must stop looking.

We dance. This is nice. We dance closer, and now we're kissing. Holy shit, I am snogging a boy in public. I have never done this in my life.

He leans in close, whispers, "Wanna come mine? I'm Mo, by the way, they/them."

I want to. I feel scared and excited and horny and pretty tipsy. Hmm, maybe I shouldn't go back with them feeling like this. Besides, I don't want to ditch Will.

I look around and see him by the door. He shakes his head sternly and leaves, followed by Michelle.

I turn back. Mo kisses me again.

I tingle all over.

I don't want it to end, but why did Will leave?

"Next time," I whisper to Mo.

They shrug, peck me on the lips, turn, and vanish into the crowd.

I hurry out to find Will leaning against a wall. He looks disappointed.

"Perhaps this mentoring was a mistake."

"What?"

"All I've done for you, and you go behind my back with someone I told you right at the start of my big night out for you, was against me."

I'm confused. Or wasted. "They only wanted to dance."

"Speak properly. He wanted more than a dance. I thought you were intelligent. You're drunk, but I'll forgive you this once."

My heart races. Not in the nice way it did with Mo. They weren't the person with the leaflets were they? Oh no, I am drunk.

"I didn't think they... he—"

"—That's right, you didn't think. I tell you what. Go back in. Let's call our friendship a day."

"It won't happen again."

He looks deep in thought. "Alright. I believe you. You are a smart lad. I've got your back, have you got mine?"

"Yes. Absolutely."

"No harm done then. Thanks for the follow, by the way."

He grins at my confusion.

He pulls out his phone, shows me my TikTok page. "You're the amazing talent behind the mask, aren't you?"

What do I say? I've kept it a secret for so long, I feel weird admitting it to anyone. I shake my head.

His smile vanishes, but rather than look apologetic, he

looks even more disappointed than he did a few minutes ago.

"Don't insult my intelligence. I know damn well you're The Enigaymatic Mystery."

"Nope."

He sneers. "If that's how you want to play it, maybe we really are done. Shame, because, as you know, I'm quite the expert when it comes to marketing, and I—"

"I know you—"

"AND I," he puts his hand up to stop me from talking, "could help you take your account to new heights, but you'd rather lie to me. TO ME. We're done. If you come to your senses, you know where I am."

He strides to the nearest cab, gets in without looking back.

What?!

Chapter 4

Aaaaaaaaand post.

I'm no longer a TikTok virgin!

Hopefully I'll soon be on one of those BuzzFeed listicles of people getting famous from the app. The partial nudity should help, which is why there was no way I was showing my face. It's bad enough living in Ming, that would make it a hundred times worse.

No idea where the blank white mask was even from, but that and *@the.enigaymatic.mystery* as my username, should be enough to keep me anonymous. And get people following.

"Ready yet lovey?" Mum calls through the bedroom door.

"Not yet." Has it been an hour since I said I was going to find something to wear? Oops. I sat down to scroll TikTok, found loads of gay guys doing a stupid new trend of putting all their clothes on, one on top of the next, cut to music. I found it so absolutely ridiculous I had to do it myself.

They all have massive followings and get loads of

attention and free stuff. I want that.

I thought I'd add one more shot at the end to try and grab a bit more attention, with all my clothes off. Back to camera of course. My bum is quite cute, and you can't see my flabby stomach. Win.

"Wear that nice sparkly shirt. I'm gonna go. I can't be late. See you there."

It doesn't even start for half an hour, what is she talking about? Ugh why didn't Rahul take me to visit his grandmother in the hospice?

Does Mum think I'm going to walk all the way to the Civic Hall, in this shirt, as though Ming isn't at the top of my list of homophobic towns to avoid?

An hour later, my video has only had three plays and no likes. I've been commenting on loads of random TikToks too. Why is nobody checking my profile out?

Do I look that awful?

Ugh. I may as well go to the party.

I grab a plain red shirt. It's Christmassy, but not too gay.

I launch the hanger across the room and leave.

I make it abuse-free. I wave to Mum on the dance floor, and find a seat away from the big window. They've not even closed the curtains. Why Shaun and Jeremy chose to have this party in the Civic Hall, right on the high street where everyone can see, I don't know.

I've been to many parties here. Everyone local has. I had my Year 11 leavers disco here. Sure it's had a coat of paint since. Or has it? I'm sure someone vommed on a chair at the disco. Looking at the stains covering the one I'm sat on, this might be it.

I keep my head turned away from the window as people stroll past having a good nose. In case they're making notes I don't want to be included in. They've probably never seen a do like this though to be fair.

This is the opposite of the usual, massively heterosexual, parties that go on here. Their idea of adding sparkle is sticking up red, white and blue bunting, fastening balloons on the walls in phallic shapes, and scattering party poppers on the tables. The men drink while the women dance and the kids are high on sugar. If it doesn't end with a punch-up, nobody has anything to talk about the next day.

Not this party. Everyone is dancing and drinking and apparently don't care that anyone could walk in off the shopping precinct and see every gay, lesbian, bisexual, trans, and queer plus plus plus. They might as well have painted targets on their backs. They'd probably do it in sequins if they did.

How do Shaun and Jeremy even know all these people? They certainly don't live around here. I don't blame them.

I pass the time commenting on TikToks. I'm up to twenty-five plays and have got seven likes, but seriously, how many times can people listen to *All I Want For Christmas Is You,* before they get fed up? The overly enthusiastic and frankly too-sparkly mob cheer once again as the twinkling intro plays for the fourth time.

I take my weed vape into the loos. Hopefully it's enough to get me through the next couple of hours.

Screams almost make me drop my vape down the toilet. I knew something was going to happen, it always does around here. I creep out of the toilet, expecting to witness a hate crime, to find it's just everyone was excited a certain Kylie song has come on.

That scream will have been heard for miles. Homophobic goose pimples will be rising all around Ming. I need another drink.

I'm distracted by an arse as I go back in.

There's a huge tree by the entrance covered in mismatched decorations. Shaun and Jeremy asked everyone to bring one instead of a gift. There's a lot of saucy Santas. I'm not sure how I feel about Leather Daddy Santa in assless chaps.

That's not the ass I'm distracted by though. Some twink-like gay in tight jeans is bent over, placing an ornament on one of the only available branches. It's a nice bum.

He stands. I turn away quickly.

Bump into a table. Stagger backwards and... yeah I'm falling.

Right into his arms.

I'm held tight. Impressive, as I'm not light. Nor thin. Nor sober.

Our eyes meet. Why is there mistletoe above us?

He follows my gaze and looks up. Oh, it's not a guy. It's a soft-butch girl with sparkly make-up and earrings shaped like those American cars with lift-up doors. She spots the mistletoe too.

Awkward.

I quickly stand up, out of her arms. "Erm. Yeah. Merry Christmas. Bye." I head to the bar.

"Merry Christmas," she says. "You alright?"

I don't want a conversation, but she did just catch me. I

turn and give a thumbs up. Ugh why did I do that? I don't recognise her. She's not related to Shaun, I've met all his family. She could be related to his husband though, because she's mixed race like Jeremy.

"You on your todd?" she asks.

"Unfortunately, no." I point over to the dance floor. *Come On Eileen* is playing, and there's a woman in the middle of the dance floor, beaming as everyone points to her during the chorus.

"That's my mum. Her name is..."

"Eileen?" The girl grins. Watches for a moment. "Awesome."

"You wouldn't think that if she was your mum."

"Better than what my rents are doing."

I follow her gaze. Two people around Mum's age stand on the outskirts of all the queers, holding hands like their heterosexual lives depend on it. A white guy dressed exactly like every straight guy dresses for a Christmas party, and a black woman, in a black pant suit and not even a milligram of glitter anywhere on her. They look like they've never seen anything as queer as this in their lives. Fair.

"I win. I'm Maya by the way."

"Benny. Did your parents drag you here too?"

She nods. "I'm only home for a few weeks and wanted to chill in my old room, get a bit of peace and quiet. Nope. Somehow anti-social."

I like her. She gets it.

"My mum pecked my head saying it would be good for me to be with my community. How rude is that? Hello, I'm 24, not a kid. So, does your family know Shaun or Jeremy?"

"Mum works with Shaun," she says.

"Mine too. She's known him..." how long? "Since I was a baby."

"My mum probably knows your mum. Does she work in the office?"

"Nosheworksinthekitchen."

"Come again?"

Grrr. Mum has never made a big deal of it, and I don't care either, but people around here have a lot of opinions. "She's the cook."

"Everybody has to eat. Personally, I love food."

Is she patronising me?

I make eye contact with my mum. She's frantically beckoning me onto the dance floor. I shake my head. She pouts her lip in a pretend sad face, puts her right hand over her heart and taps her little finger three times. I give her a small smile. I can't be arsed doing it back. Shaun grabs her hand, spins her around, and they're dancing again. Saved.

"I need booze. You?" Maya says.

The bar is in a room of its own, and it's empty. Maya gets me a strawberry cider, and a JD & diet coke for her. We sit as far away from the door to the main room as possible, because Mariah is playing again.

It's like we've known each other for ages and are catching up. It's not even like this with Rahul. I don't want to think about that.

Now I've got major FOMO. How is she a year younger than me but also living an amazing life in Manchester? She's in her final year of uni because she went late after taking a couple of years out, has a part-time supermarket job, and loves the vibe. I'd kill for that. I can't wait for me and Rahul to get out of Ming.

Oooh, if I become an influencer, I could get out faster.

She asks about my job.

"A bear, a twink, and an otter walk into a bar," I say to change the subject.

Maya follows my gaze to the three men who've walked in. "Which is which?"

"A bear is a big, hairy, older gay guy. A twink is a young, slim or athletic, cute gay guy, and an otter is a slim but hairy gay guy."

It's hilarious how seriously she's taking this in.

"I'd love to be a bear," she mutters to herself. "Which one are you?"

That's my buzz gone. The way I'm filling this medium shirt means twink and otter are totally out. I'm not hairy or masc enough to be a cub, let alone a bear.

"Great Scott, I'm rude!" She does look genuine. "Why are there all these terms for gays?"

I shrug. "Apparently the gays fought to not be put into a box, and then decided to create many smaller boxes to put themselves into."

I can't help but smile at her laugh. It's infectious.

"You're cute and funny?"

I am, yeah, but also I better be clear. "I'm gay and I've got a boyfriend."

"That's cool. Didn't want to presume. I'm queer too."

Phew. "What flavour?"

She cocks her head and takes a moment. Surely it's not that hard? I've known I was gay since I was eight.

"Well... let's go with lesbian plus."

"What does that mean?"

"Since I moved to Manchester I've been questioning a lot of things. I could be bi, or pansexual or..."

Or? What else is there?

In the silence that annoying Slade song comes on. Everyone on the dance floor cheers. I look at Maya and roll my eyes. She does exactly the same thing. We both burst out laughing.

I spot her check her phone, so do the same. I was quite enjoying her company but if she's looking at hers...

Oh my god. How has my video now had over five hundred plays and over a hundred likes? I've got my first follower too!

Now I'm feeling festive, but Maya's staring at her phone, disgusted.

"Everything OK?"

"Ever had an online troll?"

I shake my head. "I've had real life ones though."

"I've been retweeting trans moots, and using the hashtag, *Trans Lives Matter*. The past few days I've had this weirdo keep telling me I'm on the wrong side of history."

"Gross"

"Yup. He's got no followers so I haven't been arsed, but he's quote-tweeted me saying I'm being brainwashed, and it's brought a load of TERFs to my replies saying they can tell I'm not a biological female, and I'll always be a man."

I expect her to be offended by that, but for a split second I'm sure I notice a smile.

"Report... and.... block. Again. He's always picking

fights with trans people, or arse-licking accounts with huge followings."

I check my activity again. A few people have commented. Telling me I'm cute. That the mask is cool. One guy has said I should film from the front next time and... dirty bastard.

"He's worse with other accounts, mainly the trans femmes and trans women. Keeps asking horrible questions. When they clap back saying he's a nobody-bunch-of-numbers, he's like, 'One day you'll know who I am and be sorry.' Twat."

I need to lift the mood. I offer my hand. "May I have this dance?"

It's not too bad in the main room. The dry ice machine helps cover the disgusting dance floor. The red and gold metallic ribbons hanging from the helium balloons up in the ceiling give everywhere a festive shimmer. The poinsettias on the tables are pretty, especially with the candy canes and Quality Streets drizzled all over.

The outfit game is fierce. There's a lot of sequins. Lots of laughing and shrieking too, mainly from the men. Everyone looks like they're genuinely having a great time. So am I.

As we dance we start a game where for every random gay animal body type I mention, she tells me a lesbian one. She's making some of these up because no way is *Unicornette* real.

We struggle to stop laughing as our hosts go on the stage to do a speech.

Jeremy lets Shaun do all the talking, bless him. I mean, it's not like Shaun doesn't like talking. "Lez be honest.

There's nothing more important Tran family. Whatever we're connected Bi, be it blood, or through the power of queer magic, Jer and I are utterly gay-teful you're here. It's just a shame none of you dressed up."

Everyone laughs. Ugh, he's cringe.

"I even toned it down this year to give you all a chance." It's hilarious because not only is his Christmas-bauble-print jumpsuit covered in glitter, so is the ginger hair on his head and face.

"So babes, gaybes and theybes, let's Christmas this party!" Shaun shimmies his shoulders and tries his best to twerk.

Jeremy gives him a little eye roll, takes the mic, says, "Thank you all for coming," hurries off stage and puts Madonna on.

Shaun struts onto the dance floor, grabs Mum's hand. She spins into his arms and they attempt to dance to *Vogue*. Have they rehearsed this?

They're proper BFFs. I'm sure they don't feel they're being as cringe as they look.

Jeremy goes over to talk to Maya's parents. I see them instantly relax. He encourages them onto the dance floor. Well, now we're all dancing to Vogue I guess.

As the song ends I check my phone again. YES! I've got thirty-two followers.

I must be smiling too much because Mum's coming over.

"Benny, my sweet sweet boy." Yeah she's drunk. "I knew you'd enjoy yourself. Come and dance with your old mum."

I don't get chance to say no. She's already taken my hand

and pulled me onto the dance floor.

Come on, Mariah Carey again?

Oh, alright, I might as well enjoy tonight. Tomorrow I need to decide how I'm going to make myself popular on TikTok.

Chapter 5

Finally! Maya has a full day off and they're showing me their Manchester highlights.

I'm a bit wobbly though. Last night, Jacinta opened a bottle of fancy vodka to mark two-weeks until Christmas, and asked me to join.

"Did I hear drinkies?" David called, the daintiest footsteps down the stairs.

This was the first time I'd properly met him. He literally pirouetted into the lounge, grabbed the drink off Jacinta, and did a high kick. He pulled me into a hug, which felt strong but there's nothing on him, and kissed me on each cheek.

Without me asking, he told me he works at least two jobs. One on Canal Street as a drag queen (I was right, he is *Mancunoir*), and he has something to do with a queer, Black, arts project he might have said he helped set up but he speaks at a thousand words a minute.

"We'll do The Village soon. You look like you've got a

vitamin DEEEEEE deficiency. Period," he told me. "We'll kiki when I'm not working. How are you fixed for Feb?" He laughed, and stayed with us for a couple more drinks before he said, "Apols, bitches. Gotta dash. This won't tuck itself."

Zoe joined for one drink before she left to meet her friend Kate at a lesbian bar she couldn't take me to, because apparently I wouldn't like it.

I had another drink with Jacinta, until she took herself to bed, as usual, at 9.30pm.

I did a few drunk TikToks in my room. I've only gained a thousand new followers in the past couple of weeks. I need to keep pushing. 13.2k is pitiful.

Enough. I'm here with Maya.

Who I don't recognise at first, until I spot someone tapping their watch.

They're not wearing their usual oversized hoody. Today they've opted for a shirt, and damn they look good. They've had their hair cut shorter too. They're more masc than I've ever seen them.

We hug, as is our usual greeting. They smell different today. It's not her usual floral fragrance. It's sort of fruity, and there's a sweetness I can't...

"Wanna make like a tree and get outta here?" she whispers in my ear.

I do, but I don't pull away. Today is cold, I want to enjoy their warmth a little longer.

"You look great by the way," I say as we finally come apart. "Have you started the..."

"Boy juice? Nope. All this is an awesome queer barber, a properly fitted binder, and a good friend who gives me a bit of confidence."

I hope they mean me.

"Your mum still asking when you're coming home?" Maya directs me towards our first stop of the day: a load of wooden huts.

"Ugh. Every. Single. Time."

Maya has found it funny the moment December the 1st arrived, Mum has asked me that question on every phone call, email or text. I'm sick of explaining I've only got a few days off around Christmas and I'm not sure if I'm going back on Christmas Eve or the day before yet.

"She misses you. My rents were like that when I first moved out."

"Probably. She always sound sad when she phones. I'm sure her voice is getting croakier." Her cough has gone though. I guess she got it sorted, though I don't recall her telling me what happened with the doctor. Probably was the wash powder then.

Oh, it's a Christmas Market. Cute.

Maya gets us both a hot Vimto. I buy a giant bratwurst to share as we wander around.

Maya's been super busy with uni and work. We've only managed two evenings together. One at mine where we played *Cards Against Humanity* with Jacinta and Zoe, and a night at Maya's where she made me watch all three *Back to the Future* movies. She's obsessed. We watched them on their laptop, squashed on their single bed because there's an issue with one of their housemates and Maya didn't want to sit in the lounge. I didn't get home until almost 4am.

The spiciness of this sausage brings me back to the

present, but all Maya can do is laugh at my watering eyes.

Their laugh is somewhere between a witch's cackle and a deep guffaw and it improves my day every time I hear it, which has been every time we've been together.

Maya's phone buzzes. "Seriously?"

"What's wrong?"

"No rules broken. This is the fifth time I've reported my troll this week. What's the point? Look."

They show me the reply under their new-hair selfie: *You're a biological female with a mental illness and your pronouns offend me.*

"Anything I can do?" I'm not sure what I could do. I occasionally get homophobes on my TikToks but I call them out until they get bored. Most of the comments have been positive.

She types a reply, "I'll call him cis. That might get him aggy enough to say something that'll actually get him banned. Anyway, enough about trolls. Onward."

Maya points out murals as we head away from the market. Queer tiles on the floor lead us to a door in the corner of a large building.

"You'll love this place."

I'm not prepared for its quirkiness at all. It's a big old building, on many floors, selling all sorts. Costumes. Heavy metal posters. Crystals. Cannabis paraphernalia. I buy orange-flavoured rolling papers.

We head through a shop with retro T-shirts. I find one with a heart on it that says *LIKE AND FOLLOW*. I'm tempted to buy it to see if it will help me get more followers. I need to do something, I'm running out of ideas.

I shake myself out of my silly funk and catch Maya looking longingly at a *Back to the Future* T-shirt.

"Buy it."

She shakes her head. "Tempted, but I need to save." Before I can ask what for, they add, "Is there anywhere you'd like to go before we carry on?"

I shake my head. I want to see what Maya wants to show me.

They walk me through the pedestrianised shopping bit by the Arndale. Everyone is proper in Christmas shopping mode. I keep bumping into people as I look around.

"Here." Maya takes my hand. It feels like the teddy hot-water bottle I had as a kid, soft and warm. They guide my hand into my coat pocket and link their arm through mine.

"Now you can look, and I can make sure you stay safe."

Our eyes meet and their little smile matches mine, but my smile feels bigger on the inside for some reason.

I'm guided towards an alleyway. Maya gives me an enigmatic grin.

Above us, where the ceiling should be, are umbrellas.

"Look." Maya points up to the sky, beyond the brollies.

We both burst out laughing. A cloud shaped like a dick and balls.

Our laughs echo through the alleyway. It must sound horrendous to anyone walking past, but Maya's laugh makes me laugh more.

Through giggles, Maya tells me we have to get a move on otherwise the library will be closed. That sets me off again. Why is Maya taking me to a library? They grab my hand and pull. I can feel the vibration of her laughter through their fingertips and into my soul.

We stop. It's not what I was expecting.

It's like an old gothic church and castle made a building-baby.

"I study here sometimes. Wanted to share it with you."

Inside, through a gift shop and up steps. It's bright and modern but I guess I don't look impressed, because they say, "Trust me. Close your eyes."

I do. They take my hand and squeeze it excitedly. The warmth from their fingers around mine makes me feel light-headed for a moment.

They lead me forward. Even with my eyes closed I can tell it's gone darker. Colder too, and more solid beneath my feet.

It smells old. Dusty and musky but also sweet. No, that's Maya. Their fruity fragrance is oranges and... maybe vanilla. It's comforting somehow.

They whisper, "Open your eyes."

It's like we've gone back in time. Still holding my hand, they lead me slowly along the corridor. It reminds me of... Well, I don't want to say this to them because Maya has mentioned how those books they loved as a kid have been ruined, but it's like a magical school.

They lead me into rooms. Ancient books on display. I... literally... can't.

We go upstairs to the main reading room. My "Bloody hell!" echoes. Everyone looks at me. Thankfully, they all smile as though they're used to this reaction.

Books as big as a front door on some shelves. Books as old as time, it seems, on others. We've still not let go of hands. This place is so Maya.

"Knew you'd love it," they say as we find a quiet corner to do presents.

Maya's going to Jamaica for Christmas to spend time with family, so we've planned to swap presents today, seeing as it's the anniversary of when we first met.

I got them a little cheese-cutting board and knife that says, *Cheese Fiend,* because they love cheese more than seems natural.

I open mine. Awwwwww. "Did you make this?"

They nod. A little metal pin badge that says *Cute and Queerful,* in Progress Pride colours. I put it on my coat immediately.

The other gift is a little acrylic bong.

"Made that too."

"How?"

"Heard one of my exes was doing acrylic stuff for her course. I persuaded her to let me have a go."

Not me wondering why they're mentioning this ex for the first time. "Persuaded her how?"

"Nothing naughty, don't worry."

Dunno why they said it like that. Why would I be worried?

"You gonna be OK in Jamaica?"

They shrug. "Course."

I want to kidnap her so they don't have to go. I know their grandparents aren't super open to anything LGBTQ, but I'm sure Maya can handle it.

We chat about nothing as I walk them home. We stand outside their flat and for a split second it feels like the end of a date. I guess I'm ready to finally move on from Rahul.

We hug. Before I can stop myself, I say, "You hug like a boy now." Their smile goes. Shit. "That was a stupid thing —"

"It's not stupid. Been doing heaps of soul-searching lately. This binder has been deeply affirming, which was like, whaaaaaaaaat?!? So..." They go serious. I'm a bit scared. "I don't want to use female pronouns anymore."

"OK."

"And the reason I'm trying not to spend any dough, is 'cause I've spoken to my therapist... and... I reckon... I might get top surgery."

I didn't see that coming. Or did I? I can't imagine what this must all feel like to Maya. I'm proud of them. Wait, am I the first person they've told?

"What pronouns are you using then? Man ones?" Duh, man ones, what a dick.

"They/them. And I don't wanna go by Maya no more. Just M."

"Em?"

"Like the letter. For now, I'll probs change it at some point."

"Well, M, have a safe flight, and message me when you get there, and any time you need to vent."

"Prepare for hourly texts."

I head back to mine. I'm going to feel super lonely while M's away. Maybe I'll put my energy into TikTok.

I need to up my game.

It's been harder than I thought it would.

Maybe I should text him the truth.

Yes,@the.enigaymatic.mystery is me.
I'm sorry I lied to you.

***

This place is fancy AF. Will texted back immediately to say he was glad I'd come to my senses, to dress smart and meet him at this steak place.

I've not had many steaks. Mum only gets them for extra special occasions. I did order a beefsteak once at a restaurant when Ra and I were on holiday, not sure that counts.

"I knew you were intelligent." He shakes my hand and we sit.

What should I order? There are steaks with names I've never heard of before and bloody hell they're expensive, no wonder Mum hardly ever buys them.

Noticing my puzzled face, Will reaches across the table, pats my hand, takes my menu, and flags down a waiter.

"We'll both have the fillet steak, medium rare, Béarnaise sauce, and two sides of the triple cooked chips."

The waiter takes our menus, but hasn't written anything down. Will is going to go mental if this goes wrong. It wouldn't be the first time. Once, when we had coffee, the barista... He's looking at me seriously.

I follow his gaze. Am I not dressed smartly enough?

Oh! The badge on my coat.

"I'm here taking you out for probably the best meal of

your life and you wear that, even though I've explained my feelings. I'm disappointed."

I quickly take my coat off.

"I completely forgot. My friend made it."

He sighs. "That's kind of... him or her?"

"Oh. They're non-binary."

"Your friend Maya?" He's got a good memory. "I didn't realise you were still friends after everything that happened."

"Yeah. Mum made me realise it wasn't their fault."

"If indeed Maya told you the truth."

"I believe—"

"This is the problem with young gay people, they want to be anything but. In my day you had to be proud of being gay or lesbian. That's how we got our rights, but they'd rather use that horrible word. Meanwhile I'm vilified for using 'gay'. It should be getting easier to be proud of my sexuality, instead it's the opposite. I'm proud to be gay. Are you Ben?"

He's leaned in close and said this all as a whisper. I nod. I can't mess this up.

"I know you get it. How's work?"

I tell him about my projects and somehow start talking about how Mum has pestered me about coming home.

He rolls his eyes as our food comes. The steaks look good, but there's only like eight chips. Big fat stacked ones. I guess these are quality over quantity.

The meaty, salty, charred aroma floating off the steak makes my mouth water. I've never had a medium rare steak before. I hope I like it.

"She still phoning three times a week?" he asks as he pours the sauce over my steak, then does the same to his. "Eat up."

I cut into my steak. It's so soft. More blood runs out than I'm expecting. I have to eat this though.

"She is, but it's fine." I take a bite.

Wow. It barely requires chewing. It's like beef made by angels. The sauce, creamy and tangy. Swallowing makes a smile start in my stomach, and rise up to my face.

I glance at Will, he nods and winks. "You're welcome. So, how's your independent Manchester life going?"

I tell him it's been amazing, in no small part thanks to him and his generosity.

"Not a problem. You're going to do amazing things once you fully commit to being here." He leans forward and speaks quietly, "I didn't want to say this, and of course I don't think it, but that night I took you to the Gay Village, my friends found you a little bit green."

Is that why they were weird with me?

"I wouldn't worry about it. I'm impressed and someone like you could go far, with the right guidance."

He starts talking about Gale-Feng-Paisley, his company. As we finish our steaks he tells me about all the different departments and the projects they work on. It puts my stuff to shame. If I got to work at GFP, it would be a dream come true.

Our empty plates are taken. The bill comes. I feel like if I don't say something now, we might never talk about this again.

"I am trying to be more independent. Manchester is

bigger than I anticipated, and is taking a bit of getting used to, is all."

"Oh, I believe you. It's the others you need to prove it to. There's some influential people who could be great allies for you. Of course, first you need to prove your independence to yourself."

"How?"

He checks over the bill, slides it to the edge of the table, and puts his credit card on top. It's turned to me. I see it's over two hundred pounds!

"You have to cut those apron strings, Ben. You know what would be a good way to do that? Come stay with me over Christmas."

"I'm not sure my mum would be happy."

"You're a grown adult human man, Ben. But if your mother is forcing you to go home... Let me pay this bill and I'll get out of your hair. Shame though, because I am having a little get-together on Boxing Day and everyone seeing you there would stop any doubts they have about you. Do you really want to spend your days off travelling back and forth to that little town you were desperate to escape?"

"Mum keeps saying she really wants to have a proper, in-person conversation."

"I don't talk to mine. Up to you, but I've got great ideas for your TikTok, and I have time over Christmas to help you grow your account. I'm not sure when I'll have that again. How's your following coming along? You must be over twenty thousand by now?"

I wish.

What should I do?

Chapter 6

My brain takes a moment to boot up. It's quiet, unlike mornings at the house. Warm too for a change. We've reduced the heating schedule to save money.

I've never slept this well. It's been a full-on fortnight with work. I've also spent a lot of time making TikToks to put out over the next week because...

It's Christmas Day!

At least I don't have to worry about content. I've done a series called *Gifts from Gays*, basically how different labels would wrap a gift. The gay man one was fancy metallic paper, neatly folded around corners, with ribbons and bows. The gift inside was scented candles and succulents. The lesbian one was cheap paper, haphazardly wrapped, and mostly sellotape. Inside were DIY tools. The bisexual one was half fancy wrapping and half newspaper. The gift inside was a chair cushion, because have you seen how bisexuals sit?

As Will insisted, I did a trans one which had no

wrapping, just an IKEA shark plushie with a bow on top because it's what's on the inside that counts. I also did a non-binary one which had no wrapping or bows as it did not want to identify as a gift, and was just a piece of obsidian. Started as a regular rock, could've stayed that way, or become magma, or become lava, but settled on being dark and shiny. I did get a tiny bit of pushback on those two, but mostly love and likes.

I open my eyes. Will's guest bedroom. It's like I'm in a hotel. En-suite and everything.

If I was home right now, I know exactly what would happen because all my Christmases are the same. Mum would bring me a cuppa and bacon butty while she did a quick tidy. I don't miss the sound of our ancient vacuum cleaner making sure I couldn't fall back to sleep.

I'd then be called in for presents. We'd sit around listening to music until Shaun and Jeremy came round, usually late morning. We'd have pastries before we open presents with them.

Then we'd all prepare dinner which always takes hours. Any time I try and get out of it, Mum says, "*Not today, not on Christmas.*" She uses that any time anyone tries to break the yawnfest of a tradition.

After dinner we all pretend to have fun playing a board game, then we watch a film we've seen hundreds of times.

Not this year.

Mum wasn't happy. She begged me to change my mind, but I held on to what Will said. I had to do this. I text her.

Merry Christmas xxx

She phones back straight away. I can tell she's putting on a nonchalant voice, but Shaun and Jeremy stayed the night so she's not alone.

I promise her I'll come visit in the new year. She tells me she can't wait to see me and then takes a deep breath, "I want to catch up properly lovey, without a screen between us. I need to... so we can have a proper conversation."

I thank her for the six-month, fortnightly food-subscription, as well as my usual pants and socks. I opened them last night as I didn't want to bring them with me. Mum said she was going to use the John Lewis voucher I got her on the perfume she likes.

"Knock, knock." Will enters with a waft of cinnamon and chocolate, "Merry Christmas, oh you're on the phone. Pastries are ready and I've made you a cappuccino. And there's this."

He holds out a box neatly wrapped in metallic paper, with ribbons and bows.

"I'll call you later Mum." I feel Will staring as Mum tells me how much she wishes I was there but wants me to have a great day.

"I love you," she adds. If only I could do the little finger tap over the phone as Will is gesturing to hurry up.

"You too, Mum. Bye." I take the gift. "I didn't get you anything."

"You didn't have to. Come on, open it. Do you recognise the wrapping?"

It takes me a moment. "It's like the gay wrapping on my

TikTok."

He looks impressed with himself. To be fair, the one in my video took me ages. I had to find a wrapping video and watched it a dozen times before I understood the folds and tucks.

"Thank you, Will." It's a new ring light. A fancy one with different colours and effects. It's massive too. This must've been expensive.

"Do you like it?"

"I love it."

"Come on."

I text M as I follow him.

Merry Queersmas x

Will's apartment is like something from a TV show. I didn't see much of it last night, as we went out for drinks, then he got me settled in his guest bedroom and I went to sleep.

It was a weird night, though. Will has a particular type of friend. Not all the same age or race, but there's a vibe. They're all friendly and well spoken, but it's like they're holding back when they talk. Often the conversation will go silent and the topic changed.

It happened last night, until Will told everyone to, "Lighten up, it's Christmas." We talked about the price of real trees, and why it's annoying that glittered wrapping paper can't go in the paper bin.

I'm a bit confused now, though. At this time of the

morning, back home, the kitchen counters are full of food waiting to be cooked.

As if reading my mind, or maybe my face, Will says, "The food will arrive soon. Relax."

"Usually after breakfast, Mum tells us the plan, gives everyone a job, and as is tradition, puts her ABBA CD on and we get to work." Will puts on a pity smile. "Yeah, it's lame, I know."

Enjoying pastries in the lounge, he asks how I slept. I tell him I have never slept on anything so comfy. Which is true.

"You know." He puts down his Americano, raises his eyebrows, and tilts his head. "You could sleep like that every night. I've been considering taking on a lodger for a while now. Are you in?"

My mind's gone blank.

"Consider it. You said you wanted to have the full Manchester experience, and your housemates aren't giving it to you, are they?"

"I guess not." I don't know what Mum would say, but I'd love to know M's thoughts. I take out my phone, they've still not replied! I want to ask them about this.

They've not got great Wi-Fi where they're staying, so our chats have been few and far between. They're making the most of the situation, but they're struggling. I've made it my mission to send them the randomest memes every day to try and cheer them up.

"Phone away. Let's have a drink. I want to show you something."

He opens a bottle of champagne, gets his laptop, and shows me a couple of the projects his company is working on. I get excited talking about the techniques, and what I'd do differently.

"You've got a great eye," he says, as someone knocks on the door. I hadn't realised how many hours had gone, nor how drunk I am. Have we gone through two bottles of champagne? Why does Will seem more sober than me?

I don't know what I was expecting, but it wasn't a fully cooked Christmas dinner, to be delivered. Will tells me to get changed. By the time I've had a shower, which I had to ask how to use because it's super fancy, and put on different clothes as per Will's request, as he's told me I need to dress smarter if I want to be taken seriously in this industry, the table is set.

It feels weird not having a Christmas morning joint, or vape. Last time Will and I had our Thursday coffee—I'm happy we're back on them, he brought up how he doesn't like drugs, especially weed, and how they do random drug tests at his company. He said that with a wink which I expect was meant to imply something, but I was paranoid I smelled strongly of cannabis.

I've only recently found a new dealer too, thanks to Jacinta. Oh well. I've thrown the last of it away. I guess I don't smoke it anymore.

I've never had goose. We usually have a chicken, although Mum has bought the occasional turkey when she's had a good year. I can't place the herbs in these roasties, but they're the perfect balance of crispy and soft. I don't know what's in this stuffing, but it didn't come out of a box that's for sure.

It's super Insta-worthy. There's a reason I've never taken

photos of my Christmas dinners.

We eat in silence. I've never had a Christmas this quiet. Will served me my food, reminding me, "No silly chores for you today."

It's weird having no laughter around the table, but I don't know how to get the conversation going.

"So," Will says. Phew. "I loved the dating videos you did the other week. The bisexual one swiping right on every man and woman, was hilarious, although the lesbian one, where you swiped right on the first profile then searched for a house, made me laugh out loud."

I noticed all the crying-laughing emojis he did on them. I still don't know what to say to all his praise.

"Now the gay one got me thinking."

Here we go. For this one I swiped right on those with a torso pic and left on all the faces. This one is how I feel it is for me being on Grindr. I installed it a month ago, but after two weeks of absolute silence, I took my profile down.

Nobody would want my torso pic.

"You should do some videos where it appears like you're filming a dating profile video, but it's you listing all the reasons why being gay is great."

Not a bad idea. "Such as?"

"Such as, even though you're a gay man, you're still a man. Talk about how gay men come in all shapes and sizes, and can be masculine or effeminate, but you're still a man. Make it funny. I don't need to tell you that, your videos are hilarious."

He's waiting for me to say something. What do I say? "Thank you."

"You know, you could even do one where you're appealing for donations, because as a gay man you're an endangered species, because surgeons are helping erase us, yet the lesbians are all upping their numbers. I'm happy you're here, Ben. Let's pull a cracker."

I'm used to having a psychic fish toy, or a fake moustache. Will won a Harvey Nichols champagne stopper, and I got a Damson gin liqueur. We both have gold crowns, but Will said we don't have to wear them. Mum would never let me get away with that. *"No crown-less heads today, not on Christmas,"* she'd say.

By early evening I am stuffed, and we're sat on his squashy corner sofa, watching Christmas movies on his massive TV. I wish I had Mum's popcorn surprise. We always have it. A tub of popcorn mixed with many bags of chocolate. I wonder if she's made it back home for her, Shaun, and Jeremy?

The film ends, and I guess the cheesy ending is giving me the feels. Either that, or it's because Will hasn't let my wine glass be empty all day.

"Hows your follower count coming along?"

I feel like this is permission to get my phone. I notice M has replied. Their day has been a struggle.

I find a gif of a monster hugging another monster, and send it, before joining Will and telling him I'm a little over 15k. I've done a big content push over the last few weeks, and I'm glad it's paid off a little.

He whistles. "What is it you need to become a micro-influencer?"

"50k, though I'm considered a nano-influencer right

now."

"We can do better than nano." He fills my glass up again. "You have as good an eye for content as you do for design, although I thought the transgendered Christmas present one could've been funnier. I'm glad you included it though. You're a genius, and the mask is inspired. You don't even know what you've got here do you? An opportunity!" He opens up a bottle of gin, bouncing in his chair.

"For what?"

"To spread your message."

"It's just for fun."

"Don't you want to have people hang on your every word? Don't you want to be the voice of your generation? Make good money whilst you're at it. With all your followers, you have a lot of power. You could let people know what our community is really about, and how we're not falling for all this new nonsense."

I don't know what that means, but he's excited. I'm trying hard not to show how wasted I am, not after last time.

"I've got more ideas. Would you like to hear them?"

I nod. I suppose this is better than playing a board game.

He grabs a list from his little office area in the corner. It's a fancy wooden contraption that unlocks and unfolds, reveals a desk and storage, then folds away neatly.

He gives me suggestions for some of the videos I've already done, except with trans and enby characters. He goes into a lot of detail, and finds himself funny when he suggests a trans character for the duvet changing video. "The character changes the duvet from a plain black one, to a flowery one, to a plain black one again."

I don't get it, but he's already moved on.

"This would be a series called, *Just a Normal Gay.*" He's finally reached the bottom of the list. "Similar to videos you've done, but with the catchphrase, *Just a Normal Gay*. You'd do things that certain gay men do, their kinks and quirks, and pretend you're trying them out, but you keep failing because you're..." He waits for me to finish the sentence.

"Just a normal gay?"

He suggests I do one where I'm trying to do make-up and wear glitter, but keep making a mess and unable to even open the glitter. "You should also do one where you're trying and failing to be camp. Nothing else. Just lots of mincing and *yassss queen*."

I guess I've done videos similar that went down well.

He suggests I do a video where I'm looking for harnesses, dog, and pup costumes. "But the joke is, you're in the wrong shop. It's a pet store!"

He's lost me now. "I don't get it."

He laughs gently. "It's kink." He pulls a face. "You wait until Pride."

He suggests another video where I try on leather clothes. Apparently, you can get them with the arse cut out. He also said it would be funny to do one where I'm looking at jock straps, but the joke is, that's my whole outfit for marching in the pride parade.

"As long as I don't have to wear one."

"Oh goodness, no," he replies, handing me the A4 piece of paper. I say thank you. "This could be the making of you. Honestly, I'm extremely proud of you, Ben. You know what,

I hate the thought of all your talent being wasted at somewhere that isn't GFP."

Is he saying what I think he's saying?

"Listen, it might take a while, these things often can. I suggest you keep your head down at work, and I'll see what I can do. Now, drink."

***

I wake up the next day feeling horrendous. I'm in the comfy bed but I need water. I remember having more drinks, and at some point realised Mum had phoned a couple of times, so I went to the guest bedroom to phone her back in private.

I have a vague memory I was out of charge, and after plugging it in, I thought I'd have a little lie down whilst I waited. Oops. I'm still fully clothed.

I check my phone but it's not charged. I'm sure I turned the plug on. How drunk was I?

Voices force me to quickly splash water on my face in the bathroom and head into the lounge.

Michelle and her wife Pauline are here.

Visitors don't stop arriving all day. After James turns up, I head off to put something smart on.

It's all sophisticated today, and everyone, literally everyone comes to speak to me and tells me how good it is to see me. It's quite a nice ego boost.

As the party dies down, Will pulls me to one side. Most people have left, but James, Michelle, and Pauline are in the lounge, sipping port and eating cheese.

"I had another good idea for you. The T-shirt Michelle bought me inspired me." I remember Will opening the present from Michelle, but I didn't get to see the front. "You could do a series on how a gay teacher would teach different subjects. You could have the subjects on a T-shirt and teach them like a gay man. You should start by being a biology teacher."

He finds this funny for some reason. He must be drunk.

I nod, but a recent conversation with Mum flashes up in my mind. She was talking about how someone at work asked her to remove a collection tub she'd put out, as it was the Transgender Day of Remembrance. Mum refused to serve her because she kept asking when the day of remembrance for all the biological women was.

"I'll add it to the list," I say, because I don't want to be rude. Will has been so kind, but I feel like it's time for me to go. I'm at work tomorrow. I've never worked over Betwixmas before. I guess they do things differently here.

The days between Christmas and New Year, me and Mum always call Betwixmas. Days blend into one, and we've always chilled, eaten leftovers, had occasional visitors, and watched TV. Rahul even came round the year before last. He and Mum always got on well.

Our Betwixmases have been like that forever. Maybe they are a bit lame, but they felt right. This apartment and Will's friends don't feel like me. It's time to go.

"Thank you for having me, but I'm at work tomorrow, and I need to keep my head down."

"This New Year is going to be such a good year for you, Ben. Did you have any thoughts about being my lodger?"

I don't want to be rude, but this place isn't me. "Thank you for the offer. Your apartment is amazing, but for now I think I'll stay where I am."

"No problem at all. What about another brainstorming session soon to get you to 50k?"

Sounds good, although now Will knows... "Maybe I should stop using the mask? What do you think?"

Will looks at me deadly serious. Shakes his head. "Bad idea. That mask is what it's all about. You'll lose your following if you change it. The mystery is what makes it fun. You've got your own little secret nobody but me knows. Exciting, isn't it?"

I suppose it is nice having the secret, and it does make me feel good.

"Ok. Thanks again, Will."

"You're always welcome, Ben. I'll see you soon. Hopefully you'll be working for me before long. Take care."

It looks like the New Year is going to be amazing in more ways than one.

Chapter 7

Why is adulting so hard? It feels like Christmas was years ago, rather than like seven weeks. I haven't stopped.

"Well, I hope you have a nice evening with M," Mum says via FaceTime. I can tell she's annoyed with me that I've still not been home. How many times have I explained? Will has had me out every weekend meeting people from Gale-Feng-Paisley. He told me they're basically stealth interviews. Mum knows how much I want to work there.

I've met Mr. Feng, and did a Zoom with Mr. Paisley, as he lives in Canada. I've met various managers and the head of HR. It's all been nice Friday evening drinks, Saturday afternoon coffees, or Sunday brunches. I'm doing my best to impress.

It's been good fun, but Will says he has to play it carefully because they're coming to the end of the financial year, and he has to have full support if he's going to create a job especially for me.

I notice a message come in at the top of the screen.

Got all my ducks in a row, BUT... you should be warned, I'm a harsh boss. I expect all my empl...

"Please come back home soon. I want to talk to you face to face," Mum says.

I swipe the message away.

"Aren't we doing that now?"

She shakes her head, not having any of it. I know she misses me, but we can literally see each other, although for some reason Mum said she wanted to be funny, as it's my birthday, and put a filter on. So far she's been a shark, a drag queen, and she's now a horned ogre. Why she thought I'd find it funny I don't know, but she won't turn it off.

"You can always come here?" I remind her.

Her anger falls away, and for a split second, the ogre's sad. Her head tilts down, and the filter vanishes, but before I get to see Mum's face—the first FaceTime we've done in months—her head comes back up, and the filter is back.

"Maybe. Promise me you'll make time to come home soon? Right, I'm going for a lie down."

Mum's finished a lot of our calls recently telling me she's getting an early night. "Mum, it's only just gone six."

"It's a little lie down. I've had a busy few weeks, which is why I sent you money this year. I haven't had time to shop."

I don't mind money. £100 plus an extra £26 to match how old I am. Nice.

After Mum goes, I get ready. Will took me out for drinks last night, but I've kept tonight free, as M wanted to spend it with me. They've been super down since Jamaica. Being constantly misgendered will do that, but it has renewed their focus on saving for top surgery.

I suggested we stay in and make pizzas at mine. M told me their housemate said if they wanted to be a proud butch, they can. Without the need for surgery. M's tired of explaining. They now avoid her when she's in the flat.

It's going to be a good night I can feel it. All my housemates are out on romantic evenings. Zoe's meeting someone called Kay, who she met cherry picking. David's out with his boyfriend that I didn't even know he had. Even Jacinta's out. She met someone at the callcentre she works at. They're on a date, at a ghost hunting overnighter.

They all chipped in and got me a chunky, oversized snuggly hoody, because they all have one and felt sorry for me. It's toasty.

I lay out pizza bases, toppings, and a stupid amount of cheese for M. I'd never seen anyone munch a block of cheese until I witnessed them do it. Chaos.

As the doorbell goes, my shoulders drop.

"Happy birthday!"

They've casually rocked up in black jeans, tight white T-shirt, and baseball cap, like they've stepped out of a sexy American soap. Would a binder make me look this good? Even the weight they've put on since starting... what do they call it now? *AntiCIStamines*! Looks good on them. Apparently, calling it testosterone isn't cool. They certainly wear it better on their arms than my chunky wings. The upside of M having a tough Christmas, was their parents felt bad and are paying for HRT privately.

"Have you been working out?" Our hug seems extra tight today.

"Downloaded this free app for swole arms. Impressed?"

Hell yeah, I am. "You can grate the cheese then. I've only done half a block and my arms are aching."

In the kitchen, we chat about work and uni, but it feels like we're wasting time on boring stuff. So I set us a challenge to make each-other's pizza. They make mine all meats and a bit of onion. I make theirs five cheeses, pepperoni, and a ton of chilli peppers.

I should have made this a harder challenge.

We sprawl out on the sofa, scoffing pizza and guzzling Strongbow straight out of the bottle. I'm relieved to see they have their usual smile on their face. When we swap a slice of pizza, and I have to take a huge swig of cider because my mouth is on fire, all M does is laugh at me, which sets me off. Why does this always happen?

Tipsy and full, we listen to music on their phone. They've made me a playlist of my favourite songs, although they did start with *All I Want for Christmas Is You* to wind me up.

This is nice. M's lying back on the arm-rest, their bare feet on my lap.

I really want to tickle them, but they look so content. I don't want to spoil that.

I glance at my phone. Will's message!

Got all my ducks in a row, BUT... you should be warned, I'm a harsh boss. I expect all my employees to be team

*players, and to stick to the vision me
and the other owners have. Does that
sound like you?*

I glance over at M, their eyes are shut. Their little tummy rising up and down is adorable.
I text back.

Yes. Of course

I watch the bubbles appear, disappear, appear again, and the message comes through.

*I have a suggestion for a TikTok. I
noticed you're barely a thousand off
20k and I know what might get you
over that hurdle quickly. Interested?*

Absolutely!!!

*You have to do something to get
people frantically interacting.
Something spicy.*

Like what?

M moves their feet, and sits up beside me. I put my phone away.
Why are they staring at my chin?
"What? If it's pizza, it's obviously the bit I was saving."
I thought that would get a laugh, but they don't even

smile.

I sit up. "What's wrong?"

"Nothing. It's... can I?" They reach a hand to my face. I don't know what they're doing, but I nod.

They gently rub a finger over my stubble. It makes me want to laugh, but they're serious.

"What's it feel like?"

"It tickles a bit."

"No, to have."

"Annoying to shave it every day for work. Sometimes I get ingrown hairs and they hurt. Why?"

They go super quiet. I can't tell if they're sad or what.

"M?"

"Thought I might have enough boy juice for some stubble of my own by now."

M leans in for a closer look. My tummy tingles. Must be those chillies.

"I've started noticing facial hair recently. I hope when I get mine, it looks as good as yours does. Never used to like it, but I kissed this guy on New Year's Eve, who had a beard, and it felt strangely pleasant."

What! Wait? "A guy?"

M shrugs. "Now the lesbian label has gone, the plus is evolving. I mean, I've always found some men attractive, just never cishet men."

Why are they only telling me about the kiss now?

What does it mean?

"You've gone quiet. Tired?" they ask.

"Nope. I'm fine." Absolutely fine. I either need to drink more cider, or less.

They do a little shiver. I realise the heating went off ages ago.

"Come here." They lean into me as I put my arms around them.

"Sucks sometimes being me, you know?"

"I don't think you suck."

They elbow me in my tummy. Softly. "Being me, I said."

"How?" I take their hand. Squeeze it tight. They squeeze back tighter. Wow, they're strong.

"I feel like I've got myself to the station. Got on the train. Waved goodbye, but now I've no idea where I'm going. That make sense?"

Not really. "Sort of."

"I know I'm not a girl. I know I'm not cis. But right now I don't feel... I know loads of trans people. Had relationships with two trans women, and both of them knew who they were always meant to be. I've never had that." They pause and whisper, "Sometimes I don't feel like I'm trans enough." They take a stuttered breath.

"You're exactly who you're meant to be."

"So many trans people struggle with their identity. For ages. I didn't even have any gender dysphoria, until I tried the binder. I feel like I'm doing it all wrong."

I don't know what to say, but I have to say something. "I think you're brilliant. What you're doing is—"

"Don't say brave, or Doc help me, I'll smack you."

Yes! They're smiling again.

"I wasn't going to say brave, I was going to say what you're doing is showing yourself love. And you know what the greatest love of all is, don't you?"

"You know all about self-love, your housemates told me."

Cheeky bugger.

"S'not all bad," they continue. "My troll's done one. Either he's finally got banned, or found a new hobby."

We talk for a bit about their GoFundMe. They set it up on January 1st for their surgery fees, which cost how much?! They tell me it's going slowly.

"Soz again for not doing pressies, I need to save."

"I get it. Don't worry. I love this playlist."

They give me a soppy smile. "I'm enough of a present though, no?"

Yeah, they're drunk.

This silence is supes awkward.

"Oh, you'll like this." They tell me they've been tracking the changes in their voice and show me six weeks' worth of them saying, "*Roads? Where we're going, we don't need roads,*" on their phone.

"A *Back to the Future* quote? Shock."

M sticks their tongue out.

The first one is their old voice. I don't notice much difference in the next few, but slowly their voice gets a little deeper. It's pretty cool.

"You can laugh you know. It's hilarious. Like this first one, I'm a total she/her. By this one a few weeks later you can hear me slipping into they/them. I'm on track to be a he/him by Pride."

"You should put this on TikTok," I say.

Their face says it all. They won't.

One of my favourite *Self Esteem* songs comes on. We

stand up, dance, and sing it together.

Their usual orange-vanilla fragrance has something different to it today. Like a body odour smell, but not a horrible one. It's nice. Is that weird?

I'm sweating now. This fluffy hoody is warm.

Oh. Will has replied. His message comes with the happy devil emoji.

Something to force people to stop and laugh. Maybe a video about hands, or Adam's apples? Or maybe clothing choices of trans women. Or deep voices! You got something like that?

That feels a bit... I put my phone away. M is sitting right beside me, talking about how they can't wait to finish uni, and find a new place to live. I'm listening to their voice, and I can hear the difference now. It's sort of gruff, with a little croak, and it's adorable.

Is there content Will might like, in this?

I still can't get over their arms, and how cute their little podge is.

Thinking about it, this would all be a lovely date, if it was a date, which it isn't.

It couldn't be. M isn't even into guys.

Though they did say...

That doesn't mean we...

Wait.

Chapter 8

"I'll be surprised if we can get a table. We should have booked."

Thanks, Ra. Super helpful. You're supposed to be nice to me. I mean, he's not wrong. I didn't want to commit to going out to eat around here or in town. Also, Maya found me on Facebook today (which we're both only on for family) and started chatting to me on Messenger. Then it was too late to book anywhere.

The downside of being born on Valentine's Day is it's impossible to get a table.

I would've preferred to stay in and get a takeaway, but Rahul insisted we go out for dinner. I didn't particularly want to have people gawping at two gays on a date together, but once Mum said she could invite Shaun and Jeremy round and make it a big family takeaway, I decided going out was the lesser of two evils.

As we walk towards the shopping centre, he tries to hold my hand. I pull away. I do not want to be hate crimed on my 25th.

"Awww. Sod anyone who has an opinion," he says with his brown puppy dog eyes and a fake pout. He's cute, but not that cute. I shake my head. "Fine. I'll walk ahead so nobody thinks we're together."

I'm almost mad, but he's got on those burgundy skinny jeans I like. He says they're not comfy, but his bum looks amazing in them. He's probably wearing them for me. He's re-dyed his hair light pink again, too. He's not afraid to stand out.

Then again, he didn't grow up in Ming. He's not had a lifetime of it shrinking him.

I can't deny he looks particularly hot today, and he's wearing one of his trademark chunky knits. I wish I could pull it off half as good as he does, all style and sophistication. A chunky jumper makes me look fatter than I am. Like a walking ball of wool. No thanks.

As we pass the bookies and the row of three boarded-up shops, I spot a couple of drunks sitting on a bench, watching us, whispering to each other.

"Gaylords," one of them shouts.

I hurry to catch up to Ra. I want to get away, but he's turned towards them. Fucking hell, Ra. Stop! He blows them a kiss. One of them downs his can of lager and lobs it at us, luckily his aim is way off. Ra gives them the middle finger and hurries to catch up with me.

"Why?" I ask.

"Fuck 'em."

My heart races, but they don't follow. Too drunk, I assume. We approach the first of the two restaurants we have around here. A Chinese, which does a decent takeaway, but I've never been inside. Not today either. There's about six couples waiting for tables.

"Deb's it is," Ra says, as we head around the corner.

Everyone in Ming has been to Deb's and Tony's Pizzeria. It's always busy, but you can usually get a table.

Except tonight. All the windows are boarded up. A note says: *Place ransacked (again). Closed until further notice. Sorry, Deb & Tone xx*

"That's that," I say. Actually, I'll be glad to go home.

"I'm not giving up yet, Bennita," he says, with an enigmatic smile.

He leads me up the main road, towards the chippy. I forgot it has a little dining area.

As we approach it, we both stop and stare at the wall where the steps lead up above the chippy to the flats. We both hold our breath.

There's been graffiti here for decades. The first time I became aware of it was in Year 5. It's always some poor local guy's full name, followed by *is a faggot.* Through the years, the name has changed, but *is a faggot* has remained. The council used to cover it up, but it always came back. So they stopped.

We're safe. It's not either of us today.

My name appeared on there in Year 10. Rahul's two years ago, the week after we got together. He told me he ignored it until it changed. I spent the four days mine was up, anxious. I couldn't go to school because I was on the toilet every twenty minutes. Mum panicked and rang the emergency doctor, but someone told her, probably Shaun, about the graffiti.

It's a funny memory now, because she came out here with a tin of leftover white emulsion and painted over it. Then argued with a policewoman when she was caught.

My name hasn't been up since.

Good, because it made me the centre of a shit-storm of bullying, which I'm not thinking about today, thank you.

In the chippy, we take the last table. There are ten in total. All of them, except ours and one other, have opposite-sex couples at them. The only one that doesn't is a mum and three kids. Every table looks at us as Rahul pulls out my chair for me.

"Don't," I mutter under my breath.

He shrugs and sits. I'm mortified. I definitely hear laughter from the table in the far corner. I went to school with them. I cannot remember their names though. I don't give them the benefit of looking.

Instead, I message Maya and tell her all about it. She tells me I need to extra-enjoy my birthday meal to spite them. Easier said than done when the sound of one of their voices is giving me flashbacks to being called homophobic slurs at every opportunity.

Oh yeah. Maya has asked me to use the occasional *they* now.

"Bennita? I said should we get that?"

Ra points to the specials board.

It's almost as if everyone stops eating.

The room goes quiet.

I see people looking at us, but Ra is paying them no attention. He's reading about the Lovebird Special: An extra large fish, large chips, and any two sides to share.

I glance back at Maya's message. Ordering this would be a good way to extra-enjoy my birthday, I guess, but the thought of ordering it, let alone eating it together, is making me lose my appetite.

"I don't fancy fish," I lie, and order battered sausage and chips. He gets fish and chips.

I message Maya what I've ordered, but Ra is giving me a weird look.

"What?"

"Please put your phone away."

Ugh. Fine.

"Last time I ate in here, I was 21. Came with my girlfriend, Mandip."

"Ah. Back when you were straight."

He stares at me. "I wasn't straight then, like I'm not gay now. Please, babe."

"It was a joke. Soz if you were offended. Honestly, bisexuals are as bad as vegans, always telling you... *actually, I'm a vegan* or *actually, I'm a bisexual.*"

Ra glares at me. Shit, I've done it now.

I reach across the table and take his hand. His eyes widen. This has shocked him. He did not expect this. It's unprecedented.

He grins. I'm forgiven. He brings my hand close to his mouth, but I pull away before he can kiss it. That's one step too far.

I keep Maya updated as Ra goes to the toilet. They've dared me to kiss him in public. I mean, I would, but my breath smells like battered sausage now. I won't be nice to kiss.

An hour later, on the way home, it's chucking it down. We leg it back to his, as a bus drives through a puddle.

We're soaked.

It's his favourite jumper. Why is he laughing?

He takes my hands and pulls me close. He's taller than me, so as he dips his head, I know what this is leading to.

In the middle of the street, where anybody could see us?

My heart stops.

Not because it's super romantic, but because there's a group of testosteroney-looking lads watching us.

I step back.

He pulls me closer.

Our eyes lock, and this romcom moment would be one hundred percent better if it was anywhere else but Ming.

He kisses me anyway.

"Stop," I say through gritted teeth, and hurry up the street before I get the shit kicked out of me.

"Benny, what is wrong with you?" Rahul catches up with me.

"You know what's wrong. Why would you even do that?"

"Fuck sake, this again?" He storms off.

Erm, nope.

"You could've waited to kiss me at yours. We don't have to flaunt it in the street."

"I don't flaunt anything," he says, rolling his eyes.

I remind him of the time we went bowling, two weeks ago, where he wore his *Bi AF* T-shirt.

"How is that flaunting? I'm proud of myself."

"Can we save the PDA for later?"

"We barely show private displays of affection, let alone public ones."

I have no idea what he's talking about. I'm over at his all the time, or him mine. So what if I don't want to be cuddling on the sofa watching TV all the time, or holding hands across the table as we eat tea. Does that make me a bad person? No.

"We are intimate all the time."

Rahul glances around and lowers his voice. "You've barely wanted to have sex since Christmas, or spend time with me. You prefer hanging out alone now."

I would explain I've been trying to get my follower count up, but in the two months since I did my first video, I'm barely at 300 followers. He wouldn't understand, which is exactly why I haven't told him about any of it.

"That's not just on me," I say, because it's true.

He looks at me sharply, frowns, then laughs. "Not the New Year's thing again?"

Yeah, funny. I barely saw him between Christmas and New Year. He was with his family, and I was with mine. That's fine, we agreed to that. I chilled at home with Mum, and of course Shaun and Jeremy, and like everyone does during Betwixmas, we ate and drank.

So I felt like absolute shit when the first thing he said to me when we got together on New Year's Eve was, *"bloody hell, did you eat the partridge in a pear tree too?"* We don't all have a metabolism like him, able to eat anything and not put on weight. I wish I was like that, but I'm not.

"I apologised. I made a mistake and I admitted that. Have I ever said anything like that again since? No. Funny how it never works both ways with you, or did you forget what you did on the way back from Tenerife last year?"

I pull a face. All I did, and this was after I had asked him to stop hugging me in the baggage scanner queue, in front of everyone, including those stags, was joke that his bag was ticking.

"That's not the same."

His face flashes. "Really? Was it a coincidence my bag had to be checked by hand, and I was called into the body scanner and was told to remain in there for almost ten minutes?"

"I said sorry."

"Actually, you didn't."

"Fine. We're both terrible people. But blaming me for it all isn't fair."

"Do you want to be with me? You're not interested in going anywhere, or doing anything. You say you want to get out of this hell-hole, but you're making no moves to do so. You're stuck in a job you hate. Then when your mum gets on your nerves, for no reason, I might add, she waits on you hand and foot, you take all that out on me."

"I don't."

"We used to talk stuff out, but not so much in the past six months, and even less since you met this Maya person."

"I've told you she's a girl."

"What does that matter? You obviously have some kind of feelings for her, even if it's a deep friendship. We used to be like that."

"She's a girl, and I'm gay."

"You say you're gay, but you're too scared to show it, or

be proud of it, and I'm sick of it."

"Well, perhaps you should be a bit nicer to me?"

"And perhaps you should grow up. You're embarrassed to be with me. Fine, don't be with me. You're too immature to be in a relationship. Perhaps Maya can teach you how to be a better friend. I'm not doing it anymore."

My heart pounds in my chest. Shit, what have I done? I put my right hand over my heart and listen as it beats. BAMBAMBAMBAMBAM. I try to calm down. He can't be saying what I think he's saying, can he? I tap my little finger over my heart. Taptaptap. Taptaptap.

"Look. Sorry, yeah? It's not that bad."

"It is. We're done." He pauses as though he wants to say something else, then turns and walks away.

How dare he?! Fuck him then. I'd rather be with someone who wants to spend time with me, without me having to change. Someone who gets my sense of humour, and doesn't force me to do things that make me uncomfortable.

I should've known that person wouldn't be here in Ming.

I need to get out of this place.

Chapter 9

"If I didn't know better, I'd think you had a crush on her." Will winks.

I remind him, M is transitioning and isn't a girl.

"Or maybe you're secretly straight," he laughs.

I try and ignore the complexities of that. "I could be bi."

"Don't say that," he mock gasps, "you know what happened to my friend, Clive."

"Who's Clive?"

"Exactly. He chose his side, and went back to straightsville. It's clear I need to introduce you to some younger gays, because you're getting desperate, and that's confusing you about your feelings."

All I was doing was telling him about my night last week with M, as it was the inspiration behind my most recent video.

"We'll have to start meeting somewhere else otherwise. This is The Gay village. There's plenty of other places for straights."

I take the ribbing with a smile. but I don't know why, it's not like anything happened. M went home at midnight because they were on an early the next day. Maybe I should stop talking about M in front of Will in future?

Is he right about my feelings getting confused though?

"I bring good news, anyway. First, I want to say your content has been on fire recently. I love the new series."

I started a new series called, *You know you're gay when...* doing daft gay things, like, *You know you're gay when... you can't leave the house without glitter*, *...when you get turned on by a bottle of Abercrombie & Fitch Fierce*, and *...when you immediately stop scrolling the moment you see a pair of grey joggers*.

The glitter one was great fun, although Jacinta made me hoover the landing three times. Funny, she never questioned what I was doing.

I also did, *You know you're a lesbian when the smallest overnight bag you have is a suitcase*, plus a few others about tools.

The bisexual ones were mostly film and TV based, like, *You know you're bi when you're obsessed with The Mummy*.

"When are you going to do a trans one?" Will says.

"When I think of something to do."

"You're overthinking it. Your followers want to be entertained, that's why they flock to you. Make people laugh. Be provocative, nobody knows it's you. Something like, *You know you're trans when the signs on the toilet door mean nothing to you*. Or, *when you're an athlete but you're not winning with the men's team*."

He's laughing, but I'm feeling a bit awkward. "Maybe."

"Lighten up, Ben. It's a silly TikTok joke. Entertain your audience. I'm your audience and I love to be entertained by you. I loved the one you did about transgenders changing voices. I told you it would push you over 20k."

I guess so. I nod.

"You proved to me what a team player you are, and I'm a man of my word, so... Ah here she is."

He turns as Noelle, the head of HR at GFP, comes over.

"Shall we tell him the good news?" he says.

She pulls out a stack of papers.

Is this real?

"This is your official offer of employment. Have a read, and if you're happy to accept, all you have to do is sign."

I've already turned to the last page and taken the pen Will offers me, before Noelle even finishes her sentence.

My insides bubble like the champagne Will orders. I'm finally going to be working at my dream job. M's going to be buzzing for me. I best tell Mum too.

As Will toasts me, I glance at the contract. Pretty much the same stuff as I'm doing at my current job. Exact same pay too.

"When do I start?"

"That all depends on Mr. Gale." Noelle takes both signed contracts, passes them to Will.

"Now, now, Noelle. You know I don't like to do business at the weekend. Leave them on my desk. I'll get to them next week."

She gives him a huge smile, which comes across more as a sneer, but maybe that's her face. I shouldn't say she's got resting bitch face, as she has just brought my contract. Still, it's true.

As she leaves, Will watches my recent TikTok, laughing all the way through.

It's me saying the phrase, *Thanks for watching, don't forget to follow*, over and over again. Starting with me in a long wig, makeup, and speaking in a chipmunk voice, the voice gradually getting deeper, the wig getting shorter, and the makeup coming off.

I reversed it for the trans femme one.

They got hundreds of comments. Will has told me to stop reading them so I'm not distracted, which is fair because I'm trying to reply to everyone but I'm falling behind.

"Thanks again for all your help. I can't wait to start at GFP, though I've got to give four weeks' notice at my current job so..." He doesn't take the hint. He continues to praise my video.

"I can't afford to be out of work. When should I hand my notice in?"

"Tell me what new content ideas you've got."

I tell him about an idea I've got for gays, lesbians, and bisexuals playing sports.

He laughs. "I love it. You doing a trans version too?"

"I'm not sure."

"You should. You need to spice things up a bit. Keep hooking your audience in. We're aiming for 50k! You've got to keep the momentum going, but you know that."

"I'll think about it."

"Don't think too long. I've got a busy few weeks coming up. Not sure I'll have time to be messing with new contracts.

Unless something were to help take my mind away from business. Get me laughing. I do things much faster when I'm in a good mood. Do you know what I mean?"

"Did you not think the voice one was good enough? I thought that's why Noelle was here earlier?"

He looks me dead in the eye, his smile gone. "It was somewhat amusing. I now you've got more in you. Show me. I want people at my company who take risks. People who don't question a vision, when those higher up present them with it. People who respect my authority. Do you respect me, Ben?"

"Of course I do."

"That's what I like to hear. You know, there's lots of talk about trans people in sports. Could be a fun TikTok. Don't be boring like the others talking about it. Have your trans videos be about winning. Give me something like that, and you'll be handing in your resignation at your job in no time."

***

Mum's smaller, not just thinner. She's wearing makeup too. She hardly ever does.

I thought she'd run straight out to the taxi as I pull up outside home, but she waits at the door. She won't let me past without a hug. I'm sure my arms didn't fit around her this easily before I left.

She squeezes me so tight, for so long, she's exhausted when she lets go. She asks me to put the kettle on as she needs to sit down.

It's weird being back. I've been super busy working my final four weeks, plus the week of coming up with the perfect TikTok for Will. The slow-and-sleepiness of Ming takes me by surprise.

Will did want me to start at GFP straight away, but ending my old job and starting GFP fell over Easter.

I didn't think me coming home would make Mum this upset. She's already cried twice, and keeps staring at me as though I might vanish at any moment.

I fall into my pre-Manchester routine quite quickly. It's nice having snacks, although I've noticed Mum seems to have loads of organic, healthy food in. Maybe that's why she seems thinner? Still, there's plenty of Jaffa Cakes, and crisps, and it's nice not having to do my own washing for a change. She did say I could bring it home.

Mum wants me to sit with her, but she's watching a terrible show about healthy living.

I head to my room. I'm surprised she hasn't turned it into a bedroom for Shaun with the amount of times she's told me he's stayed over.

I spend the day thinking up new content ideas. Will has been suggesting more and more recently, especially after my trans sport one. I got a pair of inflatable boobs for the trans woman character, and as per Will's request, it was my character doing competitive swimming and winning.

It caused loads of debate. Loads stitched or duetted it, but Will told me I should stop watching those, nor reply to comments.

"You don't need to anymore, your followers are flocking in," he said at our meeting last week. He's not wrong. I'm

pretty sure that video was what got me over 25k.

It took me ages to get my first 5k. Literally months, even after losing my job and having more time to make content.

My notice was manic. I had loads of projects to finish, so I duetted my old content with reactions from other members of the community. I did lesbians reacting to the gay and bi ones, and vice versa. They've been surprisingly popular, though they didn't get even half the interaction of the trans swimming one.

My fave was the one where I was a bisexual, watching the gay Christmas wrapping one. I made my bi character so frustrated that he couldn't do it, being bi, that he grabbed a gay-male flag and ripped it up in anger.

Tens of thousands found that funny. To be honest I didn't even know there was a gay male flag until Will told me about it.

He thinks I'll get the golden 50k before the end of the year, and get paid to do content straight away.

I scroll TikTok on my own bed. Bliss. Watching the randomness of the content, I realise Will is right, it is just fun, not to be taken seriously. That said, I did find a new way to hack my ironing time, loads of new recipes, and a cool TV show.

My own video with the trans voice changes appears. It reminds me of the last few videos M has sent me. Their slightly-croaky-getting-deeper-and-super-cute voice makes me smile every time I listen to it. Their face has changed a little in the last month too, and even though they've been getting a few spots, which M tells me are ingrowing hairs they wish would grow outwards, they still look good.

I haven't had one this week?

Oh yeah, their grandparents are over for Easter. M has been sad in the run-up to it, so I've tried to meet them every day after my work, before they start their Tesco shift. They were only little ten-minute catch ups, but I've appreciated every minute.

Hours go by as I scroll. Mum knocks on my door about 7pm. I go find something in the freezer for tea, because she's eating weird soup she found the recipe for in a Facebook group.

Sitting down on the sofa she keeps asking if I'm OK. I keep telling her I am.

"You can talk to me about anything," she says, as she finishes her awful-looking soup, puts it down and takes my hand. "You can solve any problem with little steps."

"I'm fine, Mum. What's this diet all about?"

"Don't change the subject. You might be an adult, but you'll always be my little presh-pots, and I know when something is wrong."

"I'm OK. I'll be at my dream job next week."

"With this Will person? Are you still happy with how it's going with him?"

Why would she even ask that? I pull a face and nod.

"I just want you to be careful. I know you've been spending a lot of time with him and—"

"Mum. He's my mentor, nothing more. He's well respected in the industry, and everyone in Manchester knows him. I'm lucky he's mentoring me. Can we drop it?"

She pats my hand and smiles, then turns to watch TV as her soaps come on. She's asleep before Corrie has even finished, which is unlike her.

She wakes up and takes herself to bed. I stay up bingeing Netflix in peace and quiet, without anybody demanding it's their TV time.

In bed, I text M. They're upset, considering leaving X. Their troll has come back with a vengeance, telling M no matter how much male hormones *she* took, *she'd* never be a real man and should stop confusing gay men with lies.

I stay up texting until I'm satisfied they're OK.

I sleep in late the next day. It's comfy, quiet, and I wake up to the smell of bacon cooking.

I find Mum in the kitchen, but she's letting the bacon burn. She apologises. We eat our bacon butties on our ancient sofa, with a big cup of tea each. I finish Mum's butty because she says she's not hungry.

"I've got stuff to do in my room." I take the plates to the kitchen sink.

"Benny, have you got a second?"

"Will this take long?"

"No, love. I just need to tell you something."

My mum is so dramatic. I return.

I wait for her to talk. Instead she grabs a Jammy Dodger, dunks it in her tea, then stares into space. As she brings the dodger to eat, it falls off into her tea. She puts the tea down and bursts into tears.

What the fuck?

I've seen her cry many times, like when we went to watch *Mamma Mia*, at Shaun's wedding, and pretty much every Christmas when she gets the sherry out and tells everyone it's been another lovely day.

This feels different. My heart needs to slow down.

She buries her head in her hands, shaking with sobs. I'm getting scared now.

At last, she takes a deep breath and says, "I'm sorry lovey, I'm fine, I'm OK. Really I am."

I put my tea down and she grabs both of my hands. So fast. I don't even see her do it. They're wet with tears.

I try to say, "Mum," but my voice cracks, which starts her crying again. This isn't good, is it?

"I've been seeing a doctor."

No, this isn't good at all.

"But don't worry, they caught it. I'm going to beat this."

Everything stops.

In a single moment that feels like hours, I am frozen solid in time. My hands in my mum's. Tears fixed on our faces. Her eyes looking into mine.

And those words repeating over and over.

I'm going to beat this.
I'm going to beat this.
I'm going to beat this.

Chapter 10

I've had to get out of the house. Mum is excessively positive that her cancer has been caught early. Shaun accompanies her to every chemo session. They've been going well.

She's all I've got. I need to stop thinking about what I'd do if I lost her, but it's too quiet around here. I need to be somewhere I can escape these thoughts. Why didn't she tell me sooner? She's known since November!

I leave the house and wander around, but this hell-hole isn't helping. So, as a bus approaches, I hail it. I almost ask for a ticket to Piccadilly Gardens out of habit.

I go on TikTok. Scroll. Scroll. Scroll. I'm surprised when the bus reaches its final destination.

The shopping centre looks small now compared to the Arndale Centre, but it's loud and busy. Perfect.

I float aimlessly in and out of shops, with windows painted with flowers, or bunnies with eggs. They don't cheer me up.

I pause by the fountain. When I was little, Mum would always give me a penny to drop in for a wish.

I only have a few pound coins, my emergency bus money in case my card doesn't work. Should I waste a quid, seeing as none of my other wishes ever came true?

As I decide, I see someone who makes the hurricane in my stomach fade away.

It's M. Except it isn't.

It's not that they're wearing a skirt, a headscarf, or even make-up. It's the misery on their face. I feel like I've entered a parallel universe. This is not my M.

"Hey," I shout.

A surprised smile lights up their face. It vanishes quickly.

"This is Benny, my friend from Manchester. Benny, this is Mum and Dad, you met at the Christmas party briefly remember? Gammie and Popsy Mendoza."

I hadn't even noticed them. M's dad stands out in his jeans and jumper. Their mum and Gammie both wear colourful traditional dress. M's Popsy has colourful trousers, and a top to match his wife. I realise now, M is also in traditional clothing. I can't stop looking.

M's Dad shakes my hand, but I'm hugged by M's mum and Gammie. They're chatting a mile a minute, but I do catch something about M telling them I'm a good friend.

"I don't know what I'd do without M, to be honest."

M and their parents all hold their breath. Popsy's confused. Gammie gives me a look, like a headteacher gives to a badly behaved student.

"Her name is Maya, thank you."

"No. Their name is M," I say, but I instantly know I've done wrong. Not because the grandparents are taken aback, not because Mum and Dad seem worried, but because M is angry. At me.

"You've not even commented on her new dress." Gammie makes a noise that sounds like a tut, but scarier.

"I've never seen them wear a dress before."

M drags me aside. I can hear Gammie muttering about me being rude.

"I've told you about this." M's whispering but somehow still shouting. "I'm not out to my grandparents. Not yet anyway. It's easier this way."

Oh, yeah. "But you're having surgery soon, and you're on T."

That's the wrong thing to say. M glares at me. It's weird seeing this person so... girly, yet I know that's not at all who they are. This close, I also notice they've shaved the facial hair they've been so proud to sprout.

"I'll do it when I'm ready. Popsy has memory problems, and Gammie doesn't get it. Things are very different where they're from. You need to apologise."

"Why?"

"And call me Maya, and use she in front of them please. Can you at least do that?"

My head is spinning. I thought after our texting last night, they were feeling good.

I glance over. M's mum looks like she's calming the grandparents down.

"Do they even know you're qu... lesbian plus?" M looks down. I guess not. "I didn't realise it was like this for you."

"Why would you. You have it easy."

"Easy?"

"Benny, you're a white cis gay guy. Of course it's easier. I wish I was as privileged as you."

Privileged? I grew up in a tiny rented bungalow, in the worst part of Ming. I remember times as a kid, where Mum would make a game of us wrapping up in the lounge, with all the duvets, under candle-light, while we played board games. It was always fun. I know now those days were when she didn't have any money for the electricity meter. So yeah, what privilege?

Then again, the moment I came out, and I guess I have Shaun to thank for this, she was at the library reading queer books, or googling or mining Shaun for all the info she could about LGBTQ+ rights and history.

Ugh. I don't know if I'm annoyed or sad for M. Am I supposed to say Maya again? I really want to hug them. Her? Them?

"Just go before it gets any worse, I'll tell them you said sorry." They storm back to their family before I can reach out to comfort them.

I don't want to be here anymore.

On the bus ride home, I keep replaying the conversation with M over in my mind. Why do pronouns have to be stupid?

The moment I get home, I'm coaxed into the lounge by Mum. Shaun's here. They've got the gin open.

"Your mum's going to be OK, you know," Shaun says, before asking if I'm going to join them for whatever Netflix show they've been watching all week. They're already a season in. No thanks.

Back in my room, I feel like a teenager again. Loads of feelings, nowhere to let them out. I normally message M when I'm like this.

I momentarily consider re-installing Grindr, but to be honest, I do not want to even know what kind of gays are around here. Knowing my luck, it will be an ex-teacher.

My phone buzzes. I grab it quick in the hope it's M. Everything is going to be OK.

It's Will.

Fancy meeting for a drink?
Can't. At home, having a terrible day

He phones me straight away. "What happened?"

I tell him about Mum.

He says my mum has done such a wonderful job with me, it's only natural I'd be worried. "I never had that kind of relationship with either of my parents, even before I came out. You're unusually lucky, Ben. I'm sorry to hear about your mother. I wish I had what you two have, but I don't. Never will."

I feel bad this has brought up feelings for Will. I need to change the subject. Before I can stop myself, the stuff with M falls out of my mouth. "...I thought I was doing the right thing, but I'd forgotten what it's like with their grandparents. Now I'm sad I made them feel bad."

"You made the grandparents feel bad?"

"No, I mean M."

"See how that gets confusing? Seems she finally accepts

that too, as she's told you to use real pronouns now. You're not in the wrong, Ben."

"I don't think—"

"Did she even ask about you?"

"No."

"There you go. You sound like you're a good friend, not sure it's reciprocated. You did nothing wrong. You had nothing to apologise for."

"I should have, though."

"No. Never say you're sorry when you're in the right. You're going through something terrible. Maya didn't even ask. Cancer is no joke is it?"

"My mum will be alright."

"Let me know if she needs a specialist. I know a lot of people. I've always got your back, Ben. That's what real friends do. All this crap about pronouns and changing sex is so unimportant compared to things like this. You need to be there for your mother. No more getting distracted by nonsense. That's how a real man behaves."

I feel even worse now I've had to be told off by Will.

"Nobody is going to get anywhere, if we can't decide on who we are and stick to it. Your friend made a mockery of herself and those stupid bloody pronouns today. You're going through something horrible, much worse than having family from a backward country. I'm proud of you for not apologising. You've every right to be angry."

"I just find it all a bit confusing sometimes."

"Then channel that. Those are legitimate feelings. You know what to do with your feelings don't you? Are you angry? You should be!"

Actually, I hadn't realised how angry I was, until now.

"I feel bad for my friend too, though."

"After what she did today? I wouldn't. Make this a learning opportunity about who your true friends are. Then do something creative with it."

"I don't want to do an angry TikTok."

"Take that hurt your so-called friend has made you feel, and do something entertaining. Turn it on its head. Be your unique and funny self. 50k is getting closer. I wouldn't be surprised if you had people asking to do collabs the moment you reach it."

"I don't know what to do, though."

"I do."

An hour later, my new video is finished.

Will zoomed with me, and walked me through his whole plan—silly actions for all the different real, *"and made-up pronouns."*

For *he/him* I pull my stomach in and show off my guns. I'll edit them bigger, of course. For *she/her* I sit and cross a leg over the other, and fan myself with one hand. I stole a skirt, and a handbag from Mum to film with.

Will thought it would be funny to do a nod to *The Addams Family* with *it* pronouns, film myself in multiples for *they/them*, and then go off into the bizarre with *ze/zir, sie/hir*, and *ey/em*.

To end it, he told me I should make up some pronouns myself, and suggested I film a potato and say it's *tay/ter*.

I thought that was hilarious when I did it.

Now I'm wondering, "is this funny?"

"Turn the comments off if you're worried. At the very

least, stop reading and replying. Can you do that for me, from now on?"

"Sure. You don't think people will find it offensive?"

"You're taking it too seriously. Actually, I know a few trans people who say non-binary isn't real. If you heard the things they say about them, and non-medicalised trans people, it would blow your mind."

"Really?" I didn't even know Will knew any trans people.

"There's too many transtrenders these days."

That word makes me laugh.

"See, you agree don't you? Maybe you could do a transtrender video. I bet that would sky-rocket your followers."

"Maybe."

"I'll keep sharing the good stuff. You should consider making an X account with your TikTok name. Be easier that way. There's lots of people I like to share your content with. Anyway, get it posted. I've got the perfect person in mind I'm going to share it with."

By Sunday afternoon it's netted over thirty thousand likes, and over a thousand followers.

Still, no matter how good that's made me feel, and no comments to get bogged down with, I'm still sad about Mum.

I don't know what to do about my feelings with M, either.

Happy Easter I guess.

Chapter 11

Gale-Feng-Paisley is everything I ever wanted. My team is super encouraging. It helps that I'd already met them all through Will, at one time or another. I feel like I'm being challenged for the first time ever, plus there's loads of gays and lesbians. None in my team, unfortunately. They're all cishet men, and one cishet woman.

Mum has kept to her three calls a week. She constantly reminds me she's fine, that her chemo is going well, and she's beating it.

She always tells me she's beating it.

Will has been helpful, offering content ideas. He knows how worried I am about Mum. Some of his ideas for jokes go over my head a bit, so I've mostly done my usual silly gay, lesbian, and bisexual stuff, but I have done a few of his suggestions, including a *transtrender* one.

Tonight though, isn't about followers or content. I'm seeing M for the first time since the Easter thing two weeks ago.

I came back to Manchester feeling deflated, as if all the anger I had belonged to someone else. It was strange, but then I started my new job and my focus was elsewhere.

I knew I had to talk to M, but I didn't know what to say.

There was no way Will would give me any useful advice. He'd tell me to find better friends, not to back down because I'm not in the wrong.

I didn't want to pester Mum about it.

Then a few days later, M texted to say they regretted what happened. It lifted my mood and made everything else going on, fade away.

I told them I didn't mean to offend them, then told them about Mum.

We slowly found our groove again. We quickly got back into our regular night-texting. They've been busy with their final uni projects, and working any hours they can get.

Tonight we're hanging out, though, in a house full of LGBTQ+ people in queer fancy dress, for Jacinta's birthday. The vibe is heavy on the fun, but I've felt on edge the whole time.

Until now.

M has arrived, but I have a stomach full of wasps.

They stand at the door with a serious but sheepish look on their face, which I feel mirrors mine.

Everything goes silent. All I'm aware of is M, and my heartbeat.

I should run up to them, throw my arms around them, give them a big kiss.

I don't. That would be weird. Even if I wanted to. Which I don't. Even if they wanted me to. Which they don't.

"Seriously, you two," a purple unicorn says to me.

Her horn is white, her wig is black, and her tail is grey. Her nails are in the lesbian flag colours. I've never seen Jacinta sparkly.

She puts a hand on mine and M's shoulder, pushes us together. It's not easy in my costume.

I take in that vanillery-orangey-B.O scent.

Their arms go around me. I instantly do the same.

The wasps turn into butterflies.

I finally take in their white vest-top and moustache.

"Is that real?"

"Half and half," they say as they strut in their tight jeans. They've stuffed something down the front. I can't help but notice.

"This?" M says, following my gaze. "It's a kind of magic," they sing and pose.

"Freddie Mercury!"

M takes a bow. "What are you?"

With that, a pair of massive high heels comes down the stairs, a tight fitting dress, impressive cleavage for what is mostly makeup, and a huge hat made of flowers. "Where's my brick?" Mancunoir says.

This is the first time I've properly seen David in drag.

I let her grab me, and everyone finally understands I'm a brick, and not an odd-shaped butt-plug like a few people suggested.

As rehearsed, Mancunoir screams, "Pride is a Protest," and pushes me.

I run as fast as I can to a large piece of perspex being held by Unicorn Jacinta, and drag king Zoe. As I hit it, they pull it apart as though I've smashed it.

Everyone cheers. The party has officially started.

I don't let M leave my side all night. We chat, dance, drink, eat nibbles, and do a lot of laughing. There's many great costumes. Even though the theme was *Anything Queer*, people have gone all out.

Eventually, everyone ends up sitting in the lounge. There's people on the floor, squashed on the sofa, and stood in the doorway. M and I are wedged between the sofa and the wall.

"So I think I'm fully into guys now," M says.

"Oh, really?" I reply, but they don't answer because they're distracted.

Everyone in the lounge is talking about a big social media person, a trans woman, who has said some horrible stuff. I'm sure I've seen this woman on TikTok. Kathleen... something. She used to be a big name in TV, not an actor, but someone big. Lost their job when they transitioned. Found new fame online.

"Disgusting. What she's doing for my community is awful," says Jacinta's new girlfriend, who's dressed as the Babadook. "I have enough things to deal with outside of the trans community, but also dealing with stuff from within sets us back."

"She's racist," says a pink triangle.

"Have you heard what she said about trans people playing sport?" shouts Frank-N-Furter.

"She hates enbies too. Thinks pronouns are ridiculous," says a sheet of 1s and 0s.

Garnet's furious. "She might think she's the trans

gatekeeper, but she isn't."

"I hate how she uses the term, transtrender," Owl House's Luz shakes her head.

Sappho asks, "Why is she so supportive of she who shan't—"

"ENOUGH!" Jacinta stands. "This is a party and we're not queerphobicing ourselves tonight." She cranks the music up loud, coaxing everyone to dance. The room is full of laughter in seconds.

I can't get my pronoun and transtrender videos out of my mind now.

It was me with a shopping list, my green-screen background was a supermarket. I was buying things on a whim, like dresses, wigs, boobs, makeup, and saying things like, *I've been struggling getting opportunities at work, so today I'll be a transtrender woman.*

My follower count went up almost by a thousand within a few days. The comments and likes came in so fast, I didn't have time to look properly, what with my new job.

Of course Will loved it, he helped, but now I'm wondering if it was a good decision.

Squished together in our corner, M and I listen to the music before I say, "You're happy tonight, what's happened?"

At the same time as they say, "You're not yourself tonight, what's happened?"

"Let's go somewhere quieter," I say.

In my bedroom, we can still hear the party raging on, but with the door shut, at least we can sit side by side on the bed and hear each other.

"What's all that for?" They head to my desk. I realise I've left my ring light out, plus my box of props. Luckily, they're all under the green screen sheet.

I leap across the room like I've never moved before.

"Nothing." I grab the box before they can. "It's for work. I use it when I speak to Mum, which is why I'm sad." I don't know why I said that, but I've said it now.

Instantly, M wraps their arms around me.

I drop my head onto their shoulder. Their arms gently rub my back as I vent. I may have used Mum as an excuse, but I hadn't realised I'd been holding it all in.

Their fingers stroke my hair. It takes the worry about Mum away a little. Feeling better, I can't help but tell them about what Mum told me the other day.

Shaun had got her homemade edibles to help with her appetite, but she took one too many and had to phone Shaun, because she was convinced there was an elf hiding behind her TV.

M's laughter makes my head bounce up and down, which sets me off. This is what I want every day to be like.

"I'm pleased she's doing better now," M whispers.

"What do you mean, now?" I pull out of the hug.

"Mum told me the canteen had gone downhill, because your mum hadn't been in."

"She's only missed a couple of days." That's what Mum told me anyway.

"My mum will have got it wrong. Glad she's doing well."

I realise they haven't told me why they've been in such a good mood. I know most of their facial expressions now.

This smile means they've got amazing news.

"Your turn. Tell me." The energy radiating off them is like nothing I've ever seen from M before.

"Hit seventy-five percent."

"Of?"

They tap their chest. "I can have one and a half top surgeries."

M squees. I've never heard anyone squee in real life, but for M it's a sort of gruff-falsetto-but-voice-cracking yell, that also comes with a hip-wiggling dance, apparently.

This might be M's news, but watching them buzz is one of the best moments of my life. I wish I could bottle this up. I love M so much.

Wait. What? No! I mean as a friend, right. Right? Oh. My. God. "Let's go back and party."

By 5am there are sleeping people everywhere. I'm pleased I have my own room. M's staying over too. Surprisingly we've never had a sleepover at each other's places before.

"Grrrr. Nooooooo!"

I've got my pyjama bottoms on, but I'm topless as I hear M's exclamation. M's never seen me topless before. I feel a bit uncomfortable with them seeing me like this, because... well... it's not a great sight, but M is huffing and puffing in their new adorably-cute gruff voice.

I have to know what's wrong.

I turn. My arms covering my chest and stomach as much as I can. My cheeks burn.

They have a rucksack in one hand, in the other they're holding a tent ground-sheet. I don't understand.

"I thought this was a sleeping bag and airbed."

Now I realise M is topless too. Well, they've got their binder on, but no shirt. I can see how their curves have all but vanished. The muscles in their arms are taking shape.

Their angry face makes me snort-laugh. I quickly cover my face with my hands, exposing my chest and stomach.

A weird sensation takes over me. Normally I'd be self-conscious, but I'm not. It's like I've left my trembling body. It gives me such a euphoric buzz, I laugh even harder.

M looks at me. For a split second I see their eyes scan my topless body, then they burst out laughing too. That sets us off even harder.

Both of us, in pyjama bottoms, no tops, in hysterics.

We grab each other and sink slowly to the floor, screaming so much I get a knock on the door. Someone tells us to shut up, which sets us off again.

"You can't sleep on that."

"Where else can I sleep?"

It's laminate flooring. Good for keeping clean, but not for sleeping on. There's no other space left in the house.

Except for my single bed.

This is better than any late-night texting on our phones. Chatting next to each other about nothing, feels right. I want this moment to stay like this forever, because no matter what Will tells me about sexuality and *gender woo woo,* as he puts it, I can't help feeling the way I do.

I'm attracted to M.

And perhaps M is attracted to me? Maybe?

Should I say something? I don't want to make it weird, we've got such a good friendship. I can't be the only one feeling like what we've got could be something even better?

I tell you what, if M turns on their side to face me, I'll turn on my side to face them.

If they don't close their eyes, and look at me, I'll take that as a sign and say something.

I'm convinced M can sense my heartbeat, it's going extra fast. Surely it's going to make the bed bounce?

I'm on my back. They're on their back.

They fidget, but they don't turn their body.

But they do turn their head to look at me.

Sod the rules, I'm saying something.

"Social media's weird innit?" they say before I can even open my mouth.

"What?"

"Know my troll?"

I nod, how could I forget when it's given M a lot of anxiety.

"Well, days after Easter they replied to a tweet I did mentioning my pronoun journey, saying '*this you?*' and linked to a TikTok."

"What was it?"

"This sketch about pronouns. Have you heard of The Enigaymatic Mystery?"

Oh. I... they've... no but... what? What!? WHAT!?!?

"You OK?" they ask.

All I can do is nod.

I'm regretting drinking so much.

"Heard of them? They've got some content which I absolutely loved. Jokes about queers."

Oh my god, this is amazing.

"What you grinning at?" they ask. "It's thanks to that account my GoFundMe had such a rush. See, TERFs have some positives."

"There's something you should know about that account —" I say, then M's words finally reach my brain. "TERF?"

"Yep. They might be fooling the masses, they're not fooling me with their slow decent into transphobia."

"He's not that bad, is he?" I barely manage to say.

"He? Yeah, it's probably a guy to be fair. Surely you've seen his content getting slowly worse?"

I can't breath, let alone speak.

"I had a feeling other people might feel the same, so I shared that video they did about trans people playing sports. I also shared the pronouns one, and their recent transtrender bit. They got X outraged. Good for me, though, it got loads of people on my GoFundMe. To be honest, that's probably why it's done well."

"That's a good thing, no?"

"Funny," M says. "Know what you mean, though. Good for me, for sure. I honestly can't wait for my surgery."

"I'm super happy for you."

I sense M turn on their side to face me.

I can feel their eyes on me.

But my stomach is spinning. My head's in knots.

I roll away, whisper a dry-mouthed, "night," as I turn off the light.

I don't know how long I stay awake for, but my hangover kicks in, and M is snoring behind me, before I do.

Chapter 12

I wasn't sure my session was happening today, seeing as Will has been out of the office all morning. My whole team went with him and they were being super weird about it. I was told it was a conference, but they wouldn't give me any specific details.

I asked my manager if I could go. I'd love to attend stuff like that, but I was told Will had limited invites, "Maybe next time."

Then they all came back and Will called me up to his office. I'm pleased for the distraction to be honest. I've had M texting me about an anti-trans protest happening in St Anne's Square. M, loads of trans people, and allies have been trying to drown them out.

Will has taken his mentoring up a notch since I started six weeks ago. We now meet every Thursday in his office. He reviews my work and gives me suggestions based on his vast experience.

As is our routine now, he brings up my projects from the

cloud server where all my team's projects are stored. It always makes me nervous watching his face.

I'm currently working on three projects. One large one with the whole team, a small one I'm doing with one of my colleagues, and a tiny one I'm doing on my own. It's for a new donut-cookie hybrid shop in the city called *Lol's Donookies*. Super fun.

There's always lots of smiling. A few frowns. The odd pause whilst he gathers his thoughts. It made me nervous the first time, but I'm used to it now. I know his critiques are going to be useful.

"Hmmmm." He's weirdly more serious than normal. "I hear you're behind on this project?"

It's like the chair goes from under me. He's referring to the project I'm doing with the whole team. I'm responsible for the hashtags.

"Oh, only a little. The original hashtags didn't test well so I had to rethink—"

"Bit disappointing to hear that from your manager. I hope you're not resting on your laurels now you're in The Castle?"

The Castle is what everyone calls the office. I don't know why. I was told it on my first day and went with it. "I'm not. They were due in this morning and I've got the better ones now."

"I trust you. Just make sure you're not behind again. I've gone to great lengths to get you here. I put you with one of my best teams. Don't let me down."

I nod. I won't. I finished testing the new hashtags at lunchtime, which was twenty minutes ago. "Shall I send them over?"

"They can wait." He gives me pointers for the Donookie project, advising how the word choices can make more of an impact, and how the visuals might work better in a different colour palette.

It's amazing watching him work. He makes sure I understand his points every time. I've learned more with these sessions than I did in my whole degree.

By the time we're halfway through, I'm feeling good again. After he gives me chance to ask questions, he gets rid of the projects file, and opens up TikTok.

The sessions always end like this. It's almost a continuation of the mentoring, to be honest. He gives me feedback on my content, and tips for how I can make the next ones better.

"We have to keep 50k in mind. The pronoun one was magnificent. The transtrender one," he does a chef's kiss. "You should do more like those. What's that face for?"

How do I do this without bringing up M? "I just don't think they're funny."

"You were laughing when we came up with them. Correct me if I'm wrong, but you seemed to be enjoying yourself, and yes, I could tell even behind the mask. I know you, Ben."

I barely remember recording them. "I'm having doubts."

"You're smarter than this, Ben. Surely you've seen people talking about pronouns, and the idea of being non-binary? Actual trans people making fun of it too."

"It's just my closest..." Don't mention M. "At a party a few weeks—"

He makes me jump as he laughs. "Closest what? Come on, Ben, we both know that's not going anywhere. We need to find you a real man. You know Jeff in accounts is gay, right?"

I didn't know, but he always smiles at me when he passes.

"I'll put in a good word, shall I?" Will adds. I blush. "I don't mind playing cupid for two of my favourite gay men in The Castle. Right, we've got time left on this weekly hour I set aside just for you. My numerous project sign-offs can wait."

In our remaining time, he suggests a TikTok, with a gay and lesbian character, split screen, talking about how they're upping their numbers with straight men and women.

However, since the party, I've gone back to my old-style content, because I didn't like how M reacted to the new stuff, but they thought the old stuff was funny. "I'm working on a series with different members of the community, gays, lesbians, and bisexuals, ordering food online."

"How is that any funnier?"

"It's things like the lesbians hunting for vegan places. The gays only ordering at places with a five-star health rating. The bisexuals adding in notes to send the most attractive delivery person."

"If you've got a problem with my suggestions, tell me."

"I don't."

"What's wrong then? I'm spending hours of my time helping you. You'll be the one reaping the benefits when you reach fifty thousand, not me. What's the issue?"

How do I put into words this niggle in my stomach? "I'm

not sure if it's more hurtful than funny."

"Saying all lesbians are vegans, isn't a hurtful cliché?"

"No... It's... I don't think I'm doing anything but making light-hearted jokes."

"Then we both agree. You know I could be more hurtful, but that's not who I am. I could've been offended by some of your videos about gay men, but I saw the funny side. I always see the funny side."

"Oh. Should I stop making—"

"You're overthinking again. You enjoy your job, don't you?"

"Very much so."

"You trust my advice every week, don't you?"

"Absolutely."

"There you go. You trust me. I trust you. How many followers do you have now? Is it twenty-eight or twenty-nine thousand? Let's see. Ah, twenty-nine-point six. What we need is something big to get people interacting. What transgender content have you seen recently?"

I pause. My *For You* content has been in flux recently. It was always fellow queers full of queer joy, but recently I've had a lot of anti-trans stuff, and angry gays and lesbians.

"I don't really want to do anti-trans stuff."

Will frowns. "You don't think I'm anti-trans, do you? You know I'm not. I don't have any problems with the trans community."

It's nice to hear this, but it makes me even more confused about the content he suggests. If M thinks it's bad, what does that mean? Plus they liked my other stuff, they said it was funny didn't they! Ugh, why does everything have to be complicated?

He's looking impatient.

"There is something I've seen recently. Do you remember that celeb who transitioned? Her name is Kathleen? Maybe there's something I could do about that, unless you think it's problematic?"

"How many more times, Ben. I have no problems with transgenders, but when it comes to gays and lesbians..." He curls his fingers in, leaving two, as though he's going to flip me the V. Instead he turns his hand to the side, and snips his fingers like scissors up into the air. "Tell me more about your idea, I'm on tenterhooks."

I want this to be a good one, because I want to take a bit of time away from his ideas.

What should I suggest? Everyone at the party disliked her. Even M said that Kathleen was a bad person and deserves all the hate she's getting.

Or maybe they said all the criticism she's getting?

Maybe there's a happy medium here. "I think she'd make a good character to parody. Loads of the LGBTQ plus community dislike her."

I see him grimace for a second as I say TQ plus. I forgot.

He's full of smiles again. "I love it."

"I've got some inflatable boobs. If I find a wig like her actual hair, it could be funny?"

"Say no more. I'm going to order you one. Ben, this is brilliant. You never cease to amaze me. This idea is inspired, like all your work this week. Keep it up. You'll be running your own team in no time."

At home that evening, an Amazon parcel arrives with the

wig. A fancy silicone breast plate arrives the next day.

Over the weekend I record a few sketches of me parodying Kathleen's hate of the homeless, her odd stance on trans people in sport, and all the things she said about poor people. I decide to leave out her racism though.

My homeless one goes viral before I go back to work on the Monday. My follower count goes up to 31k.

Chapter 13

I can't believe I'm getting a lecture from my boss, on a Monday, over this. I hate this job. Could I quit my job and be a full-time content creator?

Mr. Randall thinks he's got this amazing business. It's just a design & print shop, in Ming. Occasionally we get big jobs, but it's mostly printing photos for OAPs, and weddings. Yawn.

We had this guest lecturer at uni once. An amazing guy, also super hot, who built his own marketing and design company with two friends. I knew then, I wanted to pursue this as a career.

I wish I worked for him instead. I wouldn't have to take charge on this awful campaign Mr. Randall won't stop going on about.

"It's the least you can do. All these late starts are getting tedious, Benny. If you want to keep your job, you'll do this campaign for Mr. Dormer."

So what if I've been up until the early hours doing my

TikToks and getting into work a little late? I would explain it to him, but he wouldn't know what TikTok was if someone described it to him on Facebook.

"Nathan Dormer is a homophobic twat. You didn't have to go to school with him. Get one of the others to do it." There's four of us, why me?

"Mr. Dormer is a well-respected local businessman. He's been let down by his usual company. I want him to see how great we are. You're doing it."

Ugh. I kick open the back door to get some cool air.

"Earth to big B."

I didn't realise my colleague Cai was out here having a smoke.

"What?"

"Chill, dude. Only asking wassup. Mr. R asking your availability for overtime again?"

"No. He's got me on this project for my old high school bully."

"That sucks, man. Tell him..." He flips the bird on both his hands.

"I'll have to do it." I explain to Cai how Nathan made my life a daily misery at school, even after my mum went in when we got into a fight. I punched him because he did a whole Snapchat gay slur thing against me. "I'm convinced he was the one who put my name on the graffiti wall."

"He sounds like a twunt. How can I help, Big B?"

I like Cai. He's super cool. He's got loads of tattoos and piercings. He's as edgy as it gets around here. He's really good at his job too. He started a few months after I did and has made this job more tolerable. He's got loads of experience from multiple design jobs. He's only about five years older than me.

"You should do what I do when I have to work on lame projects." His mischievous smile is too intriguing not to ask.

Eight hours later, I'm finally home. I'm straight on the chat to Maya, telling them what I did, but she's at a group support meeting for some gender thing.

Mum and Shaun are out at an ABBA tribute band in town.

I'm on my own.

I lay back on my bed, staring up at the slight damp patch in the far corner by the window. Mum has told the landlord about it, they've still not done anything. They've told us to check the gutters incase they're full. Shaun checked them, they're empty.

I decide to see what Nathan Twatface is up to on socials. He got banned from Facebook years ago. He's not on Insta. Probably got kicked off. He's not on TikTok.

I find his X, it's all business stuff. I scroll through years of tweets. Nothing problematic. He will have deleted it.

I make the most of the empty house. I record myself on various chairs, sat in odd positions. TikTok is gonna love watching how different queers sit in chairs. Ah, *Queers On Chairs* is an amazing title.

Thousands of likes, and hundreds of comments help me float through the week. Every day more come through, more followers too. I might hit 6k before the end of the month at this rate. Ahead of schedule.

I'm done on that awful project by Wednesday.

By Friday, I'm back to wedding invites. Ugh. I've been

here three years and I've never done a same-sex wedding. I don't know if that's because all the queers have escaped, or if my boss is one of those people who refuses queer stuff. I mean, it's Pride Month right now, not that anyone knows around here. Not a single flag anywhere.

"Benny! My office!" Mr. Randall growls.

I make eye contact with Cai. We pull faces.

Mr. Randall gestures for me to sit, slams something in front of me.

Nathan's leaflet.

Looks good to me.

He jabs a finger at the small print at the bottom.

What's he...

"Oh."

There, in the small print, is one of many expressions of my hatred towards Nathan, which kept me engaged during the design process. Such a fun idea of Cai's. Putting in horrible words to keep me motivated. As long as you remember to take them all out.

Oops. Where it says how they're an equal opportunity company, I missed one.

"We're a diverse company and LGBTQ+ unfriendly. Unfriendly. Do you find that funny?"

Off he goes. Nathan's had phone calls today from all over the borough, where the leaflet drops happened, accusing him of being homophobic.

I'd tell him Nathan is homophobic, but I can't get a word in.

Nathan's demanding a full refund, and reprint. My boss will have to comply, otherwise word might get out. It's only a small business. He relies on word of mouth. I've ruined that. I should be ashamed of myself accusing someone of nonsense. I'm fired.

Shit.

It's my turn to speak. I don't.

Nathan is awful. I saw what he posted on Facebook before he got banned. I'm not apologising.

I walk out, grab my coat. I'm done.

Why I chose to clear my head and walk up to the far end of Ming, I don't know. I was going to go in to the little coffee shop, more a glorified greasy spoon, until I saw Rahul sat at the double sofa in the window, sipping his caramel latte macchiato, holding hands with another guy.

He doesn't see me.

I watch for a moment. Funny, the guy he's with sort of looks like me. Well, good for him. I'm sure holding hands inside a coffee shop is super fun.

Ugh. Rahul sips his coffee, gets froth on his lip. The other man screeches with laughter. People inside turn to look, but he doesn't care. He's not that much like me, then.

I hurry home before they notice me. I smoke a huge spliff and message Maya.

Awful day

I fall asleep.

I'm woken by Mum saying, "Oh, Benny."

She's at my door, arms crossed, pity on her face. I don't know how she knows, but she does. She's apparently so disappointed in me, it's set her off coughing.

"What are you talking about?"

"Your boss just called to speak to you, but I didn't know you were home. He told me to tell you that the design software on your laptop belongs to him and you have to delete it. He pays for a certain amount of copies."

What a twat. Who even uses a landline?

"So my replacement can have it? It's rubbish anyway. Fine."

"I don't think he's taking anyone else on, lovey. Remember what I told you I overheard a few weeks ago?"

Mum reminds me of being in the supermarket queue and hearing... my old boss I guess he is now, on the phone saying business wasn't great and he's got to let someone go.

I have no memory of that. "It was an accident. Our work is always checked by another person. It even slipped past Cai. Mr. Randall gets final approval. Even he missed it."

"I did see your colleague in the same queue, actually."

"Mum, I know you don't like Cai but I do. Just leave it."

"Maybe if you apologise?"

"Haven't I been through enough? First I get dumped, then sacked, now you're pecking my head again. None of this is my fault."

Mum reaches out, takes my hand. I pull away. I can't take this right now. I stare at my phone until she leaves.

Maya replies.

What's happened?

I tell her. They approve of what I did. She had to deal

with a subtly homophobic tutor in their first year.

I love talking to Maya. It's easy. I tell them about seeing Rahul and his new camp boyfriend.

There's nothing wrong with being camp

I know there isn't in reality, but around here it's like wearing a giant sign that says *open for hate crimes*.

Wait, does she think I'm camp? We've only met once. I mean, maybe I let my hair down because it was a big old queer party, and I felt at ease with them. Also I was drunk.

I'm not camp. Nathan bullied it out of me.

I don't know what to say but they must have sensed my feelings because she sends me a video. It's of them doing an impression of what she would be like as a camp gay guy. Not in an offensive way either. Weirdly it suits them. Forgiven.

We message for a bit about Maya's meeting, which she says is giving them loads to consider, until Mum calls me in for tea.

I go through, in the hope of taking it to my room, but she's set it at the small dining table. I hate sitting on these cheap, hard chairs.

But it's shepherd's pie.

Ugh. Shaun is also here. I can see by the way he's smiling at me that he knows.

But it's shepherd's pie.

Damn, why does Mum have to make such good food when I've got the munchies? FML.

I've taken two mouthfuls before he starts. He never goes in like Mum does. I've had screaming matches with Mum before, but I'm not obligated to listen to Shaun.

"Holding on to these things isn't healthy. What Nathan did to you was cruel, but that's in the past. If you don't let things like that go, it can cause serious harm to you, mentally."

You'd think he'd get tired of discussing stuff like this all day at work.

He knows how hard it is. I can always talk to him. He won't ever judge. He wants to help, but I also need to consider that Nathan has changed.

"He hasn't. People like him never do."

"You know he has a kid in Jeremy's Year 1 class?" he says.

"So?"

"A little lad, who likes dolls, and dresses."

"Remind you of anyone?" Mum adds.

I roll my eyes. Hopefully she saw me do it.

"Nathan is fully supportive of his son. His business paid for a stack of queer inclusive books for the school, too."

Damn my body for being too stoned to move.

"That doesn't change what he did to me."

"It doesn't, but at what point is the past the past, and the new version of a person the one people remember?"

This is too much. Not tonight, not here, not about that horrible person. I wish Shaun would butt out and deal with his own stupid life. I know for a fact he hates his job. In true Shaun style, he never complains, he just goes on about how he is open to the universe to offer him something new.

It always makes me laugh when Mum tells him to quit his job first, and he's horrified. For all the ways he likes to 'help' other people, he's rubbish at helping himself. I've overheard him saying they've got a huge mortgage and couldn't afford to leave his job.

He tells me I should consider apologising. See if I can get my job back. Apparently he thinks Cai is untrustworthy too.

"NO. I'm sacked. It's done. Just shut up."

"Benny!" I can't look to see what Mum's face is doing.

"It literally just happened. Can I have one night to process?"

"I'll be here when you're ready. I know you really love that job."

For someone who's seen me grow up, he doesn't know anything about me, does he?

He's really starting to get on my tits. It's his face. He pities me.

They're both still going on about this stupid job, and poor Nathan.

Poor Nathan? Seriously? Fuck this.

"If someone had called Jeremy... if someone was racist to Jeremy, would you forgive them?"

He takes a moment. He knows I'm right. "I just want to help you. I know techniques to get your mojo back, find what it is you really want to do with your life."

What I really want to do with my life is get out of this conversation, out of this house, out of this town.

My high is gone. It's his fault.

"I'll think about it," is the only answer that will avoid a

lecture from Mum later. I take my plate into the kitchen, shove it in the sink, head to my room.

I calm myself down on TikTok, taking in all the likes and comments. I've crept up another fifty-ish followers in the last few hours, too. That makes me feel better.

Still, I message Maya to vent.

She always knows how to calm me down. Even better, they make me realise that my recent loss of boyfriend and job might be a blessing in disguise.

A friend of a work-friend is moving out of their very queer house share.

Right. And?

Why don't you...
MOVE
HERE??????????
Move to Manchesterrrrrrrrrrrrr
Get a job!!!!!!!!!!!!!!!!

What a fucking brilliant idea. I could finally escape this hell-hole.

Chapter 14

YAAAAAAAAAAAAAAAAAAAAAAAAASSSSSSS.
It's Manchester Pride.

The whole house is buzzing. Even better, M's here. David's set up his speakers, and his party playlist blasts on the landing as we all get ready.

Jacinta is quiet tonight. We've all asked what's wrong, and she says it's nothing, but she keeps looking at us, smiling sadly, caressing walls and furniture. She's weird sometimes.

It's been a good hour of narrowing down my outfit. M, and all my housemates made fun of me for not having planned what I'm wearing. I got super worried, which is why every single item of my clothing is now either on the bed, floor, or desk.

We congregate by the front door. I get told I absolutely must have glitter on me, by Zoe.

"Just a smidge."

This is not a smidge. I am covered, but Jacinta doesn't

even get the hoover out, she just shrugs. Pride really is magical.

I almost have as much glitter on as David. He's fully made up, but not in drag tonight. He makes us all link arms. Together we mince out of the house.

Will texts to tell me to have fun, and to let me know where Jeff likes to hang out. I don't text back. Part of me feels like he'd know how much glitter I have on me and disapprove.

We make our way into the city, sharing a bottle of cheap vodka. I'm tipsy by the time we've got our wristbands.

There's hugs and kisses with all the housemates as they go their separate ways. We've got plans to hang after the parade tomorrow, because they've made it clear I won't see them tonight.

I said I doubt that as Zoe is covered in UV paint, and David is wearing the sparkliest mesh top and bright pink shorts. Jacinta... she's dressed entirely in black as usual so not seeing her tracks.

They tried to get me to wear something "much gayer than that," as they told me. I don't have David's legs, so have kept them covered, but on M's suggestion I went with my more fitted top. A small-medium isn't a size I'd normally wear, but my housemates gave me tens across the board.

"Ready?" M asks, offering their hand.

I think of Will's text and the face he would pull right now if I took M's hand, so I skip ahead. "Let's gooooooo."

The Village is absolutely rammed. With one glance I see all the letters of the acronym and perhaps others I don't even know. Everyone looks at ease.

I feel it too.

I wish I could bottle this moment and carry it with me forever. It's like the opposite of Ming in every single way.

I feel fucking amazing.

We slalom through the crowd. A cute blonde guy in a jockstrap and trainers bumps into me and instantly apologises. He kisses my cheek, tells me I'm a "hot twunk," and melts into the crowd.

What even is Pride?

We join the queue for an outside bar. In front of us is a leather gay with his arse proudly cut out. For a guy that looks like he's in his fifties, he's got a cute little bum. I can't stop staring.

A fabulously rainbow-dressed woman behind me dares me to give it a pinch.

I shake my head.

"Go on, he won't mind, it's on display for a reason. Double dare ya."

In response, the leather gay wiggles his hips, pushes his bum backwards.

Neither me nor M move.

"Leave it to trans women, once again!" She gives me a cheeky wink and pinches his bum.

The leather gay shrieks with delight.

The rest of the queue experience pales in comparison.

M and I down Jägerbombs, and sip cider as we head to Sackville Gardens. M wants to quickly say hi to friends.

There's too many of them to remember all their names. I've met a couple of M's uni friends, but M tells me some are from a queer women's group they used to go to.

When M tells everyone, "This is Benny," there's a lot of oohs and ahhs.

"This is the infamous Benny?" someone says, weirding me out.

We stay a while, then M says their goodbyes.

"So, did the lesbians like me or not? I couldn't tell."

"Yeah. Duh. But you know, they're not all lesbians, they're not even all women."

"Oh, soz. Can we go do Pride now? Maybe find some guys to kiss?"

"Kulvinder's a gay guy."

M points to an Asian person, talking animatedly. He's moving so much, his shirt opens. I can see his chest scars. He's cute, especially with that stubble.

"Wanna hang with him instead?" M grins.

I'm staring too much.

I have never felt this alive. Will told me there's a nasty culture of promiscuity in The Village, which has made me feel like I shouldn't be looking, but tonight I feel like not doing so was a huge mistake.

It's amazing how being totally surrounded by your community can bring out the absolute best in people.

"Show. Me. Everything."

We're in and out of bars. We boogie on the street with strangers. I get snogged by a pansexual-beflagged guy as I wait for M in the porta-loo. We spend ages sharing chips, talking to a pup and his handler. It's surreal seeing the harness, lead, and mask, yet be talking deeply about the cost of living.

As we finish our chips, I tell M I wanna dance.

"I got you."

I follow M. Tonight seems to be all about hellos and goodbyes.

A short queue later, we're dancing to songs from musicals turned into housey bangers. It's super cheesy. I love it.

A topless Asian guy dances over to us. I try not to stare at his body. To be fair his green eyes are mesmerising. Are they contacts... or real?

We dance like this for who knows how long, then he says, "Can I kiss you?" in a hot Irish accent.

I nod.

I love Pride.

As he pulls away, I spot a weird look on M's face.

"I'm going to get drinks," they say.

Irish guy asks if I want to join him and his friends, but I'm worried about M.

I find them talking to a couple. One has a T-shirt that says *THEY*. The other has one saying *THEM*.

M points to their T-shirt. "Me too."

The pair embrace M into a huge sandwich hug. I feel like a third, no, fourth wheel. "We're not he/himists," THEY says, and pulls me in. THEY and THEM on the outside, Me and M squashed nose to nose in the middle.

This feels nice. "I kissed a random boy, did you see?"

"He wasn't random. You met him earlier. Kulvinder."

"Oh."

"Nice kiss?"

I nod. For some reason this makes M beam.

"Shall we dance?" M asks. I realise THEY and THEM

have already gone. When did that happen?

I get us shots first.

***

"I am so hungover," I say to David in the kitchen.

"Power through it, bitch," he grimaces.

"Feeling rough, gay boys?" Zoe sings from the hallway, back from her run. I absolutely hate her right now.

A shower helps, but David's right, I need to power through. I've got to meet M for the parade soon.

"Don't forget it's our housemate Pride brunch today." Jacinta reminds us as she hands us the brews she's made us all. She neither looks hungover, nor fresh and sober.

We chat over our drinks. Jacinta is strangely serious as she tells us about her evening with her girlfriend. David eagerly tells us all about his threesome in Beetham Tower.

I tell them I may have kissed a few boys and David bursts into a round of applause, which is totally inappropriate, but I love it.

Zoe is highly upset she was the only one who didn't get a kiss last night. "Oh, the pan shame! I'll make up for lost time today. I'll be the winner." She can turn anything into a competition.

Everyone has their ideal parade spot apparently, so we split up as we get into town. My hangover seems to vanish as I see M, or maybe the painkillers Jacinta gave me are finally kicking in.

They've brought Maccy Ds too.

"Lifesaver," I say.

We sit on the edge of the pavement, our feet on the road as we eat. It's weird having all the main streets closed to traffic. The crowds are forming fast, but we're at the front.

"Room to squeeze in here?" a random woman asks, gesturing at M's bag beside us.

I nod, but M says, "Our friend is joining us," then turns their back to the woman.

She walks off.

"What friend?" I ask.

"Didn't you see her T-shirt? No way she's sitting here."

I glance over to see the woman trying her luck further down, but getting the same answers of no. I see her T-shirt says LGB, then a pair of scissors, TQ.

"Is William Gale your boss?" M brings my attention back to them.

"Yeah, why?"

"How closely do you work with him?"

"Why are we talking about work?"

"Does he run the company alone?"

I tell M, Will is one of three who own the company, but they work from home a lot. "I work mostly with my own team, and Will oversees everything."

M goes quiet for a while. "Benny, you know my troll—" they start, as a Parade Marshall comes over and makes us stand behind the barrier, just as my phone rings.

It's Mum on FaceTime.

"Are you having a good Pride?" She looks better than she did last week.

"I'm having a brilliant time."

Her face lights up. She asks me about last night. I give

her a bullet list of events. When I mention the kisses, I hear Shaun's voice say, "Good on ya, Benny."

The Parade starts. It's brilliant. I show Mum the first few floats before Shaun appears and tells me Mum had to nip off and would speak to me later.

We lean on the metal barriers, our hands so close together If I move my little finger an inch to the right, it will touch theirs.

I don't though. I'm already feeling emotional due to the hangover. I've cried at four different floats, so I don't want my emotions making things even weirder between us.

I almost cry again when the parade finishes. M has to work, but started late to watch the parade with me. We hug goodbye.

It feels different.

I head into The Village to meet the housemates, but there's a commotion near one of the entrances. A crowd chants "Trans rights are human rights!"

There's a strange atmosphere. Like they're chanting out of anger, rather than to raise awareness. I don't need this today. I make my way to a different entrance and head to where the housemates are meeting.

Zoe and David give me a bright wave, but Jacinta's super-serious.

I can't believe I've almost been here a whole year and this is the first time we've all been out together.

"Are you OK?" I ask Jacinta.

She looks at us all apologetically, composes herself, tells us, "The landlord is putting the house up for sale."

Apparently she's known for a couple of weeks, and has

been wondering how to tell us. She didn't want to ruin our Pride, but she had to tell us today because the sign is going up, right as we sit here.

I'm on such a good deal there, we all are. Jacinta says it's because the landlord, an older guy who's had the house decades, has no mortgage and doesn't care about making an income.

"What are we going to do?" Zoe stutters through tears. She's taking this quite badly.

An hour later, we've cycled through finding another place to rent together, finding the money to buy the house ourselves, begging the landlord to reconsider, back to finding a new place to rent.

"There's nowhere with four rooms together." Zoe sobs again.

"I'm gagged. Period. Look." David's found our place on a house website. Is it meant to be that expensive? Even if we got a four-way mortgage, we couldn't afford it.

"It could take weeks, months even, before it's sold, and the landlord has said we are welcome to stay there until it is. There's even a chance a new buyer might want to keep us as tenants." Jacinta offers us a glimmer of hope. It seems unrealistic.

We sit in silence. Queer joy all around, us four absolutely miserable.

Before long, we've all got our phones out. Anything to distract us. David says he has to leave. I guess he's far too upset.

I head to TikTok. The fact I've crept over 40k doesn't make me feel any better.

Wait, why is Will doing a live? Has he done it by accident?

I can only see his feet. It's noisy. I put the phone to my ear.

It sounds like people are chanting at Will. Is that *Trans rights are human rights*?

Will turns to camera. "Can you hear what they're shouting at me? All I've done for the community, yet I'm the bigot? Can't anyone be a gay man anymore?"

I tell Jacinta and Zoe I have to go. I don't say why. I run to where I saw the crowd earlier.

It's even bigger.

They're now chanting, "Get out of our village!"

What do I do?

"HOW DARE YOU!" Will screams into the faces of three women and a guy who've got themselves to the front of the crowd, holding hands, heads held high. "I'M A GAY MAN. I'M A MEMBER OF THIS COMMUNITY."

"He's been going on for an hour. He commented on the slogan on that trans femme's top and it's escalated to this," a random beside me says.

I can just about see her top, *Some Women Have* is all I can read.

"This is a big group against one guy, though?"

He gives me a quizzical look. "Are you new? Have you seen his tee?"

I try, but he's surrounded.

"WHEN SOMEONE FORCES THEMSELVES ONTO ANOTHER PERSON, THERE'S A WORD FOR THAT. I'M BEING FORCED TO HAVE SEX WITH PEOPLE I

DON'T WANT TO. I DIDN'T FACE YEARS OF HOMOPHOBIA TO DEAL WITH IT FROM MY OWN COMMUNITY."

Someone shouts, "WE'RE NOT YOUR COMMUNITY," and the crowd chants it over and over.

There's so many of them, and...

Is that M?

They're gone. In their place is David. Yes, that's definitely him.

Will spots me, gives me a worried glance, turns back towards the crowd. His shoulders drop.

Those at the front shout something.

"PLEASE STOP CALLING ME CIS. IT'S A SLUR," Will yells back.

He offers me a small smile, then drops to his knees, out of view.

I see a glint of light on something metallic.

Everyone near the front gasps and yells at him.

A police siren sounds.

Will jumps up, and backs away from the crowd.

I spot David grab something off the floor, and the person who looks like M moves towards Will, then is gone from view again.

Police arrive.

Rush over to the crowd.

I watch Will turn towards them.

He steps.

Stumbles.

Goes down on the floor with a smack.

Chapter 15

It's bedlam.

More police arrive. The crowd scatters.

Will is taken away by two officers, but I lose sight of him as police escort members of the crowd away too.

Within minutes, the street's empty.

David and the M lookalike are gone.

As I walk around, I hear people saying how Will isn't welcome in our community. I hear others saying it's bad if a gay man is treated like that at Pride.

The housemate group chat springs to life. Jacinta and Zoe are worried that David isn't responding.

My first big Pride, and now I want to get out of The Village.

David doesn't respond to our messages.

I text M.

Will.

Nothing.

I find myself wandering around the city. I don't know

what to do.

Four hours later Will texts.

Home.

His apartment is busy. James is in the kitchen making brews, Michelle and Pauline are talking about how Pride should be scrapped.

Will is on the sofa, laughing with a few people I recognise from nights out. His arm in a sling.

He sees me, beckons me over. "Look what they did to me. Animals, the lot of them. Dirty animals." He looks at me.

The room goes quiet. What do you say in moments like this?

"Is there anything I can do?"

"I need to rest. Everyone out."

I turn to leave.

"Not you, Ben."

Ten minutes later, Will and I are alone, on the sofa.

"An hour I held my own against them. Just me against them all. Did you see?"

I nod.

"I thought my life as a gay man was going to get easier, after all I've been through. Same with you and the horrendous things that happened to you at school. How is it getting harder?"

Will and I have shared quite a few *war stories* as he calls them. Recalling those moments at school and uni makes my stomach twist. I try not to think about them, but when I do, it's like I'm there. All those emotions come flooding back.

"Can you see what it's like for people like us these days? I was minding my own business until they started using that horrible slur at me."

"Queer?" I whisper, I don't want him feeling worse.

"Cis. I refuse to be called that, so I told them. It made them worse."

What? Will hasn't ever mentioned anything about the word *cis* before.

"You might think I'm overreacting," he says. I'm worried he saw my confusion. "My parents and siblings would say horrible things to me growing up."

I nod to show I'm listening. He hates when people don't listen.

"They used to call me sissy. All the time. Kids at school too. I quickly learned to correct how I walked, how I talked, what I talked about. Cis is too much like that word. I won't use it, and I don't need to. Do you understand?"

"Can I get you anything? A coffee?"

"You're a good friend, Ben. I'd like that."

I struggle with the coffee machine, so he tells me what to do, unable to do much with his arm. He thinks it's fractured, but won't know until he gets his X-ray.

"I genuinely tried to have a conversation, but they wanted to cry victim. I've been silenced before. I certainly did not want to back down when I know I'm not in the wrong. As soon as they started calling me a transphobe, I knew I had lost. I tried to explain, but... well, you saw what happened."

He holds up his arm, and winces.

"They did this to me. Someone tripped me and I landed on my arm. They all lied about it, of course. Bandied together against me. That's not even the worst of it. It's a good job the police escorted me away for my own safety, they threatened me with scissors."

"Oh my god."

"Shoved right in my face, but they stopped before the police came over. They're clever like that. Someone threw banana milkshake all over my T-shirt too. Had to change it."

"Why would they do that?"

He shrugs. "Do you see what it's like for us these days? We all want to be treated fairly, don't we?"

"Absolutely."

"We all want to be free to love who we want to love, right?"

"Yes."

"You understand. I knew you would. You'll always be here for me, and help me, won't you?"

"Of course."

"Us gay men have suffered enough. You've seen what's been happening in the press. You've surely not missed everything going on in America. We have to distance ourselves from other fights. We have to protect ourselves. Like I protected you. You've seen it now, haven't you? So I've got a proposal for you. How about doing a team-up TikTok with me?"

***

I told him I'd think about it. Shortly after, James returned to take him to his private hospital appointment.

Back at the house, I'm surrounded by four people hugging me.

Wait, four? Jacinta, Zoe, David and, oh, it's M.

"We thought you were taken by the rozzers too." Jacinta pours me a cup of tea, listening to David, who was mid-flow as I walked in.

"He's all over socials now, telling lies. He's disgusting."

"Are you OK, Benny?" M's arm goes behind my back, rubbing it. I've needed this all day, but the vibe is weird.

"What do you mean, taken too?" I ask.

David goes off. He tells me both he and M were taken, along with about twenty other queers, into a van to the station.

So M was there.

"Were you arrested?" I ask.

David laughs loudly, but M shakes their head.

"Couldn't arrest any of us," M says. "Done nothing. Was all him."

"Wasn't he taken by police for his own safety?"

All four of them laugh this time.

"Don't listen to them fuckers online," Zoe says. "You're one of us, Benny, not one of them."

"He was removed from Pride and taken to the station for disturbing the peace." David grins.

"What about his arm?"

David and M lock eyes, but only for a second.

"He fell trying to get away when I grabbed the flag he cut up." David spits. "He used scissors to cut away the rainbow from the rest of the progress flag. We called him out on it. He lobbed it to the ground. Some twink tried to give him his scissors back, but by this point the police were coming. He backed away, stumbled, hit the deck like a pissed drag queen. Twat."

So he wasn't taken for his own safety? He didn't get tripped or threatened with scissors?

"I'd have kicked him in the knackers for wearing that top if I was there," Zoe adds. "How doesn't he see that the cutting of letters from the acronym won't ever stop."

Everyone agrees, except M. They look at me in a meaningful way, as though they know it was Will.

They say goodbye. They're late for work and have a lot of grovelling to do, plus they need a new work shirt, as theirs has wet yellow stains on it.

The housemates stay talking, but I need to lie down.

Who's telling the truth?

Chapter 16

The last six weeks have been a struggle. I've lost weight as I don't have any appetite. I wake up with a headache most mornings. I've started sleeping topless because by the time I get to bed every night, it feels like my T-shirts are squeezing me.

I've considered going to the doctor's, but I'm not set up here. I'd have to go home and explain to Mum why I'm back. I've started taking valerian root tablets, and CBD oil with my morning painkillers—the strongest I could get over the counter.

It's like I'm two different people living two different lives.

First of all I'm M's best friend. Things have been manic since they reached their GoFundMe target a week after Pride. I was there when they got their surgery booked. I went to the consultation with them. We've discussed everything that's going to happen and what I need to do. There's been tears, laughter, and lots of hugs. So. Many.

Hugs.

I'm also Will's mentee. He's got me on amazing projects at work and has been super supportive of my content, even though I've not been doing much recently. He keeps suggesting more ideas, every Thursday. I'm adding them to an ever-growing list.

Then there's the whole house situation. I told Will that's why I'm mainly doing reposts of my old stuff, and a few duets with silly reactions that don't take ages to edit. A few Kathleen videos too, but nothing like the ones he keeps suggesting. I want to maintain my 45 thousand followers.

I'm worried about Mum too. She's waiting for her next set of results.

I've seen loads of stuff online about Pride. Nearly everyone has the same point of view as David and M. So, despite Will sticking to his side of the story, I've suggested we pause all new-content ideas until his arm is better. It was only a small fracture, but he's still pretty shaken up.

He hasn't gone out to The Village since the incident. He says it's because he's afraid, but all I can think about is how he keeps putting off pressing charges against anyone. Refusing to tell me anything about the T-shirt he was wearing too.

He's been putting out his own content of late, mostly talking about what happened. I've seen him in meetings at work when he's being honest and sincere. His TikToks are not like that.

"Do you know what I mean?" M asks. I realise I've been overthinking this whole Pride thing yet again. I give them an apologetic look.

"I said, I know it's for my fam, but that version of me's like M 1.0. I'm 2.2 at least now. Know what I mean?"

I give their hand a squeeze. Their parents have asked M to keep their Facebook profile set with their old name and pronouns, for the sake of family living outside the UK. M hates it. Understandably so.

"Everything online is ridic," they say. "Know that TikToker I told you about?"

I'm listening properly now.

"Gone back to his old content. It's funny. Even his Kathleen vids are about how awful a person she is, as opposed to pushing out TERFy stuff."

Funny M mentioned those videos, because I've felt my audience has shifted a bit. They now give me negative comments when I do my silly gay stuff, and keep asking for the type of content Will suggests.

Although, I have had a company contact me about doing sponsored videos for them. It was something Will sorted out. An American company who do stuff for the government, but as I don't understand British politics, on Will's suggestion, I didn't get myself caught up in it. He said it was all above board, boring stuff about legislation. They want three Kathleen videos, with me doing things like story-time for kids, training for a race, and one of me pretending to be the face of a tampon brand.

The company want to pay me the equivalent of a month's wages.

"Please eat." I gesture to the Subways we bought before we got on the train. "You can't eat anything after midnight. You'll be starving later, I know what you're like."

"I'm too..." They do a little sat-down dance. We've got a table seat. I'm sat opposite M (going backwards because they hate going backwards). I glance at the two businessmen sat beside us. They're not together despite being dressed almost exactly the same. "Finally gonna have this huge weight off my chest."

They burst out laughing, which gets me giggling. Ever since the surgery was booked, M's been calling it *having a huge weight off their chest*, which they have found hilarious, but has made me groan. M is so corny.

I try to keep my giggling to a minimum, but the seriousness of the businessmen sends us both into hysterics, crying over our Subs, trying not to make dicks of ourselves.

Too late.

The closer the train gets, the more serious M becomes. I wish there was more I could do.

It's not been an easy few months with one of their housemates, who hasn't spoken to them since the surgery was booked. M's also had to leave one circle of friends because they kept saying it was sad another lesbian was being lost.

M finally eats. I try to keep the conversation light. I want them back to how they were the day they told me they had reached their GoFundMe target, and how they had *I'm So Excited* ready to play. A semi-choreographed dance to go with it.

As we get off the train, I take their hand in mine until we get to the little B&B they booked. I keep wondering if M thinks I'm being weird, but they don't let go.

We stay awake chatting, in our double bed. M keeps

mentioning how lucky they are to go private when many have to wait for surgery on the NHS.

"You're allowed to enjoy this you know. You deserve it."

We watch TV for a bit. At 1am I tell M we best get to sleep, they've got a big day tomorrow. I keep hearing my stomach rumble, which is annoying, because I'm supporting M by not eating after midnight either, but after half an hour of my tummy growls M tells me to go get a snack because they can't sleep.

I nip out to a shop across the road. I shove crisps and chocolate down my throat. I don't want to take too long.

When I get back in, M's asleep.

The next morning, everything is high-energy. M's up before the alarm, eager to go. The clinic is only around the corner.

M says hello to the surgeon and every single person that comes in to their little recovery room. Before long they're lying down on the bed.

"One hundred. Ninety-nine. Ninety-eight. Ninety-seven. Ninety..." They're asleep.

***

Almost four hours later, M's wheeled in talking about bears to the nurse.

"It's the medication. It'll wear off soon," the nurse says.

I look back at M, they're asleep again. I'm about to go get a snack when I hear M's voice.

"It done?" They're staring at me seriously. I nod. "Careful, Benny."

"What?"

"I know he's your boss, promise you'll be careful."

M's eyes are unfocussed. Dreaming maybe? "I'll be careful I promise."

Their eyes close. I go to leave, but their hand takes mine.

"I lied," they whisper.

"What about?"

"I hate him. He's the troll. I stuck out my leg when he turned."

"Go back to sleep, you need rest." This is the meds.

"Everyone saw. I made him fall. He deserved it. Don't tell anyone."

I wait for M to wake up again, but they're fast asleep.

I don't go get snacks. My head is mashed. If M did trip Will up, who's to say someone didn't threaten him with scissors too? But if Will really is M's troll, that's a huge problem. Could M have tripped Will and got all the queers to lie, like Will said?

Have I been too harsh on Will? After all he's done for me.

I stew for another couple of hours until M wakes up. Properly it seems this time.

That calm sweet face changes. Eyebrows furrow. Nose crinkles. Then their eyes snap open. The first thing they do is look down at their chest. I don't know if M's expecting to see their new body, but not only is it bandaged up, there's also a blanket over the top.

There's also a woollen throw M brought from home they like snuggling into. It got chilly in here while they were in recovery, so I carefully, very fucking carefully, I mean I have never been so careful with anything in my entire life, put the blanket over them.

So there's nothing for M to see. They're disappointed.

Their eyes find mine. "It done?" Their voice is croaky. Shaky.

"You've already asked me that," I laugh.

"Have I?" They look confused, then chuckle to themselves until they fall asleep.

Later that day, M's allowed home. I ask if they remember waking up, but they don't. They're fragile. I don't bring it up again.

***

A week later, we're back. The nurse comes in to show M the results.

"So proud of you," I whisper, as I slip out of the door.

"Hey. Come back!" they laugh.

"This is your moment, not mine."

"Please stay."

I give them a *you sure?* look. They pull a face at me. The one they always pull when I say something stupid.

The nurse cuts away the bandages. M gives me one last nervous smile, then their eyes go straight to their chest and don't move, as though they will never look anywhere else again.

I want to look at M's chest too. I know that sounds weird, but how could I not? It's all they've spoken about for months, and what they've been desperate to see all week. I'm invested almost as much as M.

But I can't take my eyes off M's face.

The bandages are pulled away. M's eyes bulge like a rabbit caught in headlights for a split second, then they soften and fill with tears, which spill down their cheeks, over their huge smile.

They bite their lip like they always do when they're too full of emotions.

I take a peek. Their chest looks sore. There's tubes from them draining liquid.

M tries to speak, finds their throat too dry, coughs. I've never seen anyone wince like that and laugh about it. Only for a moment. The laughing must be painful too. They settle on a constant cheshire cat grin.

The scars are smaller than I expected, but holy shit, what a job they've done. M has a chest. A chest like mine. Better than mine. How have they done that?

"Happy?" the nurse says as they bandage their chest back up.

"Great Scott, I am."

***

Another week or so later, M is experiencing hardly any pain and the drains are out. They constantly wear slim-fit T-shirts, and look amazing. They tell me they can't wait to get the go ahead to get in the gym so they can start toning up.

I agree. Seeing them with toned arms is certainly something I want to see. M shows me their progress every day. Why they want to spend all their recovery time with me I don't know.

Unless..?

Perhaps M does fancy me back?

A little voice that sounds like Will starts creeping doubts into my thoughts again, but I shut it down because I need to know.

I should ask, but they're healing at the moment and don't need me pestering them. No, I'll wait until they're healed.

It shouldn't take much longer. They said another month or so.

I've just now tried to help them reach for the tea bags on the top shelf and they said they could do it because, "I'm a capable man."

"So it's he, him now?" I ask.

"I still don't quite feel... I mean, I know I am. For now let's use he and they, until I feel trans enough."

I don't know what to say, so I hug him and stay silent.

But the moment he's properly healed, I'm going to ask him out.

Chapter 17

I'm spiralling.

In my mind I keep replaying Pride, conversations with Will, conversations with David, and everything M has said to me.

Who's telling the truth?

At work, I've taken on as many projects as I can manage. More than I can manage to be honest, to distract my thoughts from this repetitive cycle.

I'm on the maximum CBD dosage and go through so much codeine every week, I have to use different pharmacies because they recognise me and refuse to sell it.

This last month has been hell. I'm barely holding it together.

The few times I've seen Will at The Castle, which isn't much as he's mostly been working from home since his cast came off, he seems smaller. My mind tells me to trust him.

Whenever I go see M, he tells me he's fine, but I've noticed them wince when they do certain actions. My heart tells me to trust him.

I listen to Will talk about how his hand is still not right. He's been going for physiotherapy, and I know what happened to him isn't right.

I text M every night about silly stuff to lighten the mood. They've been getting a lot of hate on X, and I know how he's getting dog-piled isn't right.

The one time I've seen Will at his apartment though, with his friends, he's back to his usual self. The one time I tried to talk to M about what he said after his surgery, he changed the subject.

Here I go again. Replaying everything.

I've barely put out any new content recently, which is probably why I've only got a thousand new followers in a month. Will keeps suggesting TikToks. I keep saying I'm adding them to a list for when I've got time.

I've read every news article and X thread about Pride. A couple Will did an interview for, and others random queers gave their opinions on.

They all come back to the same thing: it's his word against theirs.

All I want to do is enjoy how confident M is getting. I want to get lost in his voice. It's much more masculine than mine. I want to appreciate his little beard and moustache, something I never used to find attractive on men. Rahul once grew a beard. It was horrible. It suits M though.

I want to do all that. Instead, I'm back to the replays.

Ugh, why is it all so confusing? I've looked on M's X, and can't find any proof the troll is Will, although a lot of tweets have been deleted. Will has his own account that's all work-related. Surely M wouldn't lie about that?

Yet they told me they lied about tripping Will.

I don't want all these thoughts in my head, which is why I've got stuck into work. Filled my waking hours with marketing and design.

I'm exhausted.

Mum's results weren't great. No new growth, but nothing's shrunk either. I know she's frustrated, but at least she's got Shaun. He's been there every time we've spoken.

Will has asked me if I'd like to come over to his tonight for drinks. I've told him I don't feel well. That's not a lie. I've felt shivery and heavy since yesterday. I ran out of codeine then too. I need to get to a late-night pharmacy, otherwise this weekend is going to be hell.

All the housemates are in, so Jacinta suggested, as it's Friday, we order a pizza. David's working later, so he's sat with us, half in drag (the bottom half). Zoe's got her new girlfriend, Donna, over. It's the first time we've ever met her, even though they met on the last night of Pride.

They're properly loved up. If I was feeling better, I think I'd really like her, but right now the feminist-metal music she's playing is eating me from the inside.

It seems everyone is in a relationship now. David's in two, but I still haven't worked out if it's a throuple or a polyamorous thing. I've seen both of his boyfriends—if you can call spying from my bedroom window down to the street at them, seen. They're both absolutely beautiful.

"How's M?" Jacinta asks through a mouthful of pepperphoney pizza, which isn't as bad as I thought it was going to be.

I tell her how well he's doing. Jacinta looks at me, her head tilted to the side.

"Have you fallen out?"

I shake my head. "Why would you say that?"

"You usually talk about them a bit more... what's the word?"

"Enthusiastically," David says.

Everyone nods.

"Oh. Well, we've not seen much of each other. He's recovering." Seeing as I've got everyone's attention... "He's been a bit off since that article a few weeks ago, about the guy at Pride fracturing his wrist."

"You mean transphobe," Zoe says.

"He deserved it, don't you think?" Donna says.

"He did, boo."

Really? "Deserved to be tripped over?"

For a split second, I see shock spread on David's face. "He fell, he fell. Period. He wasn't tripped at all."

"He says different." I watch to see what his face does.

"He's your boss, isn't he? You asked him?"

Everyone stops eating. All eyes on me. I guess they didn't know.

"He owns the company I work for. It's massive."

David squints at me, shrugs, and everyone starts talking about horrible bosses and how hard the job market is.

I don't even know why I said it like that. However, the way David reacted makes me think M did trip Will. If they lied about that, what else was lied about?

An hour later, as David goes to do his make-up, I say I'm going for some fresh air, but instead I text Will.

I'm coming over after all

"Long time, no see," he says, answering the door.

He pours drinks. As we make small talk about work, he plays with a squidgy ball he has to do hand exercises with.

"So, are we going to do this team-up or what?" Will asks, as he squeezes the ball as hard as he can. He winces.

"Can I ask you a question first?"

"You just did."

He smiles, but I don't want jokes right now.

"Did you get tripped, or did you fall at Price?"

His shoulders drop. He stops squeezing. "Why are you asking me that?"

"I'm just trying to get everything straight in my mind."

"Straight?" He throws the ball across the room. Smack. It hits a frame on the wall that wasn't there last time I was here. It falls off the hooks. "Been listening to all the lies online, have you?"

"No, it's not—"

"I thought you were better than that. I thought we were friends. All I've done for you, and this is what you think of me? I'm a liar, am I?"

I glance at the frame, which has landed behind a cabinet. It's a T-shirt. Under some yellow-brown stains, I can just about see the words 'LGB' on one side, and is that a pair of...

"Hey. Look at me. Have you seen how they speak about me online? One of the best things I ever did was meet you that day you got mugged. Helping you. Bringing you into my life, and my friendship circle. All my friends adore you. The team I put you with all love working with you. I did that, and this is how you repay me? Please leave."

He gestures at the door for a moment, then has to shake his hand as it's seizing up again.

"Will, I do believe you. I believe you were tripped. Honestly."

He curls up on the sofa. "I've barely heard from you since the articles went up."

"I've been busy, and there's the house stuff. Everyone is freaking out, so... I'm sorry for not being better."

"I know one way you can make it up to me."

"The team-up?"

"Come on, Ben. Let's do it. You're such an inspirational young man, and all credit to you for the following you've got, but let's grow it. I know I've helped you with your laptop, and meals out. I'd never ask for anything in payment for it. I just hope you'll consider doing this?"

The thought of doing it makes my stomach feel like it's being squeezed, but he has done so much for me.

"OK. But not yet."

"Seize the moment."

"I've got too much going on. I might have to move soon. Christmas is next month."

"How about I make at least one thing less stressful for you right now?"

I feel my eyebrows meet in the middle. "What do you mean?"

"What if I buy the house?"

I don't know what to say. Why would he do that for me?

He talks me through it, tells me he's been looking for an investment opportunity. None of us would have to move out.

How could I not do the team-up now?

He wants to do it today, but I suggest tomorrow.

As tomorrow comes, I'm back at Will's with my Kathleen outfit as he requested, and green-screen. Will ordered better lights. They're all set up as I arrive.

The wine opens as I get changed. Will doesn't let my glass go below halfway.

I tell him I'm worried about doing a live, but he assures me he will ask all the questions, as though it's an interview between him and me as Kathleen.

It's a bit of a faff having to wear this voice-changing thing under my mask, but as there's no way to edit a live TikTok, this is what I'll have to do.

He's advertised his live all day on his account. I've done it too. Seems a lot of people are going to tune in. I'm glad I'm getting less and less sober as the live time approaches.

Will assures me he's got questions I should answer as Kathleen. It's all good fun. Randomly, he's set the green-screen display as a public toilet but I'm pretty wasted now so I'm going to roll with it.

As we approach our start time, I put my right hand over my heart and taptaptap.

"Hello, TikTok. I'm William Gale. Have I got a treat for you today!"

His questions come thick and fast. So fast, I'm waving goodbye before I know it.

What did we talk about? I'm even drunker than I was that first time with Will, but it's his fault. He kept pouring.

I remember we talked about... Poor people, I think. He kept asking what toilet I would use. Yeah, he asked that a few times. Mostly it was him talking. I remember at the start he asked for my pronouns and gender, and after I said *trans woman*, he did a whole speech about how if I call myself a trans woman, why should he or anyone have to use the word cis.

Except he didn't say the word. He had it written down on a piece of card and kept referring to it as though saying the word was just too difficult.

He's on a high after we finish. His account has risen by almost a thousand followers in the little half an hour we did.

I'll check mine later. I can barely stand.

Will tells me there's loads of amazing comments, but I need my bed. He orders me a cab. I get changed and head back home.

At least I know I've got a home. The drama of having to move out is over.

I fall in bed and check my phone. My TikTok is blowing up.

I've done it. I've hit 50 thousand followers.

Chapter 18

Will has reposted the live since we did it. I haven't, nor have I watched it. I'm leaving it to do its thing, although I'm amused by how my follower count goes below, then above, 50k daily.

Will told me I must get new content out, but seeing as it's almost December and I'm super busy at work, I've put my better-performing stuff together in little compilations.

Will won't stop talking about the live. He told me X went crazy for it, and probably because I still haven't got round to making an account, he's made one for me.

He reposts all the stuff he thinks is the best. It's probably no coincidence it's all the stuff he's suggested. Apparently, I've got just under eight thousand followers. How cool.

M has been busy too, job hunting now they're fully healed. We keep saying we must get together for a proper Menny night out. That's what we call our combined selves.

In fact, I've seen something cool happening in December I'm going to book: a little winter pop-up thing with an outdoor cinema, which sounds crazy as it's freezing, but it's under cover. They provide blankets, and fluffy beanbags to snuggle into.

Back to the Future is playing. I don't think M knows. He's going to lose it when he finds out. Then, I'm going to ask him out. It's only, like, a week away, but I told myself I'd do it as soon as I saw him, in real life, after he'd healed.

I can't stop looking at my TikTok account. I have too many notifications to read, which used to make me feel amazing.

Will texts to tell me how he's been getting loads of likes on his TikTok, and comments by massive celebs, as he put it.

All your dreams are coming true.
What's next?

Now I've decided to let Pride fade into the past, as I'm never going to know the truth, what is next?

I take my CBD drops, then wash my valerian tablets down with my soluble codeine. I finally open the curtains and let the Saturday afternoon light in.

I'm surprised to see M halfway up the street.

I wave, but they don't see me. He's pacing up and down, talking to himself.

I watch him do this for so long, I hide behind the curtain when they look up to my window. I don't want them to think I've been spying.

What are they doing? He's giving himself a good talking to, but their face is more serious than I've ever seen.

They stop to rest on someone's wall, taking out their phone and watching something. I see him touch the screen as though he's moving the slider to a certain point.

He brings it up close to his face. Nods. He walks over to the house, takes a deep breath, gets to the gate, shakes his head, walks away. Down the street. He's gone.

That was weird.

I sit on my bed to replay it in my mind.

Now I think about it, he seemed nervous. To be honest, I felt a little nervous too. I promised myself I'd ask him out next time I saw him. I thought maybe it was going to be today.

What if he was coming to ask me the same question? That would be awesome. Perhaps he felt like he couldn't ask? I know that feeling. I have considered asking via text but I want it to be special.

A knock on my bedroom door.

My heart beats fast again, but as I answer, it's only Jacinta.

"Hey."

"M's at the door. They seem stressed. He's either on something, or something's happened, you need to come down."

Oh my god. Is this it?

It's happening.

I hurry downstairs. M's in the hallway, bouncing on his heels. He stops as he sees me, then sort of collapses inwards, as though all the air has vanished from their body. They take a wobbly step back. I catch him.

"Come on." If he's as nervous as me, he won't want to do

this with Jacinta in the lounge. I escort M up to my room.

"Do you want a drink, or food, or anything?"

He shakes his head. I've never seen them so quiet and withdrawn. I'm worried now he has taken something.

"You OK?" I ask. He takes a deep breath and gets balanced.

He's extra cute today. His arms folded across his chest. His tight jeans. His beard is bushier too. Sort of unkempt, rather than tidy and trim like it usually is. I'm here for it.

He looks right into my eyes. His aren't shining like they normally do, though.

Right, if he's not going to ask me, I'm going to ask him.

Deep breath. Here goes. "M, I need to—"

"The Enigaymatic Mystery," they blurt out.

"Who?" I don't know why I said that.

He frowns. Looks me up and down. As their eyes reach my fidgeting hands, I try and keep them still. What's going on?

He looks around, searching for something. They look under my desk and over to my wardrobe.

"Is something wrong? It's not the scars itching again, is it? You've not taken too much T, have you? I remember you telling me how that can make someone..."

"Make someone, what?"

I don't even know where I was going with that. I shrug.

I pat the bed beside me. It's weird being sat this far apart. He shakes his head.

"Did you see his latest live?"

My heart is racing. I daren't speak.

He's staring at me in such a weird way. OK, if he asks,

I'll admit it. It's about time he knew the truth.

"He did a live with William Gale. Your loss. Did you know he's a massive transphobe, and the one behind all those awful tweets at me? Not just me. So many other trans people."

"Will wouldn't—"

"DON'T. Don't stick up for him. That live was horrendous."

Shit.

"Made me feel stuff I've not even thought about as a newly trans guy. Ben..."

He's never called me Ben.

"The Enigaymatic Mystery is a massive TERF. Don't think he started out that way, but like a lot of shit online, things progress once someone gets an audience. He might not think he's a TERF, but after that video, I can't explain him any other way. Disgusting."

OK. Keep calm. I can get through this.

"Is it you?"

This is not the way I imagined it going. My stomach twists. My whole body feels ice cold. I keep my face still, but it's like it's been drained of every drop of blood. I feel the codeine kick in, but instead of the gentle lift I usually get, I'm sinking. Crumbling into myself.

"Answer me."

They're angry, but they appear oddly hopeful.

I know if I say yes, I will break his heart. I don't want to do that. I love him. I'm in love with M. I have been for a long time. If I say yes, I'll ruin that. I didn't think my videos were bad, but if M does...

What the fuck have I done?

Tears in his eyes now. There's only one thing I can do.

"It's not me."

He bursts into tears.

Should I hug him? Should I speak?

I instinctively put my right hand over my heart. Taptaptap. Taptaptap. What do I do?

"You know you do that when you're stressed, nervous, or anxious?" They're pointing at my little finger over my heart. I stop. "He does it too. Three times during the live. So. Final chance Is it you?"

How can I admit it now? How do I stop these tears?

"No."

M's head drops for a moment. When it comes back up, their face is red, their eyes laser-focussed on me. Filled with nothing good.

"Why? Why would you do that? The old stuff wasn't that bad, but that live one, and the more recent ones... Why would you give that transphobe your audience? When you had me in your life? Thought we were friends. Maybe more."

"Were?" I croak.

"All this for likes? Is it even true? Do you believe the shit you spout under that mask, after everything I've shared with you? Or am I the joke? A dare that's been going on for too long you couldn't get out of? What do you believe in, Benny? WHAT DO YOU BELIEVE IN?"

His voice is strong and deep now. I wish I wasn't hearing it used like this.

"I believe in you," I whisper.

"Bullshit. I came here ready to hear you out. Didn't expect you to lie. I tried to protect you all this time over your boss being my troll. Hope all your likes were worth it, 'cause those videos will come back to haunt you one day, and you know what...?" I can't move. I can't speak. "You deserve it. Whatever comes to you, you fucking deserve it. Never talk to me again."

M storms to the door, pausing as he grabs the handle.

I don't move.

They only pause for a moment, then they're down the stairs.

I hear the front door open. Slam shut.

I find the energy to move to the window. I watch as he wipes his face, takes a deep breath. He seems to have stopped crying. I haven't.

I will him to look up at me in the window.

He doesn't.

He walks away.

Up the road.

Around the corner.

Gone.

My legs won't support me anymore. I crumple to the floor and fight the tears, but I'm powerless to stop them.

Chapter 19

So much for it being the season of joy. As I pass people setting up for the outdoor cinema, Christmas trees and lights everywhere, I get a weird tightening in my chest. I have to sit down to get my breath back. I use the time to drop my codeine into a bottle of water. As it fizzes, I get my valerian pills out.

Watching M leave broke something inside me. Multiple things. My heart, for a start. I kept hoping he would come back in to my room, or come back up the stairs, or come back through the front door, or come back up the street.

How did it all go so wrong? M said himself he had laughed at the videos.

Will was helping, wasn't he? He's such a great guy. Supportive of the community. He worked for the gay and lesbian switchboard back in the day. How could my videos be offensive if he was involved?

Since M hasn't returned any of my calls or texts, (I didn't even get any typing bubbles,) I've decided I'm going to go home for the weekend.

The Castle is bustling. Everyone wears a Christmas jumper. I completely forgot that was today, so at lunchtime, sick of everyone asking me where mine was, I go get the cheapest one I can find.

I wish I felt as jolly as the twerking elf on it.

To make matters worse, now Will is back properly at work, our mentor sessions have started again. I could do without it today.

I force a smile and fake joy as he talks about my work. He layers on praise. Goes on about how much I've improved. The moment we finish talking about my projects, he's straight in on how amazing it is that I've reached 50k. "But when are you going to put out new content again?"

I shrug.

"Come on, Ben, you've wanted this moment for as long as I've known you. You can't stop now."

"I think I need to take a break."

"Rubbish. What's really going on?"

"Nothing."

"I know you, Ben, better than anyone. A problem shared is a problem halved."

The valerian isn't working today.

"I need a break from Manchester. I'm going home tomorrow for the weekend."

He turns his nose up, as though there's a bad smell. "Home?"

I nod. I need to talk to Mum. I don't know how I'll explain it to her, but I need advice.

"You can't." Will's harsh tone startles me.

"I'll be back for work on Monday, I won't miss—"

"Don't be soft. If it's the haters you're worried about, ignore them."

I wasn't worried about them until now. I've stopped reading comments because I've noticed people saying horrible stuff and also loads of positive stuff that doesn't feel positive.

"I need to—"

"No. What you need is to create new content."

I tell him I will when I've got new ideas to make content about.

He shakes his head, holds up his phone. "What's this?" He shows me our messages with all the recent ideas he's sent. They've all been about trans people and ever since... I don't want to do it. I need some time to take stock of all my content and what went wrong with M.

"I've been working really hard lately."

"I know you have, that's why you've got so many followers, but we need more."

I go to tell him I was talking about my actual job but he carries on.

"I haven't given you all my spare time to stop now. We need to keep pushing. Everything is changing, Ben. We need to keep telling it how it is. Give your support to the women whose spaces are being invaded. Prove how you want to protect the children from abuse. You've had your fun with your silly videos, now it's time to start talking about real issues."

"I don't want to do that."

He walks to my side of the desk, perches on the edge.

"Tough. Your audience wants it, and you have to give it to them. I know you're not so naïve you can't see there's a right and a wrong side of history being made. We've come too far."

"My content is just for fun."

He leans in close. "You know damn well it isn't. All the support I've given you... It's about time you started paying me back."

He stands up, between me and the door, his arms crossed.

"I will."

"Good, so get this immature idea about going home out of your head. I've got plans this weekend for you anyway. I'm throwing you a party."

I tell him I'm not in the mood for a party. He ignores me. Tells me he's inviting his most trusted friends over and wants to finally bring me into his true inner circle.

"It's time, Ben. You're coming to mine Saturday afternoon to help me set up. I won't take no for an answer. You'll enjoy it, trust me. Don't let me down, Ben. Will you be there?"

I nod.

***

"Hi, Mum," I say via FaceTime. I'd much rather be going home tomorrow, but this is the best I'm able to do.

I can only just see the edge of Mum's ear. "Can I call you back, sweetheart?"

I nod, but she forgets to end the call, leaving her iPad

against the sofa.

I can hear her being sick in the background. I turn the volume down. As I wait, I take in the little patch of the lounge I can see. I wish I was going back tomorrow. It might be small, but it's home.

I can see the edge of the TV, with one of Mum's soaps paused on it, but it's the Christmas tree that gets my attention.

Me and Mum have always gone for the, chuck-everything-anywhere approach. This tree is too symmetrical. Mum didn't do this. It has to have been done by Shaun and Jeremy.

I hear her return. "Mum," I say, but she doesn't hear me as she grabs a cushion, settles the iPad on it, on her knee. She wraps a heated throw around her. I can see the cable.

She pulls another cable from nearby. It goes under her nose. Is that oxygen?

She looks frail. Gone are her round, rosy cheeks, instead the skin looks papery and dry. Her hair is different too. A different style and colour. Almost like someone else's hair completely.

She takes a few deep breaths, takes off her oxygen, taps the screen.

"Benny, how?" she croaks.

"You didn't end the call, Mum."

"I'm sorry, sweetheart. I didn't want you to see me like this."

She checks herself in the camera, then moves the screen away for a moment. When it comes back up, she's straightened her hair and has a huge smile on her face.

"Well, this is a nice surprise, you phoning me. What's up my little presh-pots?"

She waits for me to answer. It looks like she's trying hard to keep the smile on her face. Should I tell her what's been going on?

She has cancer. Clearly, she's having a bad day.

Who else can I talk to though?

"What's happened, Benny? Are you alright?"

How does she always know?

"Mum, I've messed up with M."

"Oh, love. I bet it's not as bad as you think it is."

"He's really mad with me."

"You can fix this. Little steps by little steps. Tell me what's happened."

I'm not quite sure how I'm going to say all this. I'll have to edit as I go because... I can't have Mum hate me too.

Here goes.

I open my mouth, hoping whatever comes out isn't going to make this worse, but Mum moves her head as she settles on the sofa. I can't stop looking at her hair.

It's moved. Her whole head of hair has slipped to the side.

"Mum?" I point, but she's already spotted it in the camera.

She huffs as she moves a hand up to her hair and puts the iPad down. All I can see is the ceiling.

"Sorry, son. I won't be a minute."

"What's happening, Mum? Have you... is that a wig?"

She sighs. The image on the screen moves down from the ceiling, down the wall, and then there's Mum.

Completely bald.

"How long?"

"It was patchy, so I asked Shaun to shave it off."

"Why didn't you tell me?"

"Don't you worry about me. I feel better than I look. I'll be fine by Christmas. Don't you worry."

"You should have told me."

"You have enough to worry about by the sounds of things. I m alright. I've got Shaun helping me every night... I mean any night I need him. Tell me what's happening with M."

I can't take my eyes off her head. She can barely keep her eyes open.

"Is it anything to do with that William person you work with?"

"Why would you say that?"

"Mums know. It's the way you talk about him. It's not like how you talk about M."

"You've never met him."

"I know you idolise him and he's done a lot for you, but I'm sorry, Benny, I don't get a good feeling about him. Please tell me you're being careful. I know what you're like."

"What does that mean?"

She goes on to talk about Nathan from school. Apparently, it wasn't that he was such a bully to me that was the issue, it's that I was easily led. She mentions Cai too. Before I can protest, she's talking about one of my lecturers from my first year of uni.

"I told you, nothing happened with Mr. Kent."

"I know, lovey, but it didn't sound right when you talked about the things he said to you."

I wish I hadn't phoned now. "How was his behaviour my fault?"

"I didn't mean it like that. There's a reason he didn't return for your second year. I don't believe he left of his own accord."

"Will is nothing like that."

"Manchester is a big city, and you're so far away, but your home is always here. As am I. Please be honest with me, Benny, are things alright with Will?"

"Of course. He's been great to me. I don't need you making things sound bad. I'm not a child, and I'm not stupid." All I wanted to do was talk about M, and I get this. I'm over it.

"Let's not argue." She takes a few shaky breaths, apologises, picks up her oxygen.

"Just leave it on if you need it."

She nods. "Tell me about M. I'm listening."

I wish I had some oxygen right now. "It's fine. Just a stupid misunderstanding. I'll sort it."

"If you're sure?" I nod. "Right, well, let's talk about Christmas. You're coming home this year, aren't you."

It absolutely doesn't sound like a question. She talks about how it's going to be extra special this year. She's ordered a turkey. I'm used to a chicken. She's ordered everything pre-prepared. Things will be pre-sliced and chopped, sausages already wrapped in bacon. Pre-made stuffing. Just needs cooking.

"It will be the best Christmas ever. We will have more

time to spend as a family. Shaun and Jeremy will be sleeping over Christmas Eve this year, if that's alright? I'll still be making a trifle, though. I know that's your favourite."

"I'll be there, Mum."

"Promise?"

"I promise."

Chapter 20

Oh my god, I'm going to die. What the hell happened? My head is pounding on all sides, like something is trying to break out of my skull.

I turn to get out of bed but it's different. Bigger.

Wait.

This isn't my bed.

I unstick my eyes. The glaring light from the window stings. I notice a pint of water on the bedside cabinet. I down it.

I look around. Dark furniture. Wood-panelled walls. Expensive window blinds.

Will's guest bedroom.

I breathe away the sick that's curdling in my stomach. Is it Sunday?

I find my phone on the floor, inches away from the cable. I guess I tried to charge it but failed. I pick it up. For a millisecond I see a long list of missed calls and texts, before it dies. Ugh.

I heave myself onto the floor, headache worsening with every move. I plug it in, roll into a ball, eyes screwed shut.

Who's tried to contact me?

Could it have been Michael?

Why would he?

Oh. I remember.

I feel sick. Why did I do that?

Before I came here on Saturday, I went to his Tesco to speak to him. I waited outside for ages. He definitely saw me, because he spoke to a colleague and they looked over too.

I waited until his usual finishing time, but he didn't come out. I don't blame him, total stalker behaviour. Why didn't I just leave instead of going to customer services and asking if M was still there?

"You mean Michael?" the woman told me. That confused me.

"No. M. A bit shorter than me, facial hair, last name Emmanuel."

"Yeah, he's going by Michael now," she said. Then her face changed. I don't think she was impressed with me getting the name wrong, or she realised who I was. She simply said "He's gone. Next please."

I phoned him. Straight to voicemail. I texted. No reply. I even messaged him on Facebook, which made me feel weird as he's still going by his old name.

I thought, if only I could explain we could...

Idiot.

Maybe these calls are from Michael. I like that name, I wonder why he chose it?

I should've cancelled on Will. Ha, as if I should've at least not drunk my feelings away so hard. Last night is a blur.

What happened?

Michelle and Pauline were there. James. The manager of my team at work.

Loads of others too, but I can't picture their faces.

So much wine and champagne. So many toasts. Why was everyone desperate to talk to me?

Something about my phone too. It kept making noises, so Will took me to one side... What did he say?

Did he tell me to turn it off? No, it wouldn't be out of charge if that happened. He wasn't happy because it was a party for me. I was too distracted. What did I do with my phone then because I don't remember it making any noises or vibrating in my pocket after that conversation?

I remember after everyone left, very late, it was just Will and... It's a blank until this morning.

I've still got my trousers on, but only the T-shirt I had on under my shirt.

I head out to the kitchen.

"Afternoon. How are you feeling?"

I pull a face. Will laughs and offers me painkillers which I take gladly, because I stupidly left my codeine at home. These won't be strong enough, but it's all that's on offer.

"You were brilliant last night. You're not still mad at me for what I did, are you?"

What did he do?

Why is everyone's face weird in my mind?

Did they have their faces covered? Were they wearing

masks?

I go through to the lounge and notice several masks on the coffee-table. Ones like I wear for my TikTok.

Shit. They were all wearing masks like mine.

Fuck. Will told everyone I was The Enigaymatic Mystery, that's why everyone wanted to talk to me.

I rush to the toilet to be sick. I try to be quiet, I don't want Will to hear. Why did he do that? It was bad enough when Michael found out.

Yet, I don't recall anyone being angry. Only people saying how amazing I was, then more drinks. Even when it was just Will and I, he made sure we had one final toast before bed.

Now I've been sick I feel a bit better. Will has a coffee for me when I'm back in the lounge.

"Ignore it," he says, as my phone starts beeping. I guess it's charged enough.

He talks about last night, and mentions a CEO of somewhere I've never heard of and reminds me she said I was, *the voice of the lesbians and gays of generation zed.*

I vaguely remember meeting her. She wasn't a lesbian, though. Not many of the people there were actually queer if I remember correctly, which I'm not sure I do.

"Friends kept pestering me after our team up. It was time to tell a lucky few. Good people who are well respected and can help us. Feels good to be out in the open doesn't it?" he says.

I can't remember how I felt last night about everyone knowing. Everything was too busy to think properly. Right now though, I know it wasn't the right choice.

My phone rings again. Will tells me to ignore it as he's taking me for Sunday lunch, but I need to see if it's Michael.

In the spare room I see it's Shaun. I leave it to go to answer phone.

Oh no. All the missed calls and text are from him.

"Every night over Christmas will be like this. You better get used to it," Will says at the door.

"What?" I mumble, I'm trying to open my phone to get to the texts but my hands are shaking.

"Don't tell me you forgot you accepted my invitation? We're going somewhere warm over Christmas. You, me and my inner circle. I've already booked it off for you at work. You'll love it. Now get a shower and let's go eat."

I have no memory of that. How am I going to go abroad for Christmas when I've promised Mum I'll be home?

I get Messages open. My stomach drops so fast, I'd be sick again if there was anything left.

A string of texts, each more urgent than the last. The first one says...

Your mum had a turn, taking her to A&E.

The last one says...

COME HOME NOW

I tell Will I have a family emergency. I walk as fast as I can back to the house.

"What's wrong?" Jacinta asks. I stand in the lounge. I

don't know what to do, or what to say.

I show her the texts.

She's like a whirlwind around me. Like those shows where someone is in slow motion while everything else speeds up. She's up and down the stairs.

All I want to do is message Michael, but I shouldn't.

"Take this. Go." Jacinta shoves my rucksack at me, turns me around, walks me out the door. There's a cab waiting.

"It's taking you to the station. There's a train in forty-five minutes Get a ticket, get on it and get home. I love you. Now go. Platform two."

She was right. Platform 2.

I get my ticket.

I go to Boots pharmacy for some more codeine.

I'm on the train.

My stomach thinks I'm on a boat. My head too.

I take a few breaths to try and feel level again.

I text Will.

Gone home. Emergency with mum.
Don't know when I'll be back

I'm hungry, but I also feel sick. As I rest my head on my bag it crinkles.

There's a bottle of water, a bag of crisps, and a homemade ham sandwich. When did Jacinta do that? I don't feel like I can eat, but I need some strength for Mum. I shove the sandwich down my throat. I don't even taste it. It's an effort to swallow.

Halfway there. No reply from Will. Strange. I check it but there's no message from me to him either.

Shit. No. I didn't, did I?

Yes. I sent it to M. I better update his name in my contacts. What do I do? Do I ignore it? Do I apologise for sending it to him by mistake? Do I delete the text? Does it delete for both of us if I do that? I don't know if he's even seen...

Bubbles. HE'S REPLYING.

They stop. OK. I can't have this on my mind the rest of the journey. I copy and paste the message to Will. He replies instantly, telling me to take all the time I need.

Fields and towns go by. I'm at the door to get off before the train even stops at my station, then remember I need to wait one more stop. After I texted Shaun I was on my way, he replied to tell me Mum's at the local hospital in town.

It's agonising waiting for the train to get to the next stop. The moment it does, I run out. Jump in the nearest taxi.

It doesn't take long. Outside the hospital, I build up courage to go in, feeling like it's the end of the world.

Into the lift. Up to floor four. Doors open. Follow the yellow line to ward seven. Down the corridor Past a ward full of happy lively patients, past another full of sick patients. I hope Mum isn't in one like this.

Ward five. Ward six. There it is. Ward seven.

Half the beds are empty. One has curtains closed. I recognise Shaun's trainers underneath.

Deep breath. Please let her be OK. Please let her be OK. Please let her be OK.

Inside the curtains nobody speaks. The only movement

comes from the steady drip of whatever is in the bag connected to Mum via a tube. Shaun and Jeremy sit on one side of the bed, I stand on the other, none of us take our eyes off Mum.

I worry I'm too late, but she takes a breath. We all watch as her chest rises, then falls. Her breath sounds hollow and raspy.

I get the feeling Shaun is angry with me, but none of us have spoken since I got here. Jeremy smiled, but Shaun just nodded.

Should I hold her hand? I feel like I should.

We watch as she takes another breath. They're too slow.

"She's been asking for you for hours. You almost..." he stops as Jeremy puts a hand on his arm.

"I almost what?" I hear the rage in my voice. I don't care.

"Every time she wakes up, she asks after you."

I'm not standing for this. "I came as fast as I could. I didn't even know how ill she was. Nobody told me."

Am I in the wrong here? Mum has never told me she was this bad. Every time we've spoken, she's always been so positive, but the way Shaun is looking at me, I'm doubting myself.

"She's got through it before, hasn't she?"

Shaun shakes his head. Jeremy whispers something to him.

"You can get them. I'm staying here," Shaun whispers back.

"I want to be alone with my mum. Please." I don't want him here if he's going to make me feel bad. Jeremy nods, but Shaun shakes his head.

"She needs someone to be with her."

"I'm with her."

"You're here now. I've been the one with her all this time. I'm the one who found her on the floor. I'm the one who had to tell her you were on your way every time she asked for you."

Is there anything I can't do wrong at the moment? I look down at the floor. I don't know what to say. When I look up, they're both gone.

I take Mum's right hand. It's clinging to warmth. I wrap my other hand around it. Her little, papery-skinned hand inside both of mine. If I could donate all my body heat, all my energy to her, I would.

I wish she would open her eyes.

"Mum." It comes out as a croak. "Mum. I'm here. I'm back."

Nothing from her face, but I'm sure I feel her hand move inside mine. I wait for her to do it again.

Her face is calm. Gaunt, though. Her lips are chapped. Should I give her some water?

"Mum. I don't know what to do."

This time, I definitely feel her hand move. It twitches. I uncurl one hand and see her fingers move. Just a tiny bit. Her eyes remain closed.

I feel useless.

I kick my shoes off and get on the bed beside her. I keep her hand inside both of mine. I lay on my side, my face close to hers. I can't smell the usual Oil of Olay moisturiser she always uses, or that sweet aniseedy perfume she sometimes wears. All I can smell is a sanitised hospital. I don't want to be here. I don't want Mum to be here.

Her fingers twitch again.

"It's me, Mum. Please wake up. I need you. I'm ruining everything. I need you to wake up so you can tell me what to do."

Her lips part. Is she waking up?

"Please, Mum. I'll do better. I'll be better. I shouldn't have wasted all that time arguing with you. I should have called more. I shouldn't have gone away. Mum, please. I'll come home. I'm no use in Manchester anyway. I've ruined it all."

I close my eyes. Snuggle my face into her shoulder.

"Benny."

I jump, but I know it's Shaun. He's back to tell me to get off the bed.

"I need to be beside her."

He points at Mum.

Her eyes are open.

I jump off the bed. I don't want to hurt her. I keep hold of her hand. I can feel it shaking.

She's looking right at me.

Her breathing is shallow. I lean forward to listen, but no words are coming out. Just that rattling, getting shorter. Quieter.

"Mum. I am so sorry."

Her hand lifts out of mine. One finger points at me, then moves side to side. Her eyes look right into mine. I hope she means I have nothing to be sorry for.

Her hand drops onto her chest. She doesn't take her eyes

off me, but her lips move. A tiny smile.

I feel relieved, but as her eyes flicker to Shaun, I notice he does not look relieved.

He gives her a nod. Tears roll down his face. What's the matter with him?

Her eyes come back to me. That soft smile on her lips. My heart is racing again. She tries to speak but nothing comes out.

Shaun sobs. I've been mistaken.

Her eyes stay locked on mine.

She takes a small breath out. Takes too long to inhale again. I hold my breath with her.

Without looking away from me, her eyelids close.

My heart breaks as I breathe in.

I'm breathing alone.

Chapter 21

I lie still. No thoughts. No emotions.

Numb.

Cold.

Oh right, the heating was turned off yesterday. Maybe I should've stayed at Shaun's like he suggested, but I wanted to wake up on Christmas morning in my own house.

Christmas morning? Mourning, more like.

The house is quiet. No drone of the vacuum. No smell of bacon in the air. No tinkling of a tea-spoon in Mum's third cuppa. Not today, not on Christmas.

I pass Mum's empty bedroom. I'd do anything to see her lying there, rather than a bare mattress on an old frame.

I'm hungry. Did we pack the kitchen yet?

As I wait for my codeine to fizz, I take my valerian and CBD oil, and find half a packet of Jaffa Cakes. I take them to the sofa. It's dark with the curtains closed.

I like it, but something's missing.

I turn the old vacuum on in Mum's room, close her door,

and head back into the lounge.

The noise calms me, as does the smell of Mum's fruity conditioner as I snuggle into the headrest.

No, it's not the head rest, it's her shoulder.

"Mum?" I imagine her putting her lips to the top of my head, whispering through my hair like she used to do when I was little.

You called? I forgot she used to say that. Where did that memory come from?

"What am I going to do?"

If I was with Mum now, feeling the way I do, she would absolutely have something nice on the hob or in the oven. Lasagne. I can almost smell it.

Mum always made lasagne on bad days. Chips in the air fryer. Garlic baguette ready to go in the oven for the last ten minutes. Multiple carbs have always been Mum's way of telling me everything is going to be OK. I wish she was cooking that for me now.

Let's get some comfort food inside you. See how it feels afterwards, she'd say. She never pushed me to talk about it. Sometimes we'd eat our lasagne in silence, other times I'd go off telling her about the bully, or the exam, or how I couldn't get a boyfriend. She always listened. Always waited for me to ask her a question about it.

I could always count on the truth from Mum. The truth, carbs, and pudding with squirty cream, piled as high as she could get it without it toppling over.

I should've spoken to her about everything when I had the chance. I miss her phone calls. What I'd give to have one more. I wouldn't ask her what I should do about Michael, or

Will. I'd let her tell me about her day, what she did at work, what she was having for tea. I'd let her talk. I wish I'd let her talk more.

I wrap the sofa throw around me, bury my face into the smell and fall asleep.

I wake to the sound of Mum in the kitchen, tidying up. The hot tap always makes the pipe shudder a little. It used to scare me as a kid, because I thought it was a ghost, but Mum told me it was just the hot water tank in the loft trying to keep all the hot water for itself.

My heart skips a beat. I've realised my mistake.

Who's in the kitchen?

Jeremy nudges Shaun as I walk in.

"Did we wake you? I'm sorry, Benny. Merry Christmas."

They're organising all the food Mum ordered, which arrived a few days ago and went straight into the freezer.

"Good job this went into the fridge," Jeremy says, as he massages the turkey with herby butter, and fiddles with a pack of bacon. His hands are too greasy to open it.

"Here, babe." Shaun opens it, pulls out strips. Jeremy places them on the turkey.

"That's not how she did it," I say.

Jeremy holds the bacon out. This turkey is bigger than a chicken, but if this is the last Christmas dinner I'll ever be having here, it has to be right.

I criss-cross the bacon over the top, like Mum did every year. Something isn't right though. Not just because Mum isn't here. Something's missing.

Music.

Shaun senses it too. He finds a CD by Mum's

cookbooks, puts it into the CD player on the fridge.

We've never prepared a Christmas dinner without ABBA playing. It feels right for a moment, but as the chorus of *Dancing Queen* hits, I burst into tears.

They do too.

"You good to keep going?" Shaun asks.

"We didn't want you to be on your own," Jeremy adds.

"Not today, not on Christmas," I mutter. We all manage a laugh.

We don't eat much. It's not the same. We don't even have crackers. I wish I had appreciated all the Christmas days when I had the chance. When I think about last year it takes my appetite away completely.

After dinner, Jeremy goes into the hallway, returning with a large carrier bag.

"I found these when packing your mum's room. You know what she was like for planning ahead."

It's gifts for all of us.

Nobody moves to open them, instead they go back in the bag.

We clear the table. Jeremy puts the leftovers in tubs, as Shaun and I wash and dry up.

I open the cupboard to put the plates away, but realise there's no point. It's all going in boxes in the next few days anyway.

As I close the cupboard, the trifle bowl catches my eye, and it makes me want to go back to my room and sleep forever.

"You're coming back to ours. We won't take no," Shaun says.

Their home is normally sophisticatedly festive, but they've not even got a tree up. We watch sparkly, happy Christmas films, until I say I'm tired about 7pm. Not even Shaun's failed attempt at Mum's popcorn surprise entices me to stay.

I want this day to be over.

"Are you alright?" Shaun whispers. It's weird seeing him without a smile. Jeremy looks super sad too. Do I? I feel sad. I certainly am not alright.

I put on a smile, nod, and go to their spare room. It's mostly a mini gym, with a running machine, exercise bike, and a single bed wedged into the corner.

It's been ages since I've stayed here. Before Jeremy, Mum and I would sometimes come round. She'd share a bed with Shaun, I'd sleep in here. I don't think it was ever anything more than platonic. Shaun might be bi but he values my mum's friendship.

Valued.

In bed, I realise I've not even looked at my phone.

I find a million messages from my housemates in the group chat. I assure them I'm alright. Jacinta has messaged every day since I left.

A text from Will, too. A selfie from whatever sunny place he went to, and a—

Merry Christmas.

I cannot form the right words or get my fingers to move properly. He's been incredible since I told him about Mum. He sorted my time off so I could get the whole house boxed up. He even organised a storage unit for me.

I didn't know what to do. At all. Will did. I've not told Shaun he's paid for three months up front.

The last couple of weeks have been hard. I tried to pack Mum's room first, but I couldn't. So I started in the loft and made my way around the house. I could only do a few hours a day.

I wanted to do it all myself. I couldn't. I mostly slept on Mum's bed.

Shaun and Jeremy have helped over the last few days. Just my room and the kitchen left to go. It wasn't what I thought I'd be doing in the lead up to Christmas. The landlord has new tenants lined up for the end of this month. As Mum was already behind by two months, he wouldn't give me any more time.

I sorted the late payments. I couldn't expect Shaun to. I'll be charged for being in my overdraft, but it had to be done.

They invited me round for dinner every night, probably because we had a funeral to plan. I try not to think about the fact that Mum had already paid for it all.

I spot the gift from Mum. It's only small, wrapped in Mum's signature style; excess tape.

Opening it, I find the usual pack of socks, a box of chocolates, fifty pound in tenners, and two tickets to an LGBTQ+ Prom themed event happening in Manchester next year on my birthday. It looks fun. Expensive. I probably won't go.

My phone vibrates. In my panic, I accidentally answer.

"You didn't reply to my messages. Are you alright?" Will sounds relaxed.

I tell him I'm OK, ask how his holiday is. He tells me it's not the same without me, but I'm in his thoughts as Mum's funeral gets closer.

"I need this break. All the name-calling I've had to deal with, all the online abuse, it's taken its toll. My wrist still isn't as strong as it was."

"I wish I was anywhere but here."

"I know it's been difficult for you too, but you can't understand what I've been going through. I've tried to tell you, but you've let others get in your head. Where are they all now?"

He has a point.

"Maybe this will give you some clarity. Who else cares for you like I do? I've been through what you've been through. It's worse for me. I've got a whole cult trying to silence me. I fight on, though. I'll fight for you, too. I hope you see that before it's too late. That's if I'm still here. Merry Christmas, Ben, but I have to take my pain meds. You know where I am when you're ready to accept the truth."

***

I don't want to do this. I don't want to be here. I don't want this to be happening.

With all my suits back in Manchester, I've had to borrow one of Jeremy's. For my mum's funeral. How awful is that?

I have to sit carefully so I don't pop any buttons.

Betwixmas has been somber. I've only eaten because Jeremy makes me sit at the table and puts food in front of me. This week is usually fun, instead we organised flowers, songs, hymns, and readings.

I'm grateful Mum had talked all this through with Shaun. I wouldn't have been able to do any of this on my own. Who teaches you to organise a funeral?

I've barely slept all week. The local pharmacy told me I'd been buying too much codeine so I had to go into town to get more. I stocked up on valerian and CBD oil whilst I was there, and I grabbed a load of energy drinks as we continued packing on Boxing Day. The house is now empty. Mostly anyway. Awaiting its new tenants. It's got one more week left of being my home, but I guess it's not is it? Manchester is my home now.

I did a few TikToks to take my mind off things. I couldn't at first as everything was in Manchester. Will ordered me a new mask, green-screen, camera stand and light, had it delivered here. I could only manage a few of my old silly gay stuff.

Why do people carry coffins? It's awkward. I'm at the front with Shaun. Jeremy and a guy from work who knew Mum well, are at the back. I'm paranoid I'm going to trip up and drop her. It's heavy. This suit is hurting and these shoes are too small.

The place is full, but I can't look back at everyone.

A woman talks. Celebrant is a word I didn't want to have to learn. I was asked if I wanted to read something. I'm glad I said no. Shaun's barely getting through his poem.

I can't take my eyes off my Mum's coffin, waiting for the curtains to close and... whatever happens when someone is cremated.

"My condolences."

"I'm sorry."

"Deepest sympathy."

So many people. I only recognise a few. It's weird not having any family.

I can't get any words out. I wish I was anywhere else but here.

Back at Shaun and Jeremy's, there's a buffet and lots of people with strong emotions. Many looking sad, others smiling as they share anecdotes

As I hear someone tell Shaun "She's in a better place," I've had enough.

In the spare room, I'm getting back in jeans when the door opens. It's Michael.

"What can I do?"

I smile for the first time in ages. "Help me escape."

I follow him downstairs.

I pause as he distracts a couple in the hallway, directing them into the lounge.

He gestures me to the front door.

I'm out, running down the street.

They catch up to me pretty quickly, they're much fitter than me. It's all the working out he does. He doesn't ask where we're going.

As I reach my old front door, completely out of breath, I realise I was coming here the whole time. I let us both in.

It's silent inside. Good.

I head to the lounge. The sofa is still here as someone is collecting it on Freecycle in the next few days. We both flop on it, out of breath.

This would be nice, if the rest of the room wasn't so sad.

Clean indentations in the filthy carpet from the TV cabinet and bookshelves, both tipped as they were falling apart. Shapes in the dust on the mantelpiece from all Mum's ornaments. They're all boxed up in storage.

I don't know what to say to Michael. I guess he doesn't know what to say to me either. I'm grateful he's here, though I don't understand why.

I can't hold these tears back any longer. I bury my face in my hands.

I feel Michael's hand on my back. Warm. Familiar. I've missed their touch.

"Why did you pick Michael?" I say as the tears finally stop.

It's nice to hear their laugh again I'd forgotten how much it makes me smile.

"Dad. Was talking to him about names a while ago. He told me Michael was his choice if I had been assigned male at birth. It's not a family name or anything, he just likes Michael Schumacher. So I'm trying it. Oh, also it's he, him now."

"I was so unhappy living here, I couldn't wait to move away. Meeting you was the best thing that has ever happened to me, but I've ruined it, haven't I?"

I need to see his face. I need to know.

His brown eyes meet mine. I can smell his usual orange-vanilla scent we're so close. I want him to tell me it's all OK, but he's not moving.

"Your friendship is the most important thing to me. I don't want to lose you, Michael. Please say I haven't. I'm in love with you. I have been for a long time."

I lean forward.

He doesn't move.

Our lips, inches apart.

His eyes close.

I press my lips to his.

"Stop." He pushes himself away. "No." He jumps up. Anger all over his face.

I really don't have anyone, do I? "Please go."

I want him to refuse. He doesn't.

I scroll my messages. Not a single comment from any of my housemates. I'm sure I told them the funeral was today.

This house is as empty as my life.

You were right

Will phones immediately. "What's happened?"

I can't tell him about the almost-kiss. He won't be surprised about my housemates either.

"I am alone," is all I manage to say.

"It's not nice is it? This is why I surround myself with true friends. I always wanted you in that circle, but you put up a fight didn't you? You let them suck you in with lies. They always lie. I wouldn't need physio on my wrist if they didn't."

"You're right."

"I've done a lot for you. You've not always seemed grateful. I won't hold it against you though. You're not alone, Ben. You've got me. Nobody will support you like I do."

"Thank you, Will."

"Words are cheap. You can thank me, by getting on a plane. If you find a flight tonight or first thing tomorrow, you could enjoy our last four nights here. I promise you, you won't be alone."

After the call, I find a flight leaving first thing in the morning from Manchester Airport.

Chapter 22

My heart, body, and soul needed that trip.

Shaun and Jeremy were surprised when I told them I was going away, but were happy I would be with friends.

Five days of seafood and cocktails in the sun. Will told me absolutely no TikToks, work-talk, or, in fact, any talk that wasn't about Gran Canaria. He paid for everything too, which is good as all I had was that £50 Mum gave me. The flights were reasonable, but I've now maxed out my overdraft completely.

I didn't know how much I needed the head-space. Without it, I wouldn't have got through January as well as I have. Luckily everybody at work has let me get on with what I'm doing.

The housemates have tried to get me to sit with them in the living room every night. Jacinta might have said something to them.

I declined, every time. I don't need their pity. Will was right about them. They don't care about anyone but themselves.

My bedroom is all the personal space I own now. Shutting myself in there, away from the world, brings a little bit of comfort. That and my daily supplements.

I miss Mum.

Shaun phones me once a week. Tries to anyway, I don't always answer. He caught me at a bad time yesterday, as I had mistimed making my tea. I try to do it before, or after everyone, so I don't have to talk. I put another frozen pizza in the oven as Jacinta and David came in to cook their tea, so I jumped on Shaun's phone call to have an excuse to go back to my room.

He wanted to discuss my upcoming birthday. See if I wanted to come back. I told him I didn't. He reminded me I'm always welcome. As I didn't know what to say after that, I told him my tea was burning.

I waited to make sure Jacinta and David were finished in the kitchen. My tea should've been burned, but someone had taken it out, cut it, plated it up, and left it outside my bedroom door.

I also did a Zoom call with Shaun for Mum's will reading. I couldn't face going back for it. Shaun gets a few things. Everything else in storage belongs to me. It's all stuff though, Mum had no savings or insurance policies or anything like that.

Putting on my mask feels pointless now, but it's something to do. I do my silly little gay stuff, a few of Will's suggestions too. I've not done much content this month. I've managed about two new videos a week. The other days I re-upload old stuff.

My follower count has stayed the same, but weirdly I'm getting loads of new followers. Hundreds every day, but the following stays hovering around 50k.

"How are you doing?" Will says. We're in a little Spanish place, sort of outside, in a little alley with patio heaters keeping us warm.

"I'm good." It's true, too. I've spent loads of time with Will recently. He and his inner circle have been super supportive.

"Have you read any of the comments lately?"

He told me not to bother reading and replying while I'm grieving, but he's got my account up and seems excited.

He pauses at—

This guy speaks the truth

And—

I love him

And other positive comments, but quickly scrolls through the hate. Not fast enough though. I lose my appetite after the fifth—

He's a TERF

"This will make you smile. It only happened today. Are you paying attention?"

He brings up the X account he manages for me, shows me it's now got over thirteen thousand followers. He brings up a recent post of one of my TikToks. One Will suggested.

He shows me it's been retweeted thousands of times, but particularly by someone with millions of followers. I don't take in who, because I notice a string of comments calling me *TERF*.

"Ignore it," he says, noticing I've gone quiet. "It's a

ludicrous word that means nothing. Like *cis*. Actually, I wear the word *TERF* as a badge of honour. You should too. This is about us and our fellow same sex attracted gays and lesbians. And excuse me for being a feminist and thinking women deserve their own spaces."

Has Michael seen all these comments about me? I'll never win his friendship back if he has.

Only yesterday I went through all his tweets, keeping up to date with his life. He keeps calling out someone called *ImAGayTerf* who pesters loads of trans people, yet has been retweeted by accounts with big followers. Now I think about it, that account was also retweeted by the same celeb who shared my video.

That's not good. I need to—

"Look. This guy is a top comedian in America. He and this amazing woman who shared your other video, are the kind of people who could be good allies for you. I told you didn't I? I'm never wrong."

Will reels off more famous names. Some I recognise. They love me. They love what I do.

It's people who get hated on all the time online though. I feel like all my blood has evaporated. All my energy too.

"Pay no attention to the haters. They're the delusional ones who will soon realise they've got it wrong. I feel sorry for them. You've done good, Ben. Better than good. These fans of yours are going to change your life."

Do I want to change my life? If I were to wake up tomorrow and I was back working at the copy shop in Ming, even if Ra had still dumped me, even if my name was graffitied on the wall, I would thank my lucky stars.

What am I doing?

"Everything alright with the storage place?"

I feel like time has stopped.

"I got you a big enough unit didn't I?"

I nod. It's plenty big enough. It makes me feel sad though, thinking of all Mum's stuff sat in a metal room, but that's not what I should be thinking about.

"Are you OK with the rent? I can help you, whatever you need, say the word."

"I'm fine," I mumble.

"You know what?" He claps his hands, making me jump. "I'm going to sort you a pay increase at work. You deserve it, you've worked particularly hard this month. That way, you can have a little more money after paying rent to your evil landlord." He winks at me. "Shall we order another carafe of sangria?"

I shrug, but I can't stop looking at all these positive comments on my videos.

"They're right about you, you know. You are a hero to many gay men and women."

"My trans followers don't agree. I've been unfollowed by loads of them."

"Will you shut up about that. If they can't take the truth, they should stop forcing arguments. We didn't make it through gay liberation by being snowflakes."

"My friend said—"

"Fuck your friend. She has no respect for you. I'm the one that's here. All she's done is force her lifestyle on you. Tell me, before you moved here, were you living your life happily without all this trans nonsense?"

"I wouldn't say I was living happily."

"Don't twist my words. Our lives are getting harder of late. All they do is think about themselves. It's trans this, trans that. They don't give a shit about gay men and women. Did your friend care as much about you being gay as she did about being a trans-identified female?"

He must have done. He was focussed on his surgery for a long time, but that was such a huge deal to him.

"That right there. What you're thinking about now, I'm right aren't I?"

"It's not as simple as that."

"Yes it is. Us gays and lesbians have come a long way, and we did it by ourselves. That's why I think transgenders should be on their own. Their fight is not our fight. They're making it harder for us."

I frown. That can't be right. When Mum did all that research when I came out she said—

"You're telling me you've not seen how much more homophobia there is everywhere? We're being unfairly lumped in with them and it's not just the gays. Your poor mother noticed I bet."

"What?"

"All she must have gone through raising you alone. She did an excellent job I must say. She deserves to be recognised for that without having to appease a tiny minority. Yes?"

"Erm. Yeah?"

"I bet she didn't chest-feed you. I bet she didn't have to beg midwives to call her a mother and a woman, rather than birthing parent. Things were already tough for her. You've told me about nights she had no money for the electricity meter, or times you remember her not eating whilst you did. She's a survivor. A strong woman. She shouldn't have had to give up those words in her final months."

He tells me how he's heard that cancer wards have changed language, and how mortifying it must be for women to have to talk about their chest cancer, or have their female organs reduced to terms such as holes and external openings.

I know Mum would have mentioned that if it had happened.

She didn't talk about it though.

"You've come so far, now it's time to use your voice and your power to make sure our rights aren't taken away. You don't want your rights taken away as a gay man do you?"

"No."

"Good. Now, I've got an idea. It's going to require a few changes to your content, but I think it will be worth it." He looks at me. "I can sense your reluctance, but have I ever steered you wrong? Unlike your so-called friend and her lot who don't give a shit about your rights, there's a lot of us who aren't backing down. Do it for yourself. Do it for us and people like us. Do it for your poor mum. You know, there are people out there who want to erase the word *mother*."

I glance back at my account. There is a lot of love. More than I ever used to get.

"It might take a while to transition, for want of a better word," he laughs. "Listen. You're going to love it. There's something special happening on the 8th of March that I think

might be massive for you and your content. Interested?"
   When he puts it like that.

Chapter 23

I was not expecting this.

I decided to use the ticket Mum got me for Christmas.

Will has taken me out every night since he showed me his TikTok plan, but he's had to go to a conference in Amsterdam tonight.

Seeing as I don't have any other friends...

It really does look like a magical gay prom, but there's a massive queue. I'm stuck behind two gays about Will's age, one has spiked pink hair with flashing lights inside, the taller, bald guy he's holding hands with wears a top that has *Disco Daddy* on the front.

One night in the Enchanted Garden, an LGBTQIAAA2SP+ Prom, the sign says. Will would laugh his head off at all those letters. It is ridiculous having half the alphabet on a sign. At least it doesn't use that Q-word slur.

I present my ticket. I'm in.

Will would not go any further than this.

Above me, there's an arch, covered in signs with different sexualities and pronouns written on them. Some of them I don't even know how to pronounce.

I can imagine how Will would point out that these—what are they called, neo-pronouns? Are used by boring people who want to feel special.

Yeah, Will would've already left.

I wander past glittery trees. I dodge people on stilts dressed as giant flowers. I see people doing magic tricks. It's part fair, part gay club. It's very in-your-face.

I turn to go. Laughter makes me stop. A distinct deep-gravelly laugh. I don't know where it's coming from, but I know whose laugh it is.

Michael is here.

What should I do? I've not seen him since Mum's funeral. I've not messaged him either, but like Will has said many times, he's not my friend.

Why are my feet taking their time moving towards the exit? Great, now my way is blocked by a gorgeous sunflower-man, towering above me, sprinkling glitter on my head. He directs me to a patch of fake grass by a fountain that's full of dry ice.

Sunflower-man gestures at me to sit. He wafts a giant leaf into the dry ice, swirls it around me. I can't see anything except sunflower-man smiling above.

I hear the laugh again.

"Michael?" I whisper.

The laughing stops. Someone hurries past me. The dry ice falls back to the ground but I'm alone. Maybe I imagined it.

I listen to the DJ, dressed in a suit covered in pansies. The dance-floor is heaving, but my little grassy corner is quiet, apart from a couple of loved-up lesbians snogging, and a crying gay.

Should I go over?

His boyfriend appears. The crying gay smiles, ah, turns out he's just having a beautiful moment. I wish I was.

It's been go-go-go since Will showed me his plan. A complete reboot of my content, focussing more on how gays and lesbians need to distance themselves from trans issues.

Will had a great pitch. The event next month is going to be the start of it. I've been re-uploading my old stuff before I delete it all.

It's been nice to be reminded how I started, but Will is right, it's time for a change. He's been unbelievably supportive, he can't be wrong, can he?

Can he?

In the last few weeks I've felt like I've been in a Will tornado, but now I'm here with all these people, I do wonder...

What does that woman's T-shirt say? *Punch a TERF!* Well, if that doesn't prove what Will has been saying this whole time. Trans people shouldn't get away with this.

I mean, I'm assuming she's trans. Will told me he can always tell and will point things out to me, like hands, shoulders, facial proportions.

It's hard to say if the rude T-shirt is making her shoulders look big, or if it's her own shoulders that are big. Are her hands off? She's got a masculine face though. I think Will would be sure she is trans.

I'm definitely leaving this time.

I wind through the dance floor, which was not this busy when I was escorted by sunflower-man.

"Benny!" I'm pounced on by someone I vaguely remember from Pride. Michael's friend Kulvinder.

I glance around for Michael. He's not here. Kulvinder takes my pausing as me wanting to dance. He pulls me to his friends. They're having an amazing time. Part of me yearns to stay and see if I can feel it too.

I don't think Will would like that.

Kulvinder looks as good as he did last year, maybe even more handsome in this glittery shirt. He's got a huge bushy beard now. It makes his face look super masculine, especially with his head shaved.

He takes my hand in his big, strong, warm hands and pulls me close. His pecs are massive. I wish I had a body like him. That's never going to happen.

"Wanna present?" he whispers in my ear. I follow his gaze to a pill in his hand. "Wanna grab it, or take it the fun way?"

He puckers up. If Will was here he would make fun of me if I were to kiss Kulvinder. Well, he'd tell me I shouldn't be taking drugs, but, well, it's not a proper kiss. What would Will even make a joke about?

Also, if Kulvinder is being nice to me, that means Michael hasn't told him.

"Too slow," Kulvinder says, pops the pill into his mouth, pulls me close.

We kiss.

He slips me his tongue. I feel the pill. I'm not sure if this is the best or worst idea right now, but I've already swallowed it.

We continue to kiss. His arms move down my face, around the small of my back, and he holds me. If I didn't feel incredibly guilty, this would feel amazing.

I want it to feel amazing.

It should, but... is it me, or is Will actually here watching me?

I pull away, but nobody is watching, certainly not Will.

We dance. Michael doesn't appear.

Kulvinder introduces me to his friends. "This is Christopher, and his partner Candy, they've been together for bloody years. It's their anniversary today."

"Happy Anniversary," I say.

We talk for a bit. I'm surprised to learn that Candy is trans. Would Will have been able to tell? There's nothing masculine about her.

I notice Christopher is wearing a bow-tie in the gay male flag colours, which reminds me of a conversation Will and I had in The Village once, about a chatty gay guy and his trans girlfriend sat nearby. Will told me how it proved some sort of point, because surely a gay man isn't gay if he's dating a woman, which led into a whole monologue.

Maybe Christopher is...

Who cares? It's not my business.

I'm struggling to construct logical thoughts, and I feel the Will voice in my head is getting quieter, which means only one thing.

I'm coming up.

This music is the best thing I've ever heard. I dance with

Kulvinder, and I dance with Christopher, wow, he can move. Candy's in her own little world, arms in the air, a big smile on her face. She comes over to hug me. I don't want her to ever let go.

Everyone is having an amazing time. There's flowers and fairies and elves and sprites too. They might be real or I might be imagining them, but I love them.

I don't know how long we've danced for, but I am sweaty and tired. I still haven't seen Michael. Maybe he's not here after all. Or maybe he saw me first.

On my return from the bar, with yet another water, I stop for a moment. I feel like I'm in heaven right now. I won't tell Will about tonight.

I wish I could tell Mum though. I miss her.

It's weird how I can feel sad, but also content at the same time. I need to sit down. I spot a little stream nearby. A stream? Wait... I need to get closer. Oh, it is a stream, snaking around little grass knolls, under a bridge, and loops back around. This place is amazing. I find a spot, below fairy lights and bubbles. I lean back on a beanbag shaped like a rock.

I sip my water, and spot the woman in the *Punch a TERF* T-shirt. She's holding hands with a manly man, talking to the lesbians I saw snogging earlier.

"Ours too," she tells them. "They're only five but they've known themselves since birth, they even came three weeks early, much to my surprise because I was still working and did not expect to go into labour in the middle of a meeting."

Oh, she's definitely cis. Weird, Will says he's never wrong.

I can't help but listen. They're both bisexual, her and her husband. *Spicy straights* Will would say, seeing as they're married to opposite-sex partners.

Them and the lesbians talk about their kids. It takes me a while to register the bisexual couple only have one child, and they're non-binary.

Will calls this child abuse, but as I listen to them talk about their child, and all the beautiful things they do for them, I can't understand why Will would think that.

Also, her T-shirt is pretty funny. I can see it's a joke. Trans people get enough real abuse online, but I bet the TERFs would still go mad about this T-shirt. I know Will would. I'm not going to tell him I've seen it.

TERF isn't a nice word.

I'm not a TERF, am I?

I try and coax my fluid thoughts around that, but someone stands over me.

My heart skips a beat.

"Michael." I try to get up, but my legs won't work.

He's confused for a moment, then his face softens.

"Not using that anymore. Didn't like it. Trying, Angelou."

"Like the poet? It connects to... Bet your mum likes that."

He grins. He's the best person I've ever seen in my whole life. I love him so much.

"You alright?" he asks.

I nod. "Kulvinder gave me a pill."

"I know. Having a good day?"

"I love it here," I shout, because I want everyone to hear,

even though I'm sure everyone already knows, and agrees.

He's silhouetted by fairy lights, his face lost by bubbles, but I know exactly what it looks like anyway. I remember every detail, every changing feature.

We've not been this close for a long time. The familiar smell of his aftershave gives me goose-pimples. His arms have bulked out. He's got a vest-top on, with tie-dyed leaf shapes. He even has a bit more growth on his beard. It was tiny stubble last time. I desperately want to touch it. I bet it feels soft like a warm blanket or will tickle my fingers like those stupid feet-eating fish I once went to with Mum.

Mum.

I'm not sure she would approve of me taking drugs, but I know she'd be happy seeing me right now, like this, content. Especially after everything. She'd put her arm around me, and tell me what I need to do. Funny, I can almost feel it.

Wait! It's a real arm. How long was I daydreaming? It's Angelou's arm.

I want to stay like this forever. This place, this pill, this moment. This is where I belong.

"Can we talk?" I whisper.

"Not tonight."

"Will we be able to get past it?"

"Not yet."

"Why can't we talk?"

"Benny. Please. Today isn't the day, is it?"

"No. Today is a different day."

I should've known he wouldn't have forgotten it's my birthday.

I did feel a little bad I said no when my housemates

asked me to hang out with them tonight. They said they'd take me anywhere I wanted to go in The Village.

They'd all chipped in to buy me a pizza cooking stone for the oven, and a pizza cutter in the shape of a meerkat on a unicycle. It's ridiculous, but I couldn't stop laughing when I opened it.

I can't believe they remembered the joke. The night Jacinta opened the festive vodka, we were talking about gay body types. I said I felt I didn't fit into any of them, but if I had to chose how I felt as a gay, it would be meerkat, because I was so curious about The Village, and the whole queer scene.

I also got a package from Shaun and Jeremy. Inside was a card from them, a voucher for an American diner I'd told them I liked over Christmas, and a resin locket swirled with colours and a little bit of Mum's ashes. I told them to keep them all as I didn't know what I was expected to do with them. I'm still not sure how I feel about the locket but here it is, around my neck. My fingers touching it is the closest to a hug I'll ever get from Mum now.

I was confused by another present, until I opened it, and burst into tears.

Happy Birthday Dearest Son the card read. Inside, in Mum's handwriting, but quite messy, *I hope you have a magical day. I love you so much. Miss you. Mum xxx.*

Now I think about it, sat here, I am having a magical day.

She'd wrapped two gifts, although these were fancy so I suspect Shaun wrapped it, but Mum definitely bought them. A leather-bound diary, engraved to read *Benny's Diary*.

Inside, in Mum's handwriting, *Let it out, love Mum xxx*.

She got me a nice pen, too.

She often talked about her diaries. She wrote everything down, and pestered me for years to start one. I always said no, but I guess Mum had the last laugh, because I can't say no now, can I? Well played, Mum.

"What's so funny?" Angelou says.

I shrug.

We sit together, watching the twinkling lights, and I feel a bit of hope. We might get through this. Am I making the right choices to even have that chance though?

I don't want to think about that. I want to enjoy his arm around mine, our backs on the same beanbag, watching the bubbles pop on our feet.

Time stands still, or perhaps it moves faster than normal.

"Midnight. Have to jet." His arm snakes away from my back.

The pill is wearing off. My heart seems to be opening up an old break that was temporarily stitched back together with MDMA. "Why?"

"Wanted to give you yesterday. Happy Birthday. Rest is up to you."

"To do what?"

"Hope you work it out soon."

Every single part of me wants to follow him, but Will's voice is returning.

"See," his voice says in my head. *"Trans people are rude. He didn't need to speak to you like that, after all you've done. They're all the same."* He always tells me they're all the same.

I try to push the voice away, but he seems like he's making sense. I look around this happy place. Now, it's like nobody wants me here. I'm not sure I belong here either. Will's voice agrees, but I'm not sure his reason for me not belonging here is the same as my reason.

But the MDMA is making my curiosity for what my reason is, fade away.

This isn't the real world. Nobody here cares about me.

Will is the real world, and when I wake up miserable tomorrow, he will prove how much he cares about me.

Prom is over.

Chapter 24

"Excited?" Will asks, as our plane descends into Edinburgh.

"Can't wait." We've talked about today for months. It feels unreal that it's finally the 8th of March. All the stuff we've been working on for my account goes live tonight. There have been many late-night chats. I've slept in Will's guest bedroom more than my own bed at home.

Will has been teasing it on X. I'm up to twenty-five thousand followers. I've teased *new content soon* on my TikTok over the last few weeks. I'm floating around 60k. Amazing.

"Eat up quick. You're a mess, Ben."

He's right. I had to order a sandwich, as we've been drinking most of the day, but I can't be wasted for this event. Not that I know what it is. Will has kept it secret as a surprise.

I leave the rest of the champagne Will ordered and down a bottle of water.

I hide a wobble as we get off the plane. I'm more than a little light-headed.

I excuse myself to the toilets. Splash water on my face. Take my supplements I stashed in my bag. I'm used to taking them all now, though I've brought codeine tablets because I didn't want Will to see me fizzing.

OK. Better. I can do this. I need to do this, so Will keeps telling me.

Outside the airport, we get straight into a waiting car.

"We're going to make you a star. Everyone will adore you, even more than those that already do. I hope you're ready."

After we drive for a little while, we pull up outside a large hotel. Crowds of people are outside, with signs. With the car's music this loud, I can't quite make out what they're chanting.

The car pulls around the corner. I manage to see parts of the signs. A lot of them say *With The T*. We pull up by a back door, where a sturdy but serious man-mountain waits.

I try to look out the back window to read the signs properly.

"Look at me, Ben. This is your moment. A long time in the making. It might be International Women's Day, but this is your day. Come on."

I follow him out the cab, into the hotel. The chanting fades as the door closes.

We're led to The Bridal Lounge. Will gestures at the sign on the door, *William Gale and Special Guest.*

The room is laid out with champagne and fancy sandwiches. Will points out the bottles of Appletiser on the side that he made sure were there for me. I vaguely recall telling him how Mum always got it in for special occasions.

"Are you going to tell me what this is all about?" I notice it's 6.30pm. My posts go live from 7pm to coincide with this top secret event.

"You're the special guest. You'll never have to worry about money or anyone not knowing your name again. People who have written some of the most successful books, TV shows and films of all time cannot wait to meet you. They'll get the chance soon enough. They all will."

"Why me?"

Will holds a finger up, messes with his phone. "Are you in place?" He puts it on speaker. "This is from the hotel lobby."

Out of the phone, a chorus of people cheering and chanting "The Enigaymatic Mystery." Over and over again.

I'm starting to get a headache from all the alcohol. I pour myself an Appletiser, and Will quickly pours in vodka from a small bottle.

"Get changed. Your reboot starts soon."

He opens the door, whispers to man-mountain outside. The huge guy glances at me, nods at Will, closes the door.

Was that the sound of a lock or am I still a bit drunk?

I try the door. I can't open it for a moment.

There's a click. It opens.

"Mr. Gale will be back shortly," man-mountain says. He closes the door.

On Will's request I've brought my mask and my Kathleen costume.

Will appears ten minutes later. All I need to do is put on

my mask and I'm ready to go.

"One day you'll look back on this and realise this is where it all changed for you. You don't want to keep depending on me for promotions or living in a house I own and rent to you, do you? I'm sure you want to be able to get your boxes out of the storage place I pay for. Put them in a house you've bought yourself, don't you?"

I nod. I'm ready for whatever it is I'm doing.

I want to take a photo, but realise I can't find my phone. I ask Will if he's seen it.

He grabs his briefcase, pulls it out. Ah yeah, he made me give it to him before the flight so I didn't ruin my surprise.

"Check your TikTok," he says.

My phone rings, dings and vibrates the moment it goes back on. I'm tagged in live TikToks from inside the hotel. Mentioned in hundreds of comments saying they can't wait to meet the voice of sanity.

What?

I watch another video, filmed from the middle of the chanting crowd outside, but Will snatches my phone back.

"Mask on. Leave your phone. Let's go."

I do as I'm told. I follow him down the corridor, accompanied by man-mountain, to a small door where I can hear lots of applause and talking from the room behind.

"She's going to introduce me first, then you."

"Who's she?"

The door opens. A woman talks.

From a gap in a screen by the side of a make-shift stage, I can make out hundreds of people hanging on to her every word and looking up at her in admiration.

She's talking about feminism. Asking lots of questions about what a woman is, but my pulse is echoing in my ears. A pounding in my head, announces a hangover. I can't concentrate.

Will is introduced. He's straight on stage, waving, smiling, drinking in the applause. It's so loud that at first I don't hear him call my name, but when he tells the audience to cheer louder, and beckons me on stage, I go up.

It's like I'm a pop star.

People scream and take photos. The room is huge. Packed. There are people standing at the back.

All attention is on me. This is super bizarre.

I scan the audience. I recognise people from TV and social media.

The mask isn't great for seeing much, other than straight ahead, so I can't see the woman talking on stage. She talks about all the good I've been doing, and to look out because I've got new content going up soon.

Right this very minute in fact.

I spot a man at the front I've definitely seen on X, though I believe he got banned at one point. I think he's a famous screenwriter or something.

This doesn't feel real.

Will talks excitedly into his mic about someone called Tim and Tiff. He's having the time of his life.

Why aren't I?

All I feel inside is a knot growing bigger in my stomach. Sharp, as it snakes around my throat. It grabs my heart on the way up.

I'm sweating in this mask, yet I'm cold.

I keep focused on the audience. I don't know if it's the adrenalin, the alcohol, or the mask, but faces in the audience are changing.

That screenwriter is now Jacinta.

Behind her, two Karen looking women become David and Zoe.

Someone takes another picture. Is it Angelou?

Right in the middle a person takes notes on a pad. She changes into Mum.

My heartbeat is speeding up now. Either this breastplate is too tight, or something weird is happening across my chest.

Mum writes in the pad. Is it her diary? Is she writing about me?

My throat burns. If I move, I'll be sick. That's if anything could even get past my chest. Is Will squeezing me?

No, he's talking on the mic, but I can't hear everything. Just bits and pieces, words and phrases under the volume of my struggling breath.

"That word is a slur."

I need to take this mask off. The wig is pressing me down. The high-heels are pulling me off-balance.

I look at Angelou. He's disappointed.

So is Jacinta, David, Zoe.

Why don't they like me?

"Biological women."

Because they don't like what all these people stand for.

I spot Mum. Her heart is breaking. She hates me. She hates me being here.

"Trans radical activists."

I didn't like these people once upon a time. Why do I like them now?

This isn't who I am is it? This is all wrong.

What the fuck am I doing?

"Self-identification."

I need to get out of here.

"Supreme court."

I can barely breathe. I can't move either. I'm hot. Cold. Sweaty. Exhausted.

Frozen.

"Let women speak."

The audience applaud.

"Wave," Will whispers in my ear as he stands beside me.

I can't make my arm move. I feel him grab my wrist, lift my arm up like I'm the champion. We stay here whilst the audience gets to their feet.

Mum, Angelou, and my housemates vanish as the audience's real faces reappear for a moment, before my vision blurs.

I stagger to the side. Will puts his arm around my back and escorts me off stage. I instantly yank off my mask and collapse on a chair in the hallway.

I expect Will is going to ask me what's wrong, but he's watching the stage.

I've made a huge mistake coming here. And with all the content I've been saving for tonight.

Shit. I need to get to my phone.

I heave myself off the chair and I'm caught by man-mountain, who's appeared from nowhere.

"I need to go to our room," I croak.

"Sit, you don't look well."

No. I kick off my heels and stagger down the corridor. The farther away from the stage I get, the better I feel. As I reach our room, man-mountain says, "I'll need you to wait for Mr. Gale."

"Get out of my way."

He looks like he's going to knock me out, but I must get in. I'll fight if I have to.

My hands ball into fists. I'm ready to start hitting, but man-mountain shrugs and opens the door.

I rush to my phone. I type in the wrong passcode a couple of times.

Straight on TikTok. Sure enough I've got hundreds of new followers. I recognise at least one famous name, but I don't care right now. Only two bits of new content have gone up.

DELETE.

They've only been up a few minutes, but they've had over a thousand views already. One welcome video about my new content. One teaser video, with me holding a giant pair of scissors.

They've gone now.

I quickly go to the scheduled posts to stop the rest. There were five more videos, due to drop every ten minutes.

My heart can finally slow down.

The door opens, making me jump. It's Will.

"Absolutely brilliant. You're all anyone can talk about."

He's smiling, but his presence makes me nervous. I can't tell him I've deleted the posts. Not yet. He will find out, but I can't tell him now, in this room, with man-mountain outside.

"The after-party is happening soon. Wait until you see her house."

"I don't want to go to an after-party."

"If you're worried about people knowing who you are, don't. Your identity is safe. People have been begging me to tell them, but I've kept your secret. These are people who could do great things for you if you tell them who you are, but I understand. The things I do for you, eh?"

"I don't feel well." That's not even a lie. "I want to go home."

Will stares at me. He's deep in thought, but I can't read his face. He doesn't look angry, or happy. He's like a coiled spring. If he lets go, this won't end well for me.

He claps his hands, and I nearly shit myself. "Let me get us a flight sorted."

"Us?"

"I'm staying with the guest of honour. I've been to these parties and to be fair, I'd rather avoid the hangover and the faff for a flight in the morning. Come on."

Back in the car, on the way to the airport, he talks about how amazing tonight was, and how excited he is about my new content.

I don't want him to discover I've deleted it all, so I keep him talking. I ask questions about the event, about the hosts, about the celebrities. Anything to keep his hands away from his phone.

I manage to keep it up until we get on the flight. Our phones are turned off. I can finally relax a little. I'm physically drained, but there's no way I could sleep right now. Not with him this close.

As soon as we land, I tell him I'll make my own way back to mine. I fill him with compliments to keep him distracted, but tell him I'm going to get the train back, as I don't want to sit in another car.

We say goodbye. I keep walking until I'm on the train. I fall onto a row of three chairs. I could go to sleep right here, right now.

I don't, in case Will has followed me.

For some reason I open TikTok.

Bad move.

Thousands of comments on every post I've ever made. On Will's suggestion I'm meant to be deleting it all today.

I've lost ten thousand followers. More and more, the longer I look.

For every—

You (knife emoji) it tonight. Welcome to the family.

There's hundreds of—

TERF

Anti-trans twat

Go unalive yourself

I rush to the toilet. This feels horribly familiar. That time I got graffitied on the wall, I had abuse hurled at me for weeks in school. I had snapchat messages telling me how I would die of AIDS. I'm a paedophile. If I ever looked at a guy in school, they'd beat the shit out of me because gays are disgusting.

This is worse.

Mum helped me through all that.

I've got nobody to help me this time.

What the fuck do I do?

Chapter 25

I can't face work. I couldn't sleep properly last night. I kept dreaming I was back on that stage. I'd wake, and for a split second I could believe everything was a dream, but no, the stage had been real, and last night I had been on it.

I phone Alannah on reception to take a sick day. She mutters to someone. Will takes the phone, tells me to take the day and sober up. He laughs as he puts the phone down.

He wasn't laughing last night when he phoned to ask where my posts were. I said there was an upload error and the ones that did go up got reported and taken down. I promised I'd sort it out.

On cue, Will messages to remind me to sort the posts out, seeing as he's kindly given me the day off.

"You look like shit," Zoe tells me as I come out of my room. I don't have to worry about what to say to her because she's checked out of the conversation already and left for work.

I go to the kitchen. Am I hungry? Thirsty? I put bread into the toaster as I make myself a pint of Vimto. I down it.

I fill the glass with water again to take my supplements.

"What's the matter, Benny?" Jacinta looks concerned.

What do I tell her? She's pro everything that needs someone to be pro about it. She goes to every protest in Manchester. She will hate me if I tell her what's happened.

The toast pops up. Makes me jump. I burst into tears.

Her arms go around me instantly. David, Zoe, and I have often joked she's the mum of the house. She always rolls her eyes but never says anything. I think she sort of likes it.

She doesn't want kids, she told me that a few weeks after Mum died, as she was comforting me. She has a bad relationship with her mum, but she told me she's always felt like she's got the spirit of a mum within her. One of many spirits now I think about it. I'm sure she's told me she has the spirit of a warrior in her too. And a witch. Oh wait, no, she is a witch body and soul. I remember her telling me that. I have no idea what it means.

I don't know what to say to her. I sob in her arms.

She'd know what I should do. I can't ask though, she'll hate me. I make myself stop crying and pull away. She asks if I want to talk. I shake my head, manage a smile, take my toast and water up to my room. I have to do this alone.

I don't eat the toast. I lie on my bed waiting for divine inspiration.

I hear David return from work by the time I'm able to get myself off my bed. My mind races with ideas, none of them useful. I've decided not to take any of my supplements, especially the codeine. I don't deserve their help.

I check TikTok. I don't know why. I'm back up to 60 thousand followers. What is happening?

Most of these followers are people like Will.

What do I do?

I wish I had somebody to help me. Will said he was my only supporter but I have to get away from him.

He's so entwined in my life, though.

My whole body has pins and needles. I have to keep shaking them to feel normal.

Somebody help me!

I hate that his voice is the most dominant in my head. Telling me how proud he is of me. Telling me all the ways he's helped me. All I have to do is stand by him. Be myself. Don't let anyone take that away. Never apologise.

That's what he said, didn't he, when we talked about Angelou? I shouldn't apologise.

Oh.

I'm thick.

That's what Angelou is waiting for.

Could it make a difference? What if Angelou has seen the stuff from last night?

I still have to say sorry to him. Yes, I know I do, because the ache in my heart is fading.

No time like the present.

> *Can we meet? I know what I need to do*

***

My heart is racing. I should have practised what I was

going to say, but I wasn't expecting him to reply so fast.

Can I do this? I have to, I'm almost there.

My body is doing that thing it did last night on stage. What was it Jeremy was talking about during Betwixmas?

5, 4, 3, 2, 1 things seen, felt, heard, smelt, tasted.

I can see The Printworks. The stepping stones. A very busy pub. The cathedral.

I can see *him*.

I can feel rain as it touches my face. My jacket, keeping me dry. The cold zip, as I unfasten it, I'm suddenly too warm.

I feel my sweater under my hand as I tap my little finger over my heart.

He's agreed to meet. This is a good thing.

I hear the chatter from the busy pub. A baby crying. A busker outside M&S. She's good.

Almost there.

I smell hotdogs from a nearby stand. The Fahrenheit aftershave I've put on.

There he is. Sat on the wall where we've sat many times.

I frantically search my pockets for a mint, saved by half a packet of Polos. No idea how old they are. I shove four in my mouth and manically chomp as I walk closer.

He sees me. He doesn't smile. He doesn't appear angry either. That's a good start.

I smile as I chew.

Ouch. I've bitten my tongue. I can taste blood.

"You alright?" he says. My heart skips a beat. I've wanted to hear those words for so long. He doesn't mean them in the same way I've wanted to hear them though.

"Here," he passes me the rest of a bottle of water.

I sip it, notice blood on the rim. He frowns. I shrug, pour the rest of the water in my mouth, swish, swish, swish it across my tongue. The mint makes it cold. My cut tongue makes me wince. Good start.

He's waiting for me to speak. I don't know what to say. I need more time.

I spot a bin nearby, gesture at it as I hold up the bottle.

I've got until I get to the bin and back, to work out what to say. I can't mess this up. I have to tell him Will got in my head. I have to make sure he realises I'm not a transphobe.

I put the bottle in the bin and turn back, but my mind goes blank. All I can see is Angelou leaning against our wall, watching me. One foot on the grass, one flat against the wall, his arms crossed. When did he get a piercing in his left ear?

I can't mess this up. He looks like he's ready to listen, but I've run out of walking space and thinking time. Here I am, I have to make this right. What was I going to say?

"Hey Michael, thanks..." Shit. I've already fucked it. "Angelou. Angelou."

Angelou doesn't react. Doesn't even move an eyebrow. My mouth is dry. I can't remember words. "Let me start again. Thank you for agreeing to meet. I can't believe it took me this long to realise what it is you wanted."

He reacts now. Barely noticeable, but I can't take my eyes off him. He's taken a breath and held it. His nostrils flared.

I take a deep breath in. Let it slowly out. I glance at my feet. They point towards his. His point away towards the

Cathedral. I'm sure I saw a TikTok once, about how our body betrays how we're feeling. Does Angelou want to leave already?

I hear him breathe out, fast and hard. No need to guess what that means.

Come on, Benny, what are you doing?

I try to meet his eyes. I can't.

"I messed things up. I don't think I was ready to come to Manchester. Not mentally or emotionally. I didn't realise what I was getting into. That day you were supposed to meet me but didn't, that's where it all went wrong."

He looks away. He's fuming.

"No, I don't mean it's your fault, but that was the night I met Will. If I hadn't, none of this would have happened."

"Wouldn't it?" His voice cracks a little, like when you're holding back tears.

"Of course not. I was happy doing daft videos, but he told me I was special, that I could make a difference. I thought he was a friend."

"He is, that's the problem."

"He told me everything I wanted to hear. I looked up to him. I have since uni. I thought meeting him was a dream come true. I got to work in the place I'd always wanted to work. I never had anything as a kid, and he was so generous."

"You didn't have nothing as a kid."

"What do you mean? Of course I didn't. I only had Mum. I didn't grow up with two parents and money like you did."

"This is my fault?"

"No, I'm saying this is my fault."

"Really, 'cause so far you've said nowt."

I thought I was explaining. Haven't I? I came here to apologise and I... Oh!

"Angelou. I am so sorry for what I did. Will played me, and I was stupid enough to fall for it. I thought what I was doing was fun. I didn't realise it could be considered transphobic. I had people telling me how funny it was."

"Some of it was funny."

"Exactly. He sucked me in. Helped me when I needed him most. Used me when he found out about my videos. Oh my god, I wish I'd never met him. I've ruined everything. I was so unhappy in Ming, I couldn't wait to move away. Meeting you was the best thing that has ever happened to me. I was always there for you, wasn't I? We had a good friendship. I know my stuff was badly considered but it helped get you the money for your top surgery, didn't it?"

His eyebrows go higher than I've ever seen.

"No. I don't mean it like that. It's bad what I did. I lost my mum, lost everything, lost you, and that helped him suck me in more. Please, Angelou. You have to accept my apology. You know what those people are like, it's not completely my fault. I need you to realise, none of that was the real me. I'm the real me. The one that's always been there for you. Please. Angelou. I know you've wanted me to apologise, so here it is. I'm so, so, so sorry."

Silence. Literally everywhere. Manchester has gone quiet. Part of me panics that everyone heard my apology. I think it's my heartbeat pumping in my ears. Everything else has faded away.

His lips don't move. His brown eyes look into mine. Oh,

that orange-vanilla scent! I want him to tell me it's all OK, but he's not moving. I've said I'm sorry. This is huge for me. Why isn't he saying anything?

I feel tears forming. I blink them away.

"Your friendship is the most important thing to me. I wish I'd realised sooner. I wish I hadn't let people tell me what we had wouldn't work. I don't want to lose you. Please say I haven't. I'm in love with you. I have been for a long time."

"You fucking serious?" He shakes his head Walks away.

I hurry to catch up with him. "Isn't that what you wanted?"

"Oh no. No. No. No. Don't you dare. You lied to me, yet I hoped we somehow could get through it. I gave you plenty of chances to apologise. Still took you months. That was it? You even hear it?"

"I meant every word."

"Did you? All that shit you did online. For what? Likes? You said it was all nonsense, so why the fuck did you do it?"

"I..."

"This is going to come back and smack you in the face one day. Think this right now is bad? This is going to be the easy bit. Well, it could've been easy. Maybe your apology could've changed things. That wasn't an apology. Not even close."

If I can't make this right, what chance do I have of getting away from Will?

"Tell me what I did wrong, I'll put it right. I swear I will. I don't know how I've made this all worse? Please help me learn, Angelou."

"If you really want to do better, it's up to you, and you alone, to work it out."

"I'm not trans. I don't understand all the problems you face, so I don't know where I've gone wrong. Please just show me. Explain it to me. Teach me what I did wrong."

Angelou steps back, his hands up, palms out. Done. "It's not my job, nor any other trans person's job to do that. We don't exist to teach people like you what is right, what is wrong, and what is fair."

"I know. I know. But we're friends."

"We were. Want to do better? Find a way." He looks like he's trying hard not to cry. I can't help it though, these tears are coming whether I like it or not.

"Help me get away from him then. He owns me, Angelou. My job. My house. He even pays to store Mum's things. What am I going to do? I'm all alone."

Angelou doesn't react. "If you had the strength to do all your stuff behind my back, I'm sure you can find a way to do the same to him. Maybe you'll finally understand why I have to do this now."

"Do what?"

"Goodbye, Benny."

Chapter 26

Back home I throw myself onto my bed, curl up under the covers.

I send Angelou an apology text. I don't even get any reply bubbles. I go to Facebook Messenger and find he's blocked me.

I've really done it.

Will texts.

How you feeling?
How's everything going with the
account?

I want to tell him to absolutely fuck off and die.

Caught something. Can't deal w/TT
Give me the password. I'll sort it.
Can't. Got a violation. Appealing it!
Be back up and running by tomorrow
night. Big party at mine. Your new

*content MUST be up. Even if you have
to create a new account.*

NO. NO. NO.

OK

My chest tightens again. My insides feel like they're being compressed. I look around for five things I can see, but I need to close my eyes. A headache's growing.

I'm not going to let myself take anything for it.

Even if every inch of my body, inside and out, bursts with pain.

What feels like minutes later, Jacinta is holding a cold flannel on my forehead, telling me it's OK. My bed is soaked. I don't care if it's sweat or piss. David is cleaning up something on the floor, a wash basin full of soapy water beside him. I try to look, but it's agonising.

"I'm calling an ambulance," Jacinta says.

"Don't," I groan.

She looks at me like Mum would have done. Takes my whole face in. "Fine. Eat this." She hands me a banana.

"Not hungry."

"Please. You've either got a fever, or nasty bug. You've been unconscious for ten minutes after we heard you screaming. Don't do this to me, Benny. We're all worried about you."

I spot Zoe at the door. Not worried enough to come in, but concerned enough to be part of the group.

David pulls off a pair of Marigolds, drops them into the wash basin. He picks up a spray bottle of disinfectant, leaves.

Jacinta helps me out of bed, gets me clean pyjamas, and hands me the banana. By the time I've finished it, she's changed my bedding. The cleaned-out wash basin is on my bedside cabinet. She makes me drink a pint of Lucozade, then helps me into bed. I'm asleep before she's left the room.

This morning I feel worse. Jacinta knocks and comes in. She seems to have forgotten the knocking rule. She brings me cereal and tells me to phone in sick. I find the number on my phone, but I can't work out how to call.

"Here," she takes the phone. "I'm phoning on behalf of Benny Cedar. I'm his housemate. He's not coming in to work today as he's not well. No, I won't elaborate, nor do I have to. Thank you."

She makes me get up in the afternoon to watch trashy TV with her. Has she taken the day off for me? She's convinced I've got a nasty bug, which is why she's wearing a mask. I can't tell her this is my body punishing me for being a terrible person.

All the housemates sit with us as they get back from work. They talk about their day. I can't stop thinking about Will's party tonight.

"Don't show Benny," Jacinta says, breaking me out of my spiral.

What now?

"He needs to know, this is a community matter. No tea, no shade." David shows me his phone. I'm faced with a viral X news article: *TikTok sensation*

@the.enigaymatic.mystery helps bring the fight for LGB rights to the online generation.

Everyone looks at me to join in with their strong opinions. If they knew it was me they were angry about, they'd kill me where I sit. I think I'd let them.

"I have to lie down."

"Do you need anything?" Jacinta gets up with me. I shake my head. It's an effort to climb the stairs.

I perch on my bed. A text comes from Will.

Be ready for 8.
We're going to celebrate YOU so
HARD.

It's 6pm. If I go to that party, I'll get roped back in with his kind words.

I punish myself more on my TikTok. My follower count is now at 45k. I don't know why I still care. I have tons of hateful messages, yet somehow, these remaining followers think I'm amazing. They're giving me such love, it would be easy to miss the hate if I didn't know it was there.

Why am I even looking?

I stare at nothing, until I get another text from Will. How is it almost 8pm?

I'm sending a cab to you. You've got
ten minutes.

What do I do? What do I do? What do I do?
What would Mum say?

Little steps. What's the first step to a solution?

Don't get in the car.

Sure, but I don't even want to be here when it arrives.

OK then.

With a minute before the cab is due, I've shoved clothes into a rucksack, ignored all my housemates shouts, and I'm out the door.

At the end of the street, I pass a taxi heading to my house. I try and run, but it's too much.

I'm halfway to Angelou's before I realise that's not a step of the solution.

I turn. My body barely keeping me upright.

I get myself on a bus into the city centre. Mind blank the whole way.

I get off, straight onto a tram. Into Piccadilly train station.

I'm going home. Home? I don't know where that is anymore.

I get a ticket. There's a train in thirteen minutes.

I feel strangely numb as I get on.

I spot four texts from Will. Before he can call, I turn my phone off. I stare out the window at the darkness. I focus on the shapes, they help keep my thoughts contained.

In and out of consciousness until... I'm there.

Here.

I'm in a taxi, driving up my street before I remember it's not my home anymore.

Where do I go?

There's only one place. I tell the driver the new address.

I turn my phone on to text Shaun, and all my

notifications come through. They're all from Will. I can't look at any of them.

I turn it back off the moment my message to Shaun is sent.

I watch my old house go past. For a moment I see Mum lying on the sofa, watching TV. Actually, the sofa and TV are in the wrong place. That's a border collie and a staffie snuggled up together.

We pull up. I get out.

Their front door opens.

Shaun looks at me, concerned, Jeremy's arm around him.

On the doorstep, I pause. What are me and Shaun in this new world? I don't have time to consider because Jeremy takes my rucksack. Shaun pulls me into a hug.

It's not like we've never hugged before. He's been in my life since I was born. He's always been affectionate with me. Those hugs faded as I got older. I need this one.

I try to speak, only tears come out. I feel his chin drop onto my shoulder. His arms hold me tight. I hear him whisper something to Jeremy but we don't move. I sob in his arms on his doorstep. He lets me.

How long it's lasted I don't know, but he's gently escorting me into their lounge. I see it's been redecorated since I was last here. Dark green and pale pink. I have a vague memory of him telling me in an email. He's sent loads since Christmas. I've not replied to half of them.

The wood-burner is on. The room's warm. Safe. Jeremy brings cups of tea and biscuits on a tray as I'm taken to the settee. Jeremy always sits in the armchair by the fire. Shaun always has the settee, the left side. I'm on the right.

"Do you want to talk about it?" Shaun says as he offers me a biscuit.

I shake my head.

Shaun nods. "You mind if we finish this?" He gestures at the dramatic TV show, paused, an explosion mid-bang. Frozen faces scream.

I shrug.

The bang continues. A character yells, "Tina! No!" There's a monster too, or a zombie, or an alien. I don't know. I'm not paying attention. The chest tightening is back.

I see the TV show, but I don't watch. Eventually Jeremy goes to bed. Shaun makes hot chocolate and a Pop Tart each. Not those British ones, the American ones. Hot fudge sundae. My favourite. I wish my whole life right now was this room, these people, this hot chocolate, this pop tart.

"Shaun," I whisper.

He puts his hot chocolate down, sits up and looks at me. He doesn't say a word.

I don't know where to start. I hate myself for it all. What is Shaun going to think if I tell him?

I can't do it. Instead of words, tears come out.

"Hey, it's OK," he says.

He leaves for a moment, returns with two glasses and a bottle.

It's spiced rum. Shaun's favourite. Not mine, but the warmth down my throat into my stomach is what I need.

"We've got you. Whatever it is."

He'll change his mind if I tell him the truth. "I'm sorry I've been a dick to you."

He shrugs. "I forgive you. Another?"

I pull a face. Gross.

"Ey! Your mum bought me that for my birthday last year. Don't knock it." He laughs. I didn't know how much I needed things to be normal.

"I miss her," I manage.

"I do too."

"She'd hate me for the mess I've got myself in."

"Enough of that. She had a heart of gold and you were her whole world. Never forget that."

"You were her world too."

He takes a moment. "I was more like the moon. Close in orbit, always nearby, helping when I can, but you were her everything."

"I'm glad I got to say goodbye. I just wish she was able to say something back. I'll never know if she was proud of me or not."

"Are you bloody thick?" His words startle me. He's got a funny look on his face, half grin, half confused. "You saw her, right? In the hospital?"

"Of course I saw her. I was with her when..."

"As she left us. Her hand on her heart. Her little finger tapping."

I think back to the night. I remember holding her hand. Her looking at me. Her hand fell to her chest, then she was gone. I missed it. "How do you even know about the finger thing?"

He looks at me like I am not just bloody thick, but like I've told him the earth is square. "Are you kidding me? All these years and you think I didn't notice?"

My laugh sounds weird in my ears, like it's the first time

I've ever laughed. It sounds different somehow. Realer.

"Thanks, Shaun." Knowing Mum did the finger tap, something we started when I was in the juniors because I didn't want her to say she loved me in front of everyone, makes my heart feel bigger, my worries lighter. Tap tap tap. I love you.

"The spare room's ready. Tomorrow, it's time we went to that storage unit."

"Why?"

"There's something you need to see."

Chapter 27

The storage unit is small, but packed with boxes, labelled neatly. I don't remember doing that. It's not Shaun's handwriting either. Must be Jeremy's.

I help Shaun move boxes. The tightening that eased last night returns with full force knowing Will is paying for all this.

I should've taken my supplements before I came.

Or maybe I need to stop completely?

Shaun moves *Kitchen*, *Lounge,* and *Bathroom* boxes and finds a wall of boxes labelled *Eileen*. I wish I had been more active in the packing, then they'd say *Mum*.

All her life is in this unit. I meet Shaun's eyes. He's silently crying too.

That look is all it takes. We're full-on sobbing

The tears don't stop as I help Shaun. He moves *Eileen's Wardrobe (Summer Clothes)*. She always preferred the summer. She found old-fashioned dresses in charity shops and turned them into something new.

He pauses at *Eileen's Photos*. Mum was the kind of

person who still printed photos. She was always finding deals online for free or cheap printing. She never deleted any, even the bad ones, because she said sometimes they held the best memories. Her phone must be in a box in here somewhere too.

A shoebox makes me tear up again just as I was starting to get a grip. *Eileen's Jewellery*. Mum was never one for jewellery, except for her favourite necklace of a resin heart with a lock of my baby hair. She had a few pieces for parties. A pair of moon-shaped earrings she loved. Shaun has a pair of matching star earrings, because they always said they loved each-other to the moon and stars. Sure enough, he's wearing them today.

"Jackpot." He reveals two huge boxes marked *Eileen's Diaries*. "Help me stick 'em on the trolley."

Jeremy's got lunch waiting for us as we come back. Chicken and bacon baguettes with chips.

With every hot, spicy, juicy mouthful I swallow, another part of my body unknots.

"I marinated the chicken last night in garlic, chilli flakes, lemon juice, salt, pepper and Kalamata olive oil". With a mouthful of baguette, Jeremy heads to the cupboard to show me his fancy oil bottle.

I want to tell him it's delicious, but the smile on my face, and the sounds I'm making are enough.

Jeremy goes on to tell me about the marination process, and having to pat the chicken dry before frying. He tells me about the flavours he used on these chips. I've never heard Jeremy this excited. He's always liked cooking, but he's usually the quiet one. At least when it's been him, Shaun, me and Mum. Shaun and Mum never let anyone get a word in.

Jeremy is one of the kindest people I know. He never makes assumptions of anyone. That's sometimes led him to be scammed, but to be fair that was one time. Luckily he only sent £250 to the scammer who had hacked Shaun's Facebook and pretended he needed money.

He's never been one for getting involved with drama. It's like he refuses to force his explanations or ideas on others. If there's one person who would never ever get called out for being a mansplainer, it's Jeremy.

I wonder if he grew up in a place like this? Somewhere that made him smaller and quieter because he was gay. Must've been even harder if it was a place as white as Ming, too.

I think this is his way of saying it will all be OK.

He wouldn't say that if he knew the truth.

After lunch, Shaun and Jeremy head out. They had plans they said they could cancel, but I assured them I was OK. Which I am. Well, I'm better being here than I was back in Manchester.

My supplements help.

So here I am, in their spare room, with the boxes from the storage unit. To say they're filled with diaries is an understatement. No wonder they were heavy. I want to read them, but also I don't.

They've redecorated in here. I didn't notice last night or this morning. It's a similar colour to my old bedroom. There's a framed picture on the wall of Heartstopper. Funny, I used to have a Heartstopper poster blue-tacked on my old bedroom wall, similar.

There's also a big chunky knitted throw on the bed, like the one Mum made for me. Mine's back in Manchester, but this one is Shaun's. Mum made mine in blues and greens, his in blue, purple, and pink.

The gym equipment is gone too, replaced with a little desk and chair, similar to the one I had in my old...

Oh. I see what they've done. I don't deserve this.

I open a box. Mum's whole life contained in pages. She wrote in one every day.

I haven't started the blank diary she got me yet.

Shaun told me I need to find the final one. A diary Shaun got her, black and white striped background, with a pride-coloured A on the front. The LGBTQ+ ally flag.

Here it is. Shaun said to find the last entry. I flick through, find it halfway through the notebook. The finality of it, the fact there's no more words after... I can't read this yet.

I pick another. She's planning my thirteenth birthday. We swapped bedrooms so I could have the biggest one. I read her budgeting for redecorating. Her happiness over having money this year. Her sadness over previous birthdays where she didn't.

Hours go by. I read through another and discover I was quite a brat at fifteen. Even though Mum uses kind words, all the things I put her through bring the tightening back.

That's enough for tonight. It's supplement time anyway.

I sit with Shaun and Jeremy when they return. I can't stop twitching my leg. I need to talk to Shaun, but even when Jeremy leaves us alone to cook dinner, I can't bring myself to start the conversation.

I spot them give me multiple glances over dinner. As we watch TV after, too. I want to stay in this bubble. If I speak, I'll burst it.

I stay quiet.

I wake early Sunday with a huge stomach-ache. All my muscles tight. I have to do something. I can't stay here forever.

I turn my phone on for the first time since Friday. Ugh.

Multiple calls and texts from Will. I feel sick as I reply to tell him I had to come back here to see my doctor.

I'll be back tomorrow

I'll worry about that lie when I need to.

My housemates have filled the group chat with worried messages. I spin them the same lie. They instantly reply, full of relief and support.

I read more diaries. I skip most of the stuff that gets too personal about her. I keep my focus on the stuff about me.

I did wonder if that was super narcissistic, I now feel it's deserved, like self-harm. Every entry where Mum has been angry or sad or worried for me, I read slowly. Making myself understand what a terrible person I've always been, is the only way I'm going to get myself out of this nightmare.

I know I have to get away from William, but I don't want to stay in Ming.

I've considered running away. Leave everything in

Manchester, here, and in storage. Drain my bank account. Vanish.

I'm too much of a coward, though. I haven't even closed down my TikTok.

I take a look at my account, ignoring all notifications. I cover the follower count up. I don't want to see that today. I set my account to private. Why can't I just delete it?

Because I'm terrified Will might somehow use it against me. As long as I don't make him too concerned, I'm good.

But I have to do something that is going to affect everything between us. Of course I do. It's the only way. I just don't fucking want to do it.

I need to talk to Shaun today, but these buggers do everything together. How do you ask a pair of loved up queer men to go and do something on their own for once?

They even go to work together. They have different jobs, but they share a car. One will drop the other off and pick them up on the way home.

When they get back they hang out together. Every night. Jeremy always cooks. Whilst he does that, Shaun does the washing, or the online shop or whatever. Then they watch TV together.

What did Jeremy do when Shaun and my mum hung out?

Ah. I know. There's only one thing Jeremy does that Shaun isn't keen on: little tiny figurines of monsters. I think it's mostly *Lord of the Rings*, but I've seen *Star Trek* or *Star Wars* things. He paints them. That's what he must have done when Shaun was with Mum.

They're adorable together. I wish I had what they had. I

almost did and I blew it.

We all sit in the lounge. Jeremy puts on some spaceship thing, I can tell Shaun isn't totally into, but watches anyway. This is the most animated I've ever seen Jeremy.

"Woah. I did not see that coming. Did you?"

"I didn't babe."

I hide a smile. Shaun definitely didn't see it coming because his eyes were closed.

"That's put me in a spacey mood. Tonight's the night."

He stands up, all excited. I'm confused.

"He's talking about his models. He got the new Star Wars one—"

"Trek babe. I got the new Enterprise last month and I can tell you're not interested so I'll love you both and leave you."

I don't have any more excuses, do I!

It takes me ten minutes to finally say, "Shaun?"

Within seconds the TV is off. He's turned to face me. Anyone would think he was waiting for this.

Why won't the words come out?

I have to rip the plaster off quickly.

"Do you think I'm a transphobe?"

He's shocked. "No. Of course you're not."

He's my only person left. "I'm scared you'll change your mind in a minute."

"I won't, but I'm listening."

"I've done something bad." That's how I start. The words pour out.

Everything.

I stutter as I explain how Will is so ingrained into my life with the house, and the storage unit. I expect Shaun to tell me he would have paid for it, but he doesn't. He stays silent and listens. Like Mum would've done.

I have to pause when I mention the videos. I can't get the words out. I cry as I mention how I hurt Angelou with my content.

I hate myself for being pathetic.

Shaun puts a box of tissues between us. I use almost a full box on my tears, snot, and spit.

As it all comes out, I feel my body stop vibrating. I've done so much damage but I'm strangely calm now. "Before the car turned up, I knew I had to get away. So I came home. Well, I came here."

This is it. He knows it all. He's going to throw me out.

He's not smiling or frowning. He's usually joyful and happy. Even at Mum's funeral he was able to talk to people about the good things Mum did, and kept the energy up. This face is something I can't predict.

"I'll always be your home." He hugs me. Warm and tight.

"I shouldn't have listened to him, but I did. It's all my fault."

"All the things he's done for you, or rather, the ways he's inserted himself into your life, all those things were done on purpose, to make you feel like you didn't have a choice. There's a word for people like that."

"I got caught up in all the likes. Please don't look for my account."

"I'm too old for TikTok. So... you like Angelou?"

I tell him about the times we've spent together. How it

changed when I lied. I'm in tears again. I bury my head in my arms, curl up into a ball, and lean into the squashy arm of the sofa.

"I'll do whatever I can to help. We both will. Tell us what you need."

"I. Need. To put it right with Angelou."

"There you go," Shaun whispers. "You can't be a transphobe if this is your first thought."

"I am. I have been."

"If you want to change, you can change." Jeremy's here. I've never seen him so intense. "You can't change the past, but you can make a conscious decision to make a better future for yourself."

"Didn't you hear how awful I've been?"

Jeremy shakes his head. "I know who you are, and I know you're hurting. If you've made a mistake, I know you can put it right. You're not, and never have been a bad person. Badly led sometimes, I think."

"Jeremy!" Shaun doesn't look happy.

"I'm being honest. We both know things have been tough for him. For you, Benny. I believe you can find your way again."

"I can't do it by myself."

"Good job you've got us," Jeremy says it before Shaun does.

We talk until the early hours. They help me make a plan.

Looks like I am going back to Manchester tomorrow, after all.

Chapter 28

"Phone, text, email, WhatsApp, or Facebook Message if you need us for AN—Y—THING. You are not alone, Benny. You are our family. Do you understand?" Shaun looks at me wide eyed.

"Even after—"

"Always," Shaun and Jeremy say in unison.

As my train arrives, I whisper to Shaun, "You don't have to keep helping me you know, just because Mum asked."

He frowns so deep his eyebrows almost touch. "Eileen never asked me to do that. She always told me you'd be alright, and I believe that too. Don't look at me like that. No, she never once asked. I offered. She said she couldn't expect that of me. I said shut up you batty old faghag. She of course clutched her pearls and played the cancer card. Joking of course. She did eventually try to thank me, I told her it wasn't necessary."

I love these guys.

They wave to me as the train leaves, hand in hand. I get

a text less than thirty seconds later

Anything you need. ASK.
Please. We love you xx

Last night, Shaun said I could pack everything up in Manchester and move in with them. Jeremy said he'd come with me to Manchester and do whatever arse kicking I needed. I'm not convinced he could even hurt a fly, but I don't think he was joking.

I'm grateful they want to help, but I have to do this in person. Alone. To make sure I don't chicken out, I text Will, tell him I'm on my way back, and can we talk.

Ben! Happy to hear you're coming
back. Come over whenever. I'm
working from home today.

I change my mind about whether I should go through with it, more times than the train stops, but as I arrive into Piccadilly, I know I have to do this.

I put up a new TikTok post at the station, and go straight to his apartment.

No turning back.

At his door I'm reluctant to knock. I start to look at what five things I can see, but if I spend time on that, I'll never do it.

He always likes me to dress smart when we're together. Knowing he won't like me dressed in my jeans and hoody gives me the push I need to knock.

"You're home. Welcome back. Come in."

I swallow the sick that rises up, tap my little finger over my heart, and follow. I'm ready to tell him I'm quitting my job, and not doing any more hateful content.

"Here he is, the one and only," Will says to James and Michelle.

I was hoping it would just be him.

He offers me a glass of champagne. I down it to help my tongue unstick from the roof of my mouth.

"The future. The legend. The man behind the mask. To Ben."

Damn. I forgot he had told people.

"You know, I worked it out long before your team up on the tic tac."

"She did," Will says. "Kept it secret for you."

"It took me a bit after to get there," James says.

"Oh James," Michelle says. "We all saw how shocked you were at the party."

James puts on a *silly-me* face and shrugs.

I need to do it now, but they're filling the silence asking how my weekend was. If I'm feeling better. Talking about the weather. Discussing a new TV series.

Absolutely nothing about trans people, which feels strange because they always seem to come up. Or do they? I'm sure the topic always goes to trans people, or some problem my generation of LGBTQ+ people have caused.

I'm not here for pleasantries.

Now or never, Benny.

"I'm done with TikTok. I'm not doing any more videos."

Silence.

Their conversation ends mid-sentence.

My heart races. Stay strong.

"Why not?" The silence is broken by Will. James and Michelle are still holding their breaths.

I can't seem to formulate a single word. I shrug.

"How selfish." Michelle folds her arms, glares at me.

"It's not selfish, I'm finished."

"You can't be." James tries to glare like the others, but fails.

"He can if he wants." Will's eyes don't move from me. "If he wants to throw away all I've done for him, and all the opportunities he's got coming, he can. I don't think it's really what he wants to do though. Is it, Ben?"

All eyes on me.

Don't give in now. You can do this. Be brave, for once in your life.

"The stuff I've been doing... I'm ashamed of it. I'm not transphobic like you."

"I'm not against trans people. Show me proof of where I've said anything against trans people! You can't, can you. They can do whatever they want it just shouldn't be part of our fight, nor should it infringe on women's rights. Agree with me here, Michelle."

"I do agree. As does the supreme court. I don't want to be attacked, or raped or worse whilst using a public toilet. Do you think that's something I should be quiet about, Ben?"

"That's not likely to happen." I say this, remembering something Angelou told me ages ago, but instantly I see it was the wrong thing to say right now. Michelle looks like she's going to kill me as she darts forward. The wall is behind me, I've nowhere to go.

Inches from my face she spits, "If you think that, you are more of a misogynist than I thought could ever be possible. You don't deserve to have this man as your mentor. Apologise now while you still have the chance."

"He's not only misogynistic, he's also extremely homophobic if he thinks being gay and lesbian should be watered down because of the transgenders." James seems happy with that.

I'd laugh at how pathetic he is, but they're all blocking the only way out of this room.

Nothing to lose.

"I don't accept that." My body tingles. I feel super present right now. "I hate that I've hurt not only the trans community, but a good friend of mine." Michelle opens her mouth to talk but she can fuck right off. "Your life, your gender is not affected by trans people. I'm sorry if you've ever been attacked or abused because you're a woman."

"Yes, an adult human fe—"

Nope. "I've never had to experience that, but I have experienced hate and abuse for being gay and let me tell you, nobody needs to pretend to be anything to be an abuser, least of all queer."

They all look like I've smacked them. They hate that word. I'm glad I used it.

"Bad people will do whatever they want. Trans women do not affect what it means to be a woman, nor do trans men affect what it means to be men, not that you seem to ever talk about that. And don't make me fucking laugh about homophobia."

My chest feels lighter than air.

James is such a weak excuse of a man. I honestly do think I could kick the shit out of him if I had to. "The hate coming out of your mouth is the same as it was for gays and lesbians years ago. Even I know that and I'm not even old enough to remember it. I made a mistake doing what I did."

James' shoulders drop a little. Yeah, little twat. Michelle doesn't move, but I can tell she's out of things to say. Funny how hate comes down to very little ammo. They both look to Will.

"Feel better after your hissy fit?" Will laughs.

"I'd kick him to the kerb. He doesn't respect you, gays, lesbians or women like me. Seems he doesn't respect children either, he'd rather see them groomed. Is he a groomer too?"

I can see her eyes are daring me to say something, but what the actual fuck do I say to that?

"You are throwing away—"

"I don't care, Will. I never should have said any of it."

"Ah, but you did. YOU. Nobody made you say those things."

Well, I cannot deny that.

I expect Will to scream. Instead, he softens. "There's no repairing the damage with those lot. Why try? Did they get into your head? They have a lot of convincing arguments about gender woo woo, but you've done nothing wrong. You've seen how laws are changing, how people online are wisening up. You don't want to look back on all this one day and realise you stopped just before the revolution. A revolution you could do well out of."

I want to tell him I don't want any part of it, but no words come out.

"Benny." He never uses my real name and now I wish he hadn't. "I know it's been hard for you, with your mother, and moving here. I've always looked out for you, but you've said your bit. You've been very rude, but I know you're going through a lot. I want to keep helping you with your house, and the storage place. Let's forget about tonight. I forgive you, Benny. We all do."

"All in the past," Michelle says.

"All forgotten," James adds.

"I think the world of you. Stick with me. You'll want for nothing. In fact, you'll be supporting yourself in no time. Don't you want that? Don't you want the security and comfort you've never really had? I'll help you get it. What do you say? Shall we crack open some decent red and get your confidence back?"

All eyes are on me. I hate him but he's right, I am losing my confidence.

It would be so easy to say yes.

Don't.

You.

Dare.

"No. I'm done. I quit my job too."

Will is stunned. I take the opportunity to stride past him. Michelle goes to comfort Will. James looks like he wants to stop me, but pulls his arm back.

I did it. I'm free.

Even better, on the train here I worked out I've got

eighteen days holiday left. That's my notice period covered. I fire off my resignation email I crafted on the train, waiting in my drafts, to HR.

As I close Will's front door behind me, I catch James saying, "Have you seen his TikTok?" I don't want to hang around for Will to see that. He's going to be furious.

I slowly head back to mine. My legs are like jelly. My heart is only now beating normally, like I've run a marathon. I feel good though.

I realised on the train, my account needed to reflect who I really am, so I made my account public again, deleted all my posts. Even those daft ones I did at the start. They've all gone. In their place, a screenshot of the letter I wrote on my notes app. I found the most trending song for the background in the hope it would get to more people.

I grab myself a coffee from the first place I pass. I need the boost right now. I read my post as I sip it.

Please don't scroll on. Hear me out. The videos I posted were not representative of how I truly feel. I know I made a mistake and I'm deeply sorry. What I said about queer people, especially the trans community, was awful. I know that's not enough right now, but I hope it's a start. I do want to say that I was encouraged to do a lot of them. I'm not making excuses. I hate myself for that. I wish I had been a stronger person so I wasn't conned by William Gale. He uses many aliases online to troll the trans community on TikTok, X, and no doubt other platforms. I have cut all ties with him. I can't say he forced me to do all the videos, but the way he entangled himself into my life, made me feel like I had to. If you see anything like them online, please report them. It might not do much good. A lot of my videos were reported, but none of them were taken down as they were apparently not breaking any rules. I know, right. William Gale is a transphobe. Never listen to transphobes. We are stronger together as a community. The L, the G, the B and P with the T. The As, I, 2 spirit too. I've deleted all my posts. If you see them hanging around anywhere, don't share them. Don't be like me. Be better than me. I apologise if I've harmed you in any way. Goodbye everyone.

I see it's already been stitched and duetted. I daren't look to see if that's good or bad right now. It has had thousands of comments and over ten thousand likes.

Out of habit I check my follower count. It's just under 30k. Honestly, I don't care anymore. Well, I wish I didn't. I'm going to try to not care anyway.

Will phones as I finish my coffee. I answer and quickly cancel the call. I don't even want a voicemail from him. Before he can do it again I block his number.

It makes me smile thinking how mad he's going to be. That feeling gets me all the way home.

It's silent inside. I guess everyone is at work.

I feel sticky and gross. An extra long hot shower sounds amazing. I might even use some of that scrub David tells me I mustn't ever use because it's expensive.

As I take off my shoes, there's a knock at the door.

Not a knock, a pounding.

I freeze at the top of the stairs as a voice screams, "Answer the fucking door."

It's Will. Yeah, no way I'm answering that, especially as I'm on my own.

I would feel smug he's come all this way, raging, but honestly I'm a bit scared. It's a good job I shut the door properly. Jacinta's always telling me off for leaving it open. I double-check to make sure. Yes, it's shut.

He pounds on the door again. Swears.

I hear a familiar sound.

Wait, he isn't doing what I think he's doing, is he?

Shit.

He unlocks the door, kicks it open, spots me at the top of the stairs. I don't know what the fuck to do.

"Come and face me."

"What are you doing here?"

"It's my house, now explain to me why you thought it was a good idea to do that on your account?"

I can do this.

I can see the vase on the stairs window. I can see my pale reflection in the glass. I can see Will glaring at me. I can see the empty lounge. I can see he's closed the front door.

I touch the bannister. David's dress hanging over it. The vase on the stair window. The woodchip wallpaper on the wall.

I make my way down as he watches. I hear the third-to-bottom stair creak. I hear Will's shoe tapping. I hear my heartbeat in my ears.

I smell the plug in air-freshener by the door. I smell my own sweat.

I taste the remnants of the sandwich Jeremy made me for the train.

Deep breath. "It's my account, I'll do what I want."

"I've had thousands coming at me because of it. You need to take it down, and issue an apology immediately."

I don't think my words will come out as strong as I want them to. I shake my head.

"You'll do as I say right now, or you'll regret it."

I don't move. Mainly because I'm not sure I can.

"If you don't do it, Ben, you'll be out of my circle, and a job."

I'm laughing, but only on the inside. "I'm already out, and my name is Benny."

"I don't give a fuck about your name, or you. Delete the post, issue an apology or I'll evict you."

He can't do that, can he?

He smirks at me as though he can read my mind. "Yes, I can do that."

I take my phone from my pocket. He tells me I'm a good boy, which makes me feel so minging, even David's expensive scrub wouldn't be able to cleanse me

Also, he can't do that, not straight away. Dealing with Mum's landlord made me aware of that.

"You have to give me notice first." My body fizzes like the codeine I'll need to take when this is over.

Unimpressed, he opens his phone. If he's trying to find what the law says, he's going to be disappointed.

He puts the phone to his ear. "Hi, yes hello." He looks at

me smugly. "I have an account set up with you. William Gale. Yes, I'd like to cancel it with immediate effect. I'll no longer be needing your storage space. I believe I have twenty-eight days to collect after final payment and then you auction the contents, correct?"

No!

"Then you should know I've cancelled next week's payment. Goodbye." He puts his phone away calmly. "Do what I've asked, and we can sort this all out."

I'm desperate to tell him to go fuck himself.

All I manage to do is shake my head.

"How dare you. After all I've done. You'll be sorry. Your mother's things will be sold off. I'll be selling this place too. You and your disgusting housemates will be homeless."

I don't react. My stomach flips, but there's not much I can do about the house in this moment. I bravely walk past, open the door, gesture for him to leave.

"I've got all your old videos saved. Emails and texts too. You think you can get away with what you did? Let's see how you do when the face behind the mask is revealed."

I slam the door behind him, run up to my bedroom, jump on my bed, and scream "FUUUUUUUUUUUCK" into my pillow.

What the hell do I deal with first?

Chapter 29

They're up against the windows of the van the moment we pull up, asking about records, ornaments, books, and coins the moment we get out.

"I forgot to warn you," Jeremy says. "Don't worry, let's get the tables up to create a barrier, then we will get unpacked."

The bargain hunters watch our every move.

I suddenly feel like this is a terrible idea.

The only option, though.

I called Shaun after Will had left. As soon as I stopped shaking. He told me to come back and they'd sort it. I packed a suitcase with half my clothes. I wasn't sure how long I'd need to stay in Ming. I did consider packing everything, but Manchester is my home. I think.

I told my housemates I had to deal with Mum's storage unit, which wasn't a lie, I just didn't tell them the full story. I was hoping I'd get out before they all came home, but I faffed too much. I was surrounded by hugs, and hounded with worried questions. Even from Zoe.

They told me they couldn't wait for me to come back. They all walked out the house with me, and waved until I'd got to the end of the street and onto the bus.

Every wave back was laden with guilt.

It took us a few trips to get all the boxes out of the storage unit and into Shaun and Jeremy's house. There was no way I was letting Will win so strangers could bid for everything. This isn't any different, though.

Shaun and Jeremy didn't make it an issue, but they shouldn't have to live with rooms full of boxes, even if the loft was an option.

When Jeremy floated the idea of doing a car-boot, I wanted to scream. Shaun didn't like it either. We quickly realised there wasn't another option. I couldn't expect them to pay for the storage unit. I still need to get out of my overdraft from the rent arrears.

I spent all week going through the boxes, taking out the things I wanted to keep. Trying my best to prepare my heart and mind to let the rest of it go.

There was some good news, though.

I went on TikTok to take my mind off what I was doing and to see how people were taking my apology. I won't lie, it's more hate than love. How I've still got 20k followers I don't know.

I was surprised when Will's video came up, I thought I'd blocked him, but it was a stitch with someone laughing for three minutes. According to Will's cringe direct-to-camera monologue, my post caught the attention of the shareholders of GFP. He was called in first thing Tuesday, and sacked.

The comments on the stitch brought me life. In Will's video, which I could barely hear over the stitcher's laughing, he moaned that he's being "discriminated against," and that his "rights are being mauled by being forced to use pronouns and accept gender."

So many hateful comments for Will.

I'm still getting hate from both sides: queers and transphobes.

The car-boot has done me in. I'm knackered by lunchtime. I don't know how much we've made, but Jeremy has emptied the cash box in the van, twice. Most of Mum's clothes have gone. Loads of her ornaments I didn't know what to price everything at, but Jeremy has been on it.

I'm angry as someone haggles over Mum's old panini maker, something she treated herself to a few years ago, and absolutely loved. I did consider keeping it but I was never bothered about paninis.

"I'll give you eight quid," makes me want to smack him round the head with it. It's only priced at a tenner. Cost Mum over £100 when she bought it. But eight quid is better than nothing, and I'm tired.

Shaun's amazing with the customers. "Oh you're pressing us hard today. How about we slice it down the middle and say nine?"

Jeremy takes it all seriously. "Take a few of these out," he'll say as we get to another box. "The bigger a selection we have, the more interest we'll get. If people ask if we've got more, we can show them the rest." It doesn't matter what the box has inside, that's the rule.

In a lull, Shaun leaves. He returns with bacon butties and

teas. He tells me to go sit in the van for a rest. Part of me wants to, the other part wants to watch every last thing Mum owned, get sold.

In the van, I head to TikTok to read through replies. It's nice to see the occasional *you've done the right thing*. But for every one of those, there's at least three people telling me what I've done to Will is disgusting, and another five saying I don't belong in the queer community for what I've done to trans people.

This tea is gross. I still drink it. I reply to the queers saying how sorry I am. I am ashamed of myself. I tell the TERFs they can go fuck themselves.

Half an hour later, I've been in four reply-arguments and had a load more hate. I also get a comment with a link to a podcast.

I'm intrigued. Click.

I don't like the look of it. I for sure know it's not trans-positive, but the special guest is Will. I'm too curious.

"Hello Truthers. Welcome to 'The Harsh Truth' with me, Mr GC. That's right, GC by name, GC by nature.

I'm already regretting my decision. He sounds exactly like one of those proud-gun-carrying-white-racist-wife-beating-homophobic-pussy-grabbing-he-will-forever-be-my-president Americans. "Today I'm joined by someone in popular demand right now. I'm grateful he agreed to appear on my show. Show some love in the comments for William Gale."

"Good Evening, Mr GC," Will says.

I am lost for words as Will talks about how he's been cancelled. He says he's tried to get people to understand he's on the right side of history. He tried in his newspaper interview, his talk on some news channel I've never heard of, even with his X statement that big names have retweeted.

I go on X, find his statement. A lot of blame about The Enigaymatic Mystery, and society, but it's had a lot of interaction. I notice he's got more than 30k followers now. Ugh. I go back to the podcast.

I'm not quite sure why Will is talking to this guy? It's clear he's a homophobe. I noticed he did a podcast with members of that homophobic church, but Will is happy to share his opinions.

"I dated one once, you know. Of course I didn't know she was a trans-identified female at the time. I felt forced into doing something I didn't want to do."

He's such a liar. He told me about this. He faked feeling sick to get out of the date and ghosted the guy.

Now he's talking about drag queens. How it's a disgusting art form and a danger to kids. I'm about to turn off when he mentions me.

"I did everything for The Enigaymatic Mystery, Mr GC. I took him under my wing. He was brought up by a single mum, very poor, had nothing. I saw a lot of myself in him. I didn't want him to end up wasting his potential. I merely wanted him to achieve something, and get himself out of a lifetime of poverty. That was a mistake. He was ungrateful and he cost me my business."

"You're a hero," Mr GC says. "Tell me about his old videos you found offensive."

Will talks about how he found my first silly gay videos

harmful. I've had enough. I go back to the car-boot.

By the time we're packing up, I'm drained. Physically, but mostly mentally. There's still so much left. We make plans to do another one tomorrow.

At theirs, Jeremy goes through the freezer for something for dinner, but I want to thank them for their help. I go get chippy.

I walk past the print shop. It's no different. Same signs in the window. One of which I designed three years ago.

There's a light on. They must be doing a last-minute print. I turn to go, but my old boss sees me. I watch him go through a series of emotions. *Who's that? It's Benny who used to work here. I had to let him go. Oh, his Mum died. Aww, Benny.* He gives me a small wave.

I wave back. He'd probably give me my old job back if I asked. When we were sorting the order of service, Shaun got them printed here. He told me Mr. Randall had sacked Cai months ago for poor behaviour. Nobody has seen him since.

Could I do my old job again? I debate this as I get to the chippy, but as I pass the graffiti wall and see the name of the poor guy who *is a faggot* this week, I realise I do not belong here anymore.

As it happens, after we eat our chippy, I get an email from GFP. It seems I'm going to have to go back to Manchester anyway.

I'm woken early on Sunday. Another car-boot. I don't even mind all the early-birds now, I just want to get this over with, get the stuff sold, and do whatever I need to do next.

Shaun isn't full of jokes today, but Jeremy keeps our spirits up. By lunchtime we've not much left. I find myself scrolling TikTok. I call out a few more transphobes. Apologise to more queers. It's making my chest feel tight again.

I head to X.

I want to read Will's statement properly, but I'm distracted by a trending hashtag, *#WilliamGalePatheticTERF*. Oh he's going to be furious.

I spot a tweet from him saying he's being targeted. That this is abuse.

I scroll on to find what seems to be the start of the hashtag.

Someone called *Star Emmanuel* has done a reaction video about Will's podcast. I have to watch this.

His voice makes my heart leap, and immediately sink. He might have changed his name, his voice might be deeper than I last heard it, but it's him.

Listening makes me feel close to him. Star? I like it.

For every comment Will makes, Star calls him out, or proves him wrong, or generally makes a mockery of him.

"Wanna talk about right side of history do you?" Star says, throwing facts and figures about the support the trans community has. If the retweets and likes are anything to go by, and this has gone more viral than anything I've ever created, it seems Star is right that the gender criticals are just the ones that scream the loudest, despite being few in number.

He laughs at Will being cancelled. Talks about real abuse that members of the queer community have faced.

I hold my breath as it gets to the bit where Will mentions my TikTok account, but Star says he's not going to talk about the rest of the podcast. He reminds people, "Hate only has power if we give it power." He signs off with a big smile.

Am I allowed to be proud of him? He will have been out of his comfort zone doing that, but he was super eloquent.

I'm glad so many people are calling Will out, sending him loads of crying-laughing emojis.

As I click on Will's account, it goes private.

Ha!

"We've done as good as we're going to do." Jeremy makes me jump. He's right. Nobody is looking anymore. All the good stuff has gone. We pack what's left into boxes. Shaun says he will take it to the charity shop in the week.

He asks if I want to do it, but I tell him I have to go back to Manchester. They're not happy when I tell them why, but I assure them I'll be OK.

Jeremy cooks lasagne for dinner. When I comment how much it tastes like Mum's, he tells me he found her recipe inside one of the cookbooks when he was putting them out at the car-boot.

The food gives me a warm fuzzy feeling inside.

Shaun and Jeremy have been amazing. For the first time in a while, I feel calm.

That all changes as I get on the train back to Manchester.

Chapter 30

"You've been a TERF this whole time?" David spits. "Do you also think I'm a paedophile because I do drag?"

Jacinta doesn't speak. She gives the most disappointed look I have ever experienced, even from Mum.

"The fact you didn't tell us when that awful, horrendous man bought the house, proves how selfish you are." Zoe sticks a middle finger up at me, turns her back, and goes to her room.

I've just come in. How do they know?

"What you've done is a disgrace to our community. It's a good job we have to get out in a few weeks, because none of us want to live with you anymore." David looks at me with disgust as he storms upstairs.

"We comforted you. All those times we saw you hurting, and it was this wasn't it?" Venom in Jacinta's eyes and voice.

I want to do better. Lying isn't going to get me anywhere. "I honestly regret it all. I am going to make this right."

"You can't."

No. I probably can't. "I'll try."

"If you needed help you should have come to us. To me."

"I didn't think I needed help. I won't ever make that mistake again."

"I don't have any more spoons to give you, Benny. I'll be civil for these last few weeks, but I won't talk to you again."

Fair. "May I ask one question?" Jacinta nods. "Who told you?"

Jacinta's confused for a moment. As she sees I genuinely don't know, she grabs her phone.

I get a message from our housemate WhatsApp. It's a link for an article. Jacinta leaves the group. Above the message I see David and Zoe have already left.

I spot the eviction notice on the wall. Four weeks is all we've got. I spent a week of it in Ming. Three weeks to decide what the hell I'm going to do.

In my room I click on the article.

It's like the floor has spun me upside down. I don't know which way is up, and I feel sick to the depths of my soul.

I take an extra large dose of CBD and my valerian, whilst I get my codeine fizzing.

It's not enough to make me feel better about what's happened.

My secret has been revealed.

Will outed me.

Everyone knows it was me behind the mask. I would have known if I had listened to the rest of the podcast. This transcript of the conversation has my photo at the bottom.

The same picture as on my GFP ID card.

My chest tightens, worse than ever before I feel sweaty. Sick. My stomach seems to be pulling my entire body to the floor.

How the hell am I going to get through these next two weeks?

My heart feels like I've just drunk a pint of red bull. Are the walls moving in or is my vision going weird?

Calm the fuck down.

OK. I see my bed. A bed that felt like home not so long ago. It's now the last place I want to be. That's not helping. I see my box of filming stuff. I must get rid of that. I see the dark clouds over Manchester from my window. Fitting. I see my closed bedroom door. I don't think I'll see anyone even if I kept it open. I see my open laptop with the email that forced me to come back.

I touch the box of filming stuff as I tip it into a bin-bag, ready to be thrown away for good. I accidentally touch the Kathleen wig, the last thing out of the box. I touch the empty lunch bag that Jeremy made. I touch my laptop with the email that forced me to come back.

I hear David and Jacinta whispering in Jacinta's room, in serious tones. I hear rain hitting the window hard. I hear my heart pounding in my ears at the thought of the email that forced me to come back.

I smell the remains of the tuna sandwich that Jeremy made. I smell the effects of my nervous stomach, over the email that forced me to come back.

I taste bile at the back of my throat, because my housemates... I guess they're not mates anymore, know the truth, and I'm stuck here.

All because of this stupid email from HR telling me if I don't come back and work my two weeks' notice, I'll be made to pay back wages and holiday pay.

I thought I had eighteen days of holiday left, but apparently eight of my twenty-eight were for bank holidays. I told them that still left ten, because I worked all this out. I took two days to go with Star for his surgery. Five days Will booked for me over Christmas when we went to Gran Canaria. One day off for my birthday, and Will persuaded me to take two days off so we could have an extra long weekend brainstorming content before that event. That's ten I've used. Eight bank holidays. Ten statutory leave days left.

However, although Will said he would sort the two weeks I took when Mum died, they were counted as holidays. I never should have trusted him. If it wasn't for the stupid way I'm paid two weeks in advance, and two weeks in arrears, I wouldn't be here.

I can't afford to pay it back. I'm still in my overdraft from paying Mum's landlord. The bank wouldn't extend it. I tried.

I could use the five-hundred and twenty-seven pounds and twenty-two pence we made at the car-boot. All Mum's clothes, the little trinkets she'd bought over the years, and none of it was worth much. I can't bring myself to do that. It's just sitting in a tin at the bottom of my rucksack.

I told Shaun and Jeremy I had to work my notice. I can't have them thinking I've made even more of a mess of things.

Besides, I deserve to face whatever it is these two weeks

at GFP are going to bring. Then I'll have another week to decide where I'm going to live.

I've brought some of Mum's diaries with me. I'm glad I did because I cannot sleep.

Monday morning, everyone in the house turns their back on me, so I leave early and take the long route to work.

I have to force my feet to take me into The Castle.

Everyone glares. I know now how many transphobes work here, but it's not just them, it's all the queers too.

"Mr. Cedar." Noelle from HR beckons me into her office as a couple of my old team leave with boxes. They look like they want to kill me.

"What's going on?" I ask.

"Since the board voted to remove Mr. Gale as CEO, the other managers are cleaning house. Your old team has gone. Proud of yourself?"

That's amazing. "So, why am I here?"

I can see how much she hates me. Of course she would, she's good friends with Will.

"All this needs digitising." She gestures at a stack of boxes.

"That's not my job."

"You'll find your new contract, that you begged Mr. Gale for, says your job is whatever other duties we ask. This is your job for the next two weeks. Or you can quit, and set up a direct debit for your wage return."

This feels worse than having my name on the graffiti wall. Worse than all the abuse I get online. Worse than having to sort a funeral for my own mum and selling all her things.

I totally deserve it.

Star told me I'd get my comeuppance.

Everywhere I go, I get filthy stares. My actions have either caused redundancies, they think I'm a TERF, or I should be ashamed for what I've done to Will.

Noelle sits me in the very open middle of The Castle.

Serves me fucking right.

At lunchtime I need to get out. I queue in a sandwich shop. The people in front start whispering. One of them turns. A heavily tatted person with spiky red hair, points at his badge in trans flag colours that reads *He/Him*, and says "TERFs aren't welcome here."

The person he's with says, "Not so vocal now are you? Come on, say your awful shit to our face."

The manager glances from behind the counter, "Get out my shop."

With every single customer looking at me either with hatred or confusion, I go buy a meal deal from Boots. I needed to go to the pharmacy anyway.

Back to my desk, my rucksack has been filled with the contents of the kitchen bin. Coffee grinds, banana peels, tea bags and the remains of a chocolate milkshake.

I see many people smirking. I go to empty my bag, but Noelle shouts across the office, "Your lunch break is over. If you're in work, you should be working, or it's cause for dismissal, and then you'll be invoiced for those wages you stole."

I sit with a stinking bag for the rest of the afternoon.

After a long day, I'm back at the house. There's a note on my door telling me not to use the kitchen when others are in there, and not to use the lounge at all.

This room is my only sanctuary now.

Tuesday. Getting called "a dirty fucking shitstain orphan who'll never work in this industry again" is one of the nicest things I overhear. This job is all I've ever wanted to do, now I've lost any future in that too. What do I have left at this point?

I take my bag with me everywhere I go now. I get lunch at the furthest place I can get there and back to. I focus on work to avoid the looks.

On the way home I buy myself a second-hand kettle from the charity shop, a load of Chinese pot noodles, crisps, chocolate, a loaf of bread, and butter. I even buy plastic cutlery and paper plates.

Wednesday. I've lost count of the times I've been called a TERF, a snake, a liar, and a rat. As I return from lunch, I find my computer acting funny.

"Corrupted files," Noelle tells me, adding I must have done something wrong. She reminds me all files need to be digitised by the end of next week.

I suspected something like this might happen. Luckily, even though they only gave me access to one drive, they missed my access to the old team's cloud. They're all gone, so Noelle had nobody to point it out. I've been saving all the work to that too.

I go home via the pharmacy and fill up on all my supplements.

Thursday. I barely hear the snide remarks now. It's every time someone walks past. Every. Single. Time. I concentrate on the digitising. On the way home I get a pack of the strongest sleeping tablets the pharmacist recommends. I've barely slept since being back.

When I get into work on Friday, there's spit on my monitor. When I come back after lunch, my chair has been taken. I'm told there's no more available. I'm forced to prop up my monitor and keyboard on the boxes, and work standing up.

I'm exhausted by the time I get home. I dread to think what's going to happen next week.

I can't even relax this weekend. I get home to another note on my door. The housemates are having a farewell party with friends. I've been told not to come anywhere near it.

I'm too scared to even use the toilet. I take the risk as I hear them playing Lily Allen's *Fuck You* song. I can hear the chorus sung much louder than any other part.

Shaun and Jeremy phone. They've done this every night, but I can't face them tonight. I text them to say I've got a migraine. Not a lie. Headaches have been constantly coming and going every day.

I can hear them talking about me downstairs. I don't know what they're saying, but it's enough for Jacinta to ask them all to change the subject. I take a sleeping pill and cry myself to sleep.

Saturday, I get up early, take a rucksack with one of Mum's diaries, and head out. I'm gradually reading them all. I still can't face the final one though. I also take the diary and pen she got me for my birthday. Maybe today will be the day I start it?

A bus and tram get me out of town. I wander from cafe,

to bar, to waterside bench.

I listen to the rest of the podcast that Will did. I wish I had done it last week and known he named me.

I head over to TikTok. I need to start making this right.

I reply to more hate.

I tell the queers how sorry I am.

I tell the TERFs how horrendous they are.

I get into an argument about drag story time. I tell them there's nothing insidious with it, but more people pile on telling me how I'm sexualising children. I fight back, reminding them it's not trans people or drag queens harming children.

I get into two different arguments about trans people using toilets. Even when I tell them how cis women have been murdered when someone thought they were trans, I didn't seem to be winning.

I put up another written post on my account.

> *I support ALL the trans community. From the kids, right up to the adults. Every. Single. Person. I'll never make the mistake of harming any of the queer community ever again. I am so, so, so, sorry.*

It feels weird how I've still got 15k followers.

I consider sleeping outside somewhere tonight, but it's freezing. I head back to the house, and sneak up to my room.

Sunday morning. I hear people moving outside my room, sellotape being used. Someone is moving out. I don't know who. I daren't go look.

I spend the day replying to more hate, reporting the many calls for me to unalive myself, and threats of harm and rape.

Monday. I sleep through my alarm. Ugh. Another week of torture.

I don't shower. I spray myself with deodorant instead. They're not having the benefit of me being late.

At my workstation I find the word *pedo* printed hundreds of times. I ignore it to start on my files to find my keyboard doesn't work. I'm typing but all I can see are red squiggles.

It takes me a while to realise someone has set my typing colour to white.

The comments have gone up a notch. I'm called groomer, paedophile and child abuser. I'm called TERF, transphobe and gay traitor.

After lunch my monitor is covered in stickers saying *No more transing away the gay*. Noelle tells me if I don't clean them off I'll be charged for damaging property.

When I leave, I discover stickers on my jacket saying *Diversity's winning by silencing women*. Not stuck on. Glued on. I rip my jacket getting them off.

It's quiet in the house. I notice Jacinta in the lounge but nobody else all night. There's no wigs or drag stuff anywhere, nor is there any vegan stuff in the fridge.

I reply to more messages, but keep getting tagged in the same post.

Click.

"Well, Ben Cedar, I hope you're happy getting your trans-identified friends to abuse me. For those that are unaware, and those intelligent enough to pay no attention to the horrendously cruel space we call social media, I've been ground zero in a campaign of cancellation. For a number of weeks now, bad actors, fake accounts and liars have harassed me. I have had people abuse me in the street, and due to the sheer number of trolls online, been unable to speak my side of the story. You may have seen the horrendous video by someone who calls herself Star, this week at least. She thought it would be funny to create a horrible hashtag against me. Other people have supported her too. So I want to ask if you're happy now, Ben? You did all this, and you're going to regret it. Mark my words you'll regret it."

I take a sleeping tablet, but lay awake most of the night feeling like I'm drowning.

Tuesday. It's a struggle to get myself dressed and out the door.

I feel like people know who I am everywhere I go. Maybe the people eating breakfast in the window of Costa just gave me a random dirty look, but the people I opened the door for in M&S definitely knew me. They sped up towards me, stopped, gave me a look of pure hatred, and went to a different door.

Is this what Manchester is for me now? I can't live the rest of my life with my hoody up and head down. What other option do I have? I cannot face going back to that concrete hell-hole, doing my old job, living in a spare room.

I don't belong anywhere.

I find a spot to sit before I go into work and read another of Mum's diaries to take my mind off everything. She talks about not having the money for the electricity meter. I must be about five. I remember these moments as being a fun game, with us wrapped in blankets, surrounded by candles, playing board games. Mum talks about how ashamed she is. I don't want to read any more.

I get to work and type, type, type. I'm so used to people walking past and saying something horrible, I don't even flinch.

I work through my lunch break to get as much done as I can. At 5pm I email Noelle with the files I've done so far. It's about three quarters of it all, maybe slightly less. I'm worried she's going to find my cloud files and delete them. I CC everyone in the building with the link to the files too, surely there's at least one person here who is on my side? What happened to Jeff?

"You know it's a breach to take files home," Noelle says as she beckons the security guard over.

"I didn't take anything home."

Unfortunately, it's not the chilled Asian guy who is pleasant to everyone, it's one of Will's friends. A huge, thick-necked white guy who I'm pretty sure has called me *fag* every morning this week, but never loud enough for me to record him, although what would even be the point?

"Check his bag for GFP property. He got all that work done fast. Too fast."

He empties my bag over the desk. It's a few snacks, the diary Mum got me for my birthday and Mum's diary. He picks it up.

"Be careful with that," I say before I can stop myself. Now he knows it's important.

He shakes it hard, puts his fingers inside the pages.

Grabbing. Ripping. He wants a fight. I have to let him destroy it. There's pages all over my desk.

"You can go," Noelle says to me. I'm happy she's disappointed, but I want to get out.

As she walks away, the security guard dregs up phlegm from the pit of his stomach and spits on Mum's open diary.

I throw everything in my bag and get the hell out.

The moment I get around the corner, I take Mum's diary out. There's spit all over the page. I grab a tissue, dab it as carefully as I can, but Mum's words are being smudged with the sticky green mucus.

I look at the torn out pages. I want to feel sad about it, but I don't.

This last week and two days has been hell. Nothing is going to get any better is it?

I have ruined everything because I am worthless.

I take a deep breath. I know what I have to do.

A calmness fills my body, taking the constant tightness away.

In the nearest off-license I buy the cheapest vodka and head home, to my pathetic room, with thoughts of my sleeping pills and a good long sleep.

I stop for a homeless person. It's not much, but I've got two tenners and a few quid in change. I give them everything. Including my emergency bus money. They're grateful and want to talk but I want to get home as fast as I can.

I head back the long way. One final tour of the city.

Over a bridge I stop to stare into the fast-flowing water below. I take out the diary from Mum. I'm not going to need this. I almost drop it into the river but I throw it in a nearby bin instead.

I end up near one of the big theatres. I never did come see anything. I notice an ad for a forthcoming show. *Mamma Mia*. Well, that's a sign isn't it.

OK Mum. I'm coming.

Chapter 31

"Benny Cedar!"

I freeze as I hear my name. I want to go home and be done, but there's something familiar about the voice.

Pink hair. Knitted jumper. Skinny jeans.

"What are you doing here?" I blurt out as he comes over.

"Nice to see you too." Rahul's hair is longer, but nothing else has changed.

"This is weird."

"Is it? You live here, don't you?" How does he know? "Something's wrong, isn't it!"

"I'm fine. Why are you here?"

He beckons someone over. "This is my girlfriend Su. We've come to watch whatever musical it is that's on at the Opera House."

"You hate musicals."

"I know!" He's still got that gorgeous smile.

"I'm trying to make him more cultured. This has taken a year of persuading."

They've been together a year? Good for them.

"Su, this is Benny."

She gives me an *ahhh this is him* look.

"Well, enjoy the show. I've got to go. Bye, Su. Goodbye, Ra."

I've got a plan and I'm going home to—

"We've got a while yet if you want to catch up?"

"Do you really want to catch up? The way things ended... we've not seen each other for years."

"Correction. I saw you at your mum's funeral. My condolences, by the way."

"I didn't see you."

"Sat at the back. I did come to the wake, but you vanished with someone and you never came back. I liked Eileen."

Su gives me one of those sympathetic smiles you give people when they bring up dead relatives.

He puts a hand on my shoulder. I melt a little. Not in the way I would with Star, but it feels nice. I wish I hadn't treated him so badly.

Well, I may as well go out on a positive.

"Ra, I need to apologise for the way I treated you. The things I said... my behaviour was... I wasn't in a good place while we were together. I don't think I've ever been in a good place. I don't mean to imply it was your fault. It wasn't I've never known who I am. I took that out on you. I said things about you being, you know, liking guys and girls."

"You can say bisexual," he says, with an encouraging smile.

I feel a little grin happening. "Bisexual. I want to apologise for that. You've always known who you are. You were a great boyfriend. If things had been different, if I had been better... Sorry, Su, for being cringe. No, I didn't deserve you. I truly am sorry, Rahul. I wish we could have stayed friends."

"Is that not what we are?"

"No point being friends with me now."

He takes my hand. Something unknots in my stomach. "I accept your apology."

"You wouldn't if you'd seen the stuff about me online."

Rahul's confused. Su isn't. A flicker of memory passes over her face. She's seen it. She glances at Rahul, and the way he looks at her, I know he's seen it too.

"Honey, we'll be late." Su holds out her hand for Rahul. He takes it. She leads him away.

At least I got to say sorry for something.

He whispers to her, she whispers back in a serious tone, walks away.

Rahul comes back.

"You've seen it, haven't you? I'm so ashamed."

He nods. "I also saw your final TikTok. I know you, Benny. I don't know why you did it, but I know your heart is in the right place. Do you honestly regret everything you did?"

I nod. I can't speak or I'll start crying and never stop.

"I believe that. The old Benny would never have said sorry to me. I'm impressed. If you truly want to change, I know you can do it. Reach out if you need to talk. I can't say the same for Su. Her sister and best friend are both trans. I'm not sure she could forgive you."

"Could you?"

"I can, I will, and I am forgiving you. Take care, Bennita. I hope you find out who you are, because he's going to be amazing."

His arms go around me. Our cheeks touch. A moment of his familiar warmth, peppery fragrance, soft squeeze.

He kisses my cheek, winks, darts after Su.

When my uncles phone that night, for the first time since I returned, I mean it when I tell them I'm OK. For a moment I consider starting the diary I rescued from the bin, but I'm going to wait until I've got something good to start it with.

Wednesday. I buy a pair of cheap earbuds, wear them all day at work. I see the reflection of people mouthing furiously at me, but all I can hear is calming lo-fi.

Thursday. An email goes around with an autotune of me as Kathleen from my live with Will, but knowing tomorrow is Friday prevents my chest from feeling too restricted.

I get home to find Zoe packing up a car. I keep my head down and return to my room. I eat pot noodles and bread but I feel like I'm on the way up.

I'm determined not to let this final day keep me down.

Friday. 5pm. I send Noelle my files. It's all uploaded. She seems surprised but after going through it twice, she has to admit it's all there.

I leave the building for the final time. I'm free.

Now what? I don't have a job. I have to be out the house in one week.

I spend Friday night replying to the trolls. It's nice to see positive comments. I cry when I see Rahul has left a comment to tell me he believes in me.

I read through another of Mum's diaries. She talks about how hard it was when I was born. Apparently I was poorly. She struggled for a while. She says it helped that my Uncle Shaun moved in and helped pay the rent for a while. I didn't know he did that.

He helped look after me whilst Mum went back to work, doing whatever jobs she could do, that would allow her to spend as much time with me as possible.

Well Mum, I need to find a new job too.

I spend Saturday looking for local jobs, and somewhere to live, but everywhere wants a deposit, and proof of income. I also can't find a single marketing and design job locally.

On my way back from the bathroom I accidentally knock David's door open. I've never seen inside. It's empty now but something catches my eye behind the long curtains. Half a joint.

In my room, I open the window, pull the curtains behind me and lean out as far as I can.

I'm crying? Pathetic. What the hell are you crying for?

I look at what five things I can see, but I realise I don't need to do that. I'm not feeling anxious, I'm just feeling feelings. I need to channel this.

> Dear Star. I am sorry. Truly, honestly, deeply sorry. I know what I did was appalling. I take full responsibility. I regret all the hurt I caused you and the

> queer community. Mostly I regret losing our friendship. I am going to do everything I can to put that right because I was not the friend you deserved. I hope one day we can talk in person, and find even a small spark of our friendship again. Until then, I am sorry from the bottom of my heart.

I stare at the text.

Minutes pass.

An hour passes.

By midnight I realise this text is nothing. He deserves more. I delete it and head to his X.

It's gone.

As far as I can tell from the hashtag, he was hounded by Will and his gang, and eventually banned. Not Will, Star.

Will has got a ton of new followers. My account he set up is tagged in loads of tweets from them and him.

I try several times to guess his password to log in to delete it. I eventually give up.

I wake up in the early hours. Racing heart. Sweating. On the verge of hyperventilating. I'm panicking my text to Star has ruined everything. I check my phone.

I deleted the message. I never sent it.

It takes me a while to get back to sleep.

The next afternoon I wake up and creep downstairs. It's quiet. I peer into the lounge and the panic comes back. We've been burgled.

The TV and DVD player are gone. Even the wifi router. I rush into the kitchen. No microwave, no pans, no cutting board, no toaster. Nothing in the cutlery drawer except the small set of four knives, forks, spoons and teaspoons I bought ages ago.

A note.

Gone to my new place. I'll be back Saturday for the landlord inspection. I'd rather you weren't there. Seeing as Saturday is the last day of our tenancy, you've no reason to be. Post keys through letterbox when you leave. I'll sort final bills and take what everyone owes from returned deposits. Any refunds I'll email you.

Jacinta.

Back in bed, I stop myself crying the moment the tears come. Enough, you stupid idiot. This is all on you. Every single last stupid fucking thing is your fault. Only you can sort it all out.

What am I going to do? I have to find a job. I have to find a place to live. I have to buck myself up. I have to apologise to Star. I have to...

No. I don't have to do all that at once.

OK, first thing: stop living like a hermit.

I take my toaster down to the kitchen. I'm in this house alone, I do not have to make toast like a saddo in my room.

The next day I shower, head out to the charity shops. I find a saucepan, frying pan, and a little pack of cooking utensils. On the way back, I get cooking oil, a pack of eggs, a pack of reduced chicken, salt, and pepper. I take the last of my CBD oil. I've already run out of valerian pills, but I think I can cope without them. I did try and stop the codeine but I felt like I had the flu all day, so I took some and have made a mental note to deal with that slowly.

First step done.

After a lunch of eggy bread and oven chips I found in the back of the freezer, I move to the next step.

I had to come to a coffee shop. A rough local one, I'm sure no queer people have ever been into. With no internet at home, I had no choice.

Two hours in, I can't find any marketing or design jobs. All I manage to do is bookmark a load of fast food, restaurant and bar jobs.

Seriously, Benny! Give up. Go back to Ming.

No.

What other choice have you got?

I'll find a job.

There's nothing out there you want to do.

I'll keep searching.

You've got five days. You won't find anything.

I take out Mum's diary and flick through. My eye catches an entry where she lost her job and is worried about Christmas.

It's so hard finding something that can work around Benny in nursery. Shaun's got his own place now and has offered to help but he's got a new girlfriend to think about. They're so sweet together. However, I saw in the post-office window people are looking for cleaners. Well, I can clean. I've taken a note of all the numbers and tomorrow I'm going to phone them all.

She spent months cleaning other people's homes. She cooked for a few clients too, found she enjoyed it, and put a sign up in the post office asking if anyone wanted meals cooked. She cooked for a year before she got the canteen job. I never knew that.

Thanks for the advice, Mum.

Create the job I want.

By Friday I have a website and portfolio of work I did in Ming, the good stuff anyway. All the way up to the projects I led at GFP. I did worry they might ask me to take it down, but they have to see it first. I'll worry about that if and when they ask.

Plus, having to go to a cafe to do it, got me out the house.

Now I need clients, or at least testimonials. "But first I need to find somewhere to live," I say to Uncle Shaun when he phones for his nightly catch up.

"You've always got a room here," he replies.

I go silent. I hear Uncle Jeremy in the background mutter something. Uncle Shaun mumbles something back.

"Hi Benny, it's Jeremy. You don't want to move back here, do you?" How do I answer that? "The silence says it all. You probably don't remember my Aunt and Uncle. They live in North Manchester. It's not as close to the city centre as you are now, but they've got a spare room they rent out. It's not much, but they are lovely and remember you from the wedding. We can afford to pay your first month's rent."

I try and keep the tears out of my voice as I thank them. Before I know it, they've arranged to pick me up tomorrow, to take me.

I can't expect them to pay my rent.

By the time I go to bed, all my stuff packed, I've phoned four restaurants, a McDonalds, a KFC and a bar near to Uncle Jeremy's Aunt and Uncle's house, to see if they've got any jobs going. I get a yes from all but KFC.

Things are looking up. They're looking up from a low point, but I'm holding onto that as I stand here, Saturday morning, ready to leave.

Seeing the empty room reminds me of moving out of Mum's house but I'm not going to cry today.

As Uncle Shaun knocks on the door to take me to the next step of my journey, I'm wobbling.

I open the door, ready for my uncle's hug. I need it.

It's not Uncle Shaun. Nor Uncle Jeremy.

It's not even Jacinta.

I shut the door, but he puts his foot in the way.

"This is my house. Be careful."

I want to smack him in the face. My hands turn into fists on impulse.

"Unwise," Will says, noticing. "It's my right to charge for anything I feel needs redecorating or repairing."

I have a feeling he deliberately turned up early to catch me here, which means he knew I was still here. Fucking stalker.

I move my bags to the front door, ready to go. My uncles will be here any minute.

He makes a show of getting out a pad and pen. "You need to stay for my assessment."

"Jacinta's doing it."

"She's not here. I don't have time to wait. I might have

questions. Do you want me to charge everyone?"

I follow him around all the rooms, but I refuse to make eye contact.

In my room, he tells me he wants the laptop back he gave me ages ago.

I go downstairs to get it, but I realise it still has some of my work on it. It's all backed up to an external hard-drive, but I don't want him getting access to anything personal.

I open it to delete everything. He tries to grab it, but I don't let go.

"Do I need to phone the police?"

I give him the laptop.

"What's that?" He gestures to a mark on the kitchen tiles.

I wipe it off with my sleeve. "Are we done?"

He stands by the door. I'm trapped.

I try to sidestep but he holds out his arm.

"You think you ruined me with my dismissal, don't you? I should thank you for how my life has changed. I'm getting into places I never thought I could. All I did for you, you never once thanked me. Ungrateful little bastard. I wish I had left you mugged on the street when you first got here. I wasted so much time on you. I'll never get that time back. Are you going to give me that time back?"

My back is pressed against the fridge. He comes closer. Peers down at me. He's angry. Crazy. I've never seen him like this. He slams the notepad down. I notice it's got nothing written on it at all, just doodles. I can smell his breath, garlicky and minty. I don't want him to touch me.

His hand reaches out, but he jerks back. Someone drags him out of the kitchen.

It's Uncle Jeremy, his phone recording in his other hand.

I have never seen him do anything like this. He wouldn't even harm a fly.

"Time to go," he says to me.

I run to the front door. I find Uncle Shaun watching in shock.

"The laptop. It's got all my files on it."

"Wait in the car." Uncle Shaun strides in.

I hear all three of them raise their voices.

My uncles walk out.

"Tell Ben he won't be getting his deposit back."

Uncle Jeremy turns to him, holds up his phone. "Come near him again, or do anything to affect these kids you chucked out, and this recording will go to the police."

What the hell? Is Uncle Jeremy a gangster now?

He shouts over to ask me the password for the laptop, which I realise he's holding.

Jacinta walks around the corner. Looks at me and Uncle Shaun. She frowns, concerned, goes towards the front door.

"That's Jacinta. She's here for the check-up."

Uncle Shaun hurries toward her. "Hi hun, they did the check-up early. It's all good. You don't need to go in."

Jacinta looks like she is going to protest, but she takes in Uncle Shaun's serious face. She peers into the house to see Will huffing and puffing, but not daring to come out. She looks back at me, worried.

I give her a small smile.

She blanks me. Walks away.

"Wiped. Everybody in," Uncle Jeremy barks as he hands Will the laptop. I know he doesn't mean to sound so demanding, he's obviously running on adrenaline, but I don't argue.

Uncle Shaun gives Uncle Jeremy a raised eyebrow and a cheeky little smile. Uncle Jeremy tries to return the look in a super masculine way, but it comes out super camp.

All of us, including him, burst out laughing as we drive away.

Chapter 32

Uncle Jeremy's Aunt Pearl and Uncle Sid are the cutest people ever. They made me feel so welcome. On the way over, Jeremy told me how they've struggled recently to get a new lodger and were over the moon when he asked if they were open to me moving into their little terraced house.

Uncle Jeremy didn't say what the struggle was exactly, but he hinted. They're black and in their 70s. It seems they just want to live a quiet life.

My room is bigger than my previous one. Pearl and Sid have an en-suite, so the main bathroom is all mine.

They don't know what I've done. Uncle Jeremy told them my rented house was sold and my job went bust. It doesn't quite feel fair that they have absolutely no reason to think I'm awful.

They're gay friendly, as you'd expect when their favourite nephew is gay. Their words. Tiny Pearl has already told me how she used to go out with her gay friends back in the day when you had to knock on a secret door and give a password.

I've been super busy since I arrived last week. I had interviews for all the jobs I applied for. All of which said no, except a restaurant in the town centre that has offered me a trial shift for tonight. It's only a ten-minute walk away, too.

I've kept building my website. Sid has a desktop computer they use mainly to contact relatives on the other side of the world. It's slow, but it does all I need it to do. I've been contacting loads of LGBTQ+ businesses in Manchester to see if they're open to free design and marketing work in return for a testimonial.

So many companies ghosted or said no, probably because I decided to be honest and put my name on each email.

Three companies got back to me. I've offered to do a pitch for each of them. They're all in Manchester city centre. For some reason, I decided to arrange them all for today.

"Here you go, sweetie," Pearl says as she puts a bacon butty in front of me. I was going to have cereal, but who can resist this? I've got my own little cupboard my uncles helped me fill with food before they left. I felt like I was going shopping with my two dads, with Uncle Shaun reminding me to get healthy stuff, and Uncle Jeremy telling him off, saying I can have whatever I wanted. I felt bad I couldn't pay. I'm not getting out of my overdraft any time soon. I spent the car-boot takings on the first month's rent.

"Good luck, Benny," Sid says as I put my plate in the dishwasher. He shakes my hand and slips me a tenner, "for the bus fare". I try to tell him I don't need it, but he's staring at me as though declining would dishonour his whole family. I love them both. I am glad they know nothing about what I've done. I keep reminding myself that was old Benny. As long as he stays old, they don't need to know anything about him.

My first pitch meeting. There's an atmosphere already. It's a small trans charity helping towards transition costs and support. I'm in here with the manager, assistant manager, one of the crisis team members, and one of their service users. They're all trans.

My hands shake as I show them the mock-ups I printed out at the local print shop. Whilst there, I did ask if they had any jobs, but they didn't.

I see them side-eye each other. I know that's not because I'm stuttering through this pitch.

This place was the one I spent the most time on. They do such good work, but their website is clunky. Star actually looked into this place when he was saving. He didn't meet the criteria, though. I remembered him saying how rubbish the site was, so I've focused on two main things I can help them with: marketing the services to potential funders, and navigation ease on their website for service users.

I do my ten-minute pitch in under seven minutes because I'm nervous as shit. Now they're passing the mock-ups around, not taking anything in.

The service user, a serious-looking guy with an awesome handlebar moustache, holds one of the mock-ups in his hand. "Can you tell us..."

"Thank you," the manager interrupts him. She's a petite woman, but she holds herself in a way that makes her seem much taller.

I have a feeling he wasn't going to ask what she thinks he was going to ask.

Fuck it. I'm prepared for this.

"I wish I hadn't done any of it."

They all look at me and communally take in a big breath. Not one of them asks me what I'm talking about. They know.

"I hurt a lot of people, and I am deeply ashamed. I don't want to ignore my past, but I do want to move on from it. My mum recently died. That's not an excuse, that's me telling you I've got no-one to fall back on for help. I love doing this job. If I can do it whilst putting some love back into the world and back into the queer community, all the better. What you're doing here is brilliant, and if there's any chance forgiveness is on the table, I will make sure I earn and deserve it."

Silence. It feels like forever.

All I can hear is my heartbeat galloping in my ears.

"We need to consider this," the manager says.

"Thank you for your time and for this chance," I stutter. I grab my bag, rush out.

I can't look back. I feel like crying, but I've got another interview to get to.

The second interview doesn't feel as bad. It's an organisation for queer people to socialise. I pitch to the manager who's a friendly-looking gay bear, his beyond femme lesbian assistant, and one of their trans board of directors. He hasn't cracked a single smile.

Their website is already pretty good, but I felt it was lacking in visual impact.

"And in that third image you can see how the words focus on the joy of the social aspect of the events, rather than the activities themselves."

"Are you open to feedback?" the big gay bear says with a smile. I nod. He glances over to the trans guy for a moment. "Why the hell did you think we would take you on after what you did? You know we are open to everyone in the community, cis and trans."

All three of them glare, awaiting an answer.

"I hurt a lot of people, and I'm deeply ashamed. I don't want to ignore my past, but I do want to move on and find a way to gain the trust of those—"

"You will never gain the trust of the trans community or this organisation." The trans guy stands. "We didn't think you'd turn up. You've got balls on you, I give you that, but you can absolutely fuck off."

He collects all my mock-ups. Rips them up. Drops the pieces to the ground.

I collapse on a bench in Sackville Gardens. I'd rather be a bit further away from Canal Street, but my next pitch is around the corner. It's somewhere amazing.

I go through the pitch in my head, but laughing distracts me.

I look up. Two people hold their phones up. Are they filming me?

I walk away but someone shouts, "Face me, you coward."

It's Will.

"Stop filming me."

"It's our right, groomer."

"What do you want?" I don't want to say his name.

"So you love transgenders now, do you? After all the stuff you said about them online. Go on, admit what you said."

He's trying to rile me up. It's working.

"I've already admitted I did it and admitted it was wrong. What more do you want?"

Other people watch now. A small group come closer. They seem to be enjoying it as Will lists all the TikToks I did against the trans community.

I notice people across the canal, watching with their drinks. They whisper to each other. Surely they can't also be supporters of Will?

They're not coming to help, even if they aren't.

"This will be going up on all my socials. I've got more followers than you ever had, you know. I've got all your videos saved, they're not going away. Never."

"Good for you."

"It is good for me. All of them support me and what I stand for."

"You don't stand for anything."

"I stand for women, children, and the appalling way lesbian and gay teenagers are being forced to transition."

I turn to leave, but there's more people blocking my way.

"Leave me alone."

"I will now I've said my piece." He turns to the camera, smiles, steps close to me and whispers in my ear, "I can't say the same about my followers."

He turns back to the cameras and talks. I hurry away as fast as I can.

I'm glad this final interview is right at the edge of The Village.

I almost didn't come. I may have spent the least time working on this pitch, but I'm determined to do it. It's a company called *Manchester Independent Trans Youth*. They do amazing work with trans kids but need serious help with their marketing.

I'm in the room with the two managers. Lucy, a tall Asian trans woman, and Nick, a black non-binary person with a beard, long hair, and who's pretty in a masculine way. I feel a weird sense of déjà vu, like I've seen Nick before

I also have about fifteen trans teens and tweens watching me.

"You haven't quite captured our programme in these, but you're close. I can tell you've put a lot of thought into them," Nick says. They've put the mock-ups up on a wall for all to see.

"These suggestions for website improvements though are spot on," Lucy says. "We've done a lot of the work ourselves to save money, but our strengths aren't in web design."

"I thought the website was user-friendly," I say, which makes them both smile.

"Our only... how do I put it...?" Nick says.

"Concern?" Lucy adds.

"Yeah, well... not quite concern. As a trans organisation we have a lot more to consider than just our own image, if you know what I mean."

OK. Let's hope this goes better third time around. "I understand. I know what I've done has hurt a lot of people and I'm ashamed—"

"Did you mean to hurt us?" I'm cut off by one of the teens.

"What made you do it in the first place?" a tween says.

Every single pair of eyes, including both managers, stare at me. "I carry a lot of shame for everything I did."

"Yeah you've said that on your TikTok."

"Tell us why you did it in the first place."

"And why we should accept your apology."

I wasn't expecting questions like this. Then again, I wasn't expecting kids.

"Why did you choose that Kathleen woman to impersonate?"

"Why did you do any of it?"

A chorus of yeahs. I want to run as fast as I can out the door.

"Let him speak," Nick says.

"I did it because I mistakenly thought it was a good idea at the time." I don't know why I said that, but now I've said it, I'm more shocked nobody has gasped in surprise. "I don't want you to think I'm passing blame onto someone else."

"Who?"

"That Will transphobe?"

I nod. "I decided to reach out to places like this, because I'm trying to do better. I spent a long time hiding behind the lie I told myself that it was all *him*. I know it wasn't."

"Yeah, I've posted some cringe stuff."

"Not transphobic stuff though."

"Close. But no."

Being honest sucks. "I put my trust in the wrong person.

That's all on me. But I don't want that to be the way I'm seen for the rest of my life."

"Is that why you deleted your videos?"

"Except the apology one."

"Some apology, he had to write it down. Why didn't you say it?"

"I only saw the last few."

"I've got them all saved."

"Me too."

"Show me."

Will was right, my past is never going to go away.

I can't give up because of that. "I'd rather you saw me as I am today. I do honestly want to work for your organisation."

"For feedback for your business though."

"True. I'd prefer not to have to face those videos ever again though. That doesn't mean I've forgotten about them. Every day I think about them. I'm not that person any more."

"Do you hate trans people?"

The question comes from a young trans masc who reminds me of Star, which makes my heart break even more. What if Star thinks that too?

If he did... I'd rather I was—

No. You can't guilt yourself. You knew the road would be bumpy, well here are the bumps, and none of it is to do with anyone except yourself. Own it.

"Not then. Not now. Not ever. I hoped me being here today might show you I'm trying to be better."

"How come that Will guy is still profiting off all your

content?"

"Let's wrap up question time," Lucy says. "Thank you, Benny. We'll be in touch."

I can't stop thinking about Will now. He's always going to be there. How can I ever escape my past?

Oh god, this is like what Uncle Shaun was saying before I came to Manchester, about my old bully. He said he'd changed and I said he couldn't. That doesn't bode well for me, does it!

All the way back to... home, I guess, I feel like I've wasted my time today.

I don't get to dwell on it for long. Trial shift.

I finish at the restaurant at 1am. It was busy, but it went well enough to be offered more shifts. I even made twenty quid in tips.

In my bedroom, I can't sleep. I'm knackered from shadowing the staff, learning menu items, and polishing cutlery, but my mind won't let me sleep.

I wanted today to be amazing. Part of me hoped it would go so well, I could start my diary at last with something good. Nope.

The teens have affected me the most. I remember what it was like being their age in my town, how awful it felt, and there I am, the cause of their hurt. No wonder they kept asking me questions.

One question in particular sticks in my mind. My lame written apology.

It feels weird setting up for a video. I don't have any of my old stuff. My phone is propped up on my headboard. The desk lamp on my face.

I stumble my words a couple of times and restart, but this is the one.

"Hey, TikTok. It's been brought to my attention that my previous apology wasn't good enough. I want to be honest with you. As you can see, no mask, and no voice modulation. This is me, Benny Cedar. I made and posted all those videos and I deleted them because not only am I ashamed of them, but because there's enough hate in the world. I put my trust into the wrong person, but I don't want to talk about William. He is still harming the trans community, and I want nothing to do with *him* again. I'm not going to talk about why I posted them, because I want to move forward. So let me start by saying, I apologise to anyone that has felt ashamed, hurt, or been abused because of my videos. I apologise from the bottom of my heart. The world is hard enough for us all in the community without me making it worse. I assure you this will never happen again. Without going into too much detail about my personal life, I should have spoken to my closest friends and family about it when things felt wrong. I did not do that. Things were difficult enough with family stuff, but let's say I missed my chance. I hurt a close friend too. A trans friend if you can believe I had such a friend. I should have spoken to him, but I was stupid to believe in someone else I thought had all the answers. I did eventually open up to someone in my family. Someone who is like a father, a big brother, an uncle, and a friend. I am eternally grateful to him and his husband for all their help. I promise to do better. Thank you for listening, and my heartfelt apologies once again."

I post it before I can change my mind. Relieved, I finally

fall asleep.

The comments flood in. There's a lot of hate.

The next day, I reply to as much of it as I can, telling them how my support of trans people doesn't take anything from women nor does my support of trans kids mean I'm abusing them.

My heart lifts a little as comments say I'm brave. I feel weird someone has commented about my mum dying. Randomly, that has got almost four thousand likes.

A few days later, I get an email from the trans charity to say they couldn't take the risk of me doing anything harmful again.

I'm knackered by the weekend. I'm on a split shift today but there's a three hour gap. I've come back for a quick nap. Sid has made me food even though I've told him I'm happy to cook my own. He's an ex-chef. His food is amazing, if a little too spicy for me. I know who would love this though.

The thought of Star makes me lose my need for a nap. I head to TikTok, find I'm tagged in something. I have to unblock Will to discover it's the video he took the other week.

It's got thousands of likes and positive comments.

I scroll through them, but when I come to the tenth comment saying they're going to find me and make me pay for abusing kids, I decide that's enough.

As I put my phone away, it rings.

"Is that Benny? It's Lucy from *MITY*."

I'm lost. "Mighty?"

"Manchester Independent Trans Youth."

"Oh, OK. No worries. I understand."

"Understand what?" Lucy chuckles. Didn't she tell me no? "We've discussed it, and we want to give you a chance."

What the hell? They're giving me the job? I mean, it's all free, it's not like I'm going to be doing my last restaurant shift anytime soon.

"Are you serious?"

"I am. We adored your mock-ups. Even though some of the young people weren't sure at first, once your video went around they all changed their mind. It was brave of you to be so vulnerable. We had a huge discussion yesterday about cancel-culture and second-chances. One of our mission statements here is to let people be who they want to be."

I feel like I could walk on air. "I can make any changes to the mock-ups you want, and get them over to you in the next week."

"Well, about that..."

Chapter 33

"Hey, TikTok. I had my second session with the young trans people this week. They're finally warming to me. I wasn't as terrified this week either. They were super welcoming, considering... you know."

I'm careful not to mention anything that could identify *MITY* or its service users. I want to keep doing this job, even if it is only once a week.

I pause the recording, find the green screen effect, put up a background of comments I'm going to talk about.

"I'm super grateful for all these kind comments. I also got a few saying what I'm doing is performative. Isn't all social media performative? It's not like I've filmed what I've been doing, or who with, but I can see how these videos might come across that way. I'm not doing these videos for you. They're my way of keeping myself in check."

When Lucy suggested I come in and work with the kids on the website, teaching them as we go, I leaped at the chance. I told her I wouldn't let her down. She said she knew I wouldn't, she could see how passionate I am.

There was a little funding for it too, enough for my bus fare and a takeaway on the way home. I was worried the restaurant wouldn't let me have every Wednesday evening off, but I told them I could work any other day, including all weekend.

I put the background back to normal, carry on recording.

"And to those that say I'm grooming these youngsters," I don't put those comments up in the background, "you have no clue what it means to understand yourself, do you? Bore off."

The young people are amazing. In the room it's like a switch is flicked. Outside, many of them hide themselves inside hoodies. At *MITY*, they are their authentic selves.

I want to talk about how amazing they are. How curious they are about marketing and design, but I don't want to say anything that could identify them and cause more issues.

Last week, the kids had loads of questions about my old content, until Lucy told them to stop. I said I didn't mind, I wanted to be open. I did regret that. I was exhausted from answering questions by the end of the session.

This week, they were more interested in power words and SEO. That tired me out in a different way. I impressed myself with what I knew though. Who knew I'd enjoy teaching?

I finish my video by thanking everyone for their time and for the positive comments. I really wanted to name Rahul for his clapping hands emojis and the single pink heart, but I'd definitely be accused of being even more performative.

***

"Hey, TikTok. To the supporters on last week's video, thank you so much. I am not doing this for the praise, but I won't deny seeing people be positive about me, helps me breathe a little easier."

I wish those comments and likes didn't make me feel like this. It's pathetic, but likes have been there for pretty much my whole life, how am I meant to stop needing them?

"It's easy to think that everything about being trans is hard and horrible, but hearing all the trans joy from the young people is amazing."

I wish I could share some of the stories the kids tell me. I never would. We had to stop for about ten minutes today after Leo, a tiny trans masc who looks like he's about ten but he's almost sixteen, and has the thickest Welsh accent I've ever heard, told me about coming out to his grandparents.

Maybe it was the way he told it, or his accent, but he had us all in hysterics acting out how they reacted.

I said I wish I was young again so I could come to *MITY*, but as Leo said, I'm not trans. This got a few others debating it, saying I might be or could be one day. I told them I don't think I'd be allowed to be trans after what I've done, and quickly changed the subject.

"We need more joyful queer stories. It's easy to think the hate is the majority, but let me tell you, those pathetic and cruel pieces of..." I'll edit in a little poo emoji there, "just shout the loudest. They're jealous. They think we shouldn't be experiencing any joy at all. Yeah, you know who you are, you keep commenting in your silly little groups of fake names. Do you have nothing better to do than make pathetic attempts at spreading hate?"

I thank everyone for the positive comments again. I hope Ra knows it means so much that he continues to comment every week.

As I upload, I notice I've got stacks of new private messages. Judging by the first few words of each, none of them are nice. I slide them all to delete.

I drop some codeine into water. Cutting it out is a slow process. I read one of Mum's diaries until my body has unclenched.

***

"Hello, TikTok. It's meant the world to me, those of you who have left nice comments on last week's video. They took a little time to find but I appreciated them all." I appreciated them so much, I thanked every single one individually, whilst replying to every hateful comment with *grow up*.

"I feel blessed that the young people have warmed to me, but it makes me even more disappointed in myself for what I did."

No-one brought anything up about it tonight, for the first time ever. I took that as a tiny little achievement.

"The haters have been out in force, spamming my videos. Don't they have anything better to do? To those of you that have repeatedly called me a..." I point upwards, at the end of the video I'll add in the words, *grXXmer* and *pXXdo* so I don't get my video taken down by saying them, "and how you wish me to be unalive, know that you only see my life through this little rectangle. You don't know who I'm working with, what I'm doing, or where I'm doing it, so you need to shut up and worry about your own pathetic life. If you think helping kids be their authentic selves is harmful, you're the problem here, not me."

I don't want to tell them how many replies I've had saying they're going to find me and make me pay. Mainly because I'll be accused of lying. Also, truth be told, I don't want to count them.

I'm glad the restaurant has had me on constant split shifts due to staff illnesses, it's helped distract my mind.

With my painted on smile, I'm not letting them see they've got to me, I talk a little bit about queer joy again. If only I was feeling it as much as the kids do when they get to their safe space every week.

"Keep believing in yourself and living your truth, it makes the queerphobes and transphobes furious. Good. They don't deserve happiness. They are complete wastes of space. Just do everyone a favour, and get off TikTok."

I finish the video by sticking up my middle finger.

Sid's made a Caribbean stew. It's delicious, but with all these new comments and private messages appearing, I've lost my appetite.

***

"Hi, TikTok. To those that have continued to threaten me

since my video last week... I'm not scared of your pathetic comments. You're all absolutely disgusting humans."

I delete and re-record it, but it's still not right, I sound terrified. I have to make it sound convincing. I am not letting the phobes see they're getting to me.

Third take. Good enough.

"I know what I did was wrong. I'm working on being better, but I don't deserve the messages I've had. These are from last week's video."

I green-screen the background and put up the comments. It took ages to get them edited together, even longer to blur out all the death and rape threats and comments calling me a groomer and paedophile. There were almost nine hundred comments in total, all mostly saying the same thing. They can't even come up with their own replies.

"I've also had lots of people saying they support William. If you support someone as terrible as that, you must be a lovely person. Don't worry, I'll keep calling out the haters. Let's see how brave they really are."

After I've uploaded, I realise I didn't say goodbye. I'm not doing it again. My hands wouldn't keep my phone still. If they continue to shake this much, maybe I should get a new stand.

Before I turn the light off, I check my replies.

I've been stitched.

Should I be watching this before bed?

Click.

I see someone play the end of my video, then pop up on screen. He's an awful looking thug whose face makes me feel sick, even without him saying he's going to come find me to show me how brave he is.

I report it straight away. Block.

I've been so good, barely taking my codeine this week, but tonight I don't even hesitate before popping two into water. The fizzing helps calm me a little.

Good job I've still got those sleeping tablets. I'm going to need one tonight.

***

I've tried six times to do a video. I keep stuttering or getting my words mixed up.

I've had to prop my phone up on a pile of Mum's diaries because my hands are tight, sweaty fists.

It took all my energy to get through tonight's session and not let the kids see what a week of constant, cruel comments and messages has done to me.

I daren't even look at my messages right now. They keep coming.

Lucy asked if I wanted to go for something to eat after the session, I politely said no. I've barely had any appetite for weeks. I've lost weight. I've not even eaten the restaurant food, and that's made by a chef trying to get a Michelin star.

I'm back taking codeine, valerian root tablets, and CBD again.

Whenever Sid has cooked, I move it around my plate, trying to squish it into the smallest space. I put it in the bin when nobody is looking.

I need to do a video to prove to them they're not getting to me, but first I need to get rid of this headache I've got from clenching my jaw.

Another message has come through. I'm going to tell them they're absolute scum and—

It's a link to a TikTok live. Oh, this might not be horrible. Click.

A pale, bruised face makes me jump. It's that horrible thug from last week.

"So come down, the details are in the comments. Let's show him."

Comments come up. People wish they could come. They hope he teaches Benny a lesson.

The tightening wraps around me like never before.

"Ehhhh, lad. Safe innit," thug says as a gammony-looking white guy, who looks like him except ten years older, appears. They bump fists. Older thug shows his bag. He's got a dozen eggs.

I can't move. It's a struggle to breathe.

I can barely hear the nonsense they're talking, because of the blood-rushing sound in my ears.

Another guy turns up. A black guy who looks like a teenager.

Thug is shocked nobody else has come. "We'll be back in a bit." The live ends.

Should I phone the police?

They don't really know where I live, do they?

I pull up TikTok on the cheap tablet I bought a few weeks ago. It's second-hand but is decent enough for what I need it for.

I dial 999 into my phone and keep my thumb near the call button.

It's not long before a new live starts. The three men say hello, show what they've got. Thug has a hammer, gammon shows his eggs again, the teen has fireworks.

"Right, who wants us to do this? Give us a like."

Likes appear. They keep coming.

I spot a few saying they're going to be reported, this is wrong, but not many.

I can't watch the comments anymore. They're coming up to a row of shops that are familiar. As they turn the corner, there's a row of terraced houses.

Oh my god, they do know where I live.

WHAT THE FUCK DO I DO?

They laugh as they edge closer. The screen is kept tight so I can't tell how far away they are. In the background they pass a skinny tree. I remember Uncle Jeremy had to pull up outside a tree the day they brought me, as there was no spaces outside Pearl and Sid's.

How far down is that tree?

Six houses away?

I count the terraced houses behind them.

1. 2. 3. 4.

"We're here," thug says, close to the screen. There's a bush behind him that's too familiar.

I need to phone the police.

I hurry to the top of the stairs. There's no window on the landing here. I can't look out to the front.

I have to warn Sid and Pearl first.

Oh my god, what if they get in?

I creep down the stairs as the thugs get their weapons out and peer around the bush.

"I hope he's home," gammon says.

Pearl and Sid are on the sofa. The curtains are closed, but the front door is right there.

I watch as they creep closer to the front of the house. Thug's face fills the screen, shows a bit of the door, puts his finger to his lips. "Shhhhh."

I can't let anything happen to Pearl and Sid.

I don't care what they do to me.

I watch thug use the hammer to gently tap on the door.

OK. I have the power of surprise. I'll open the door and... and... AND?

"Catch," thug turns the camera. The teen catches the hammer, faces the window.

Thug's face appears. He makes a fist, knocks on the door.

Pearl glances over.

"I'll get it," I rush down the stairs.

Thug fiddles with his trousers as the others laugh. He puts his groin to the letter box.

No.

I grab the handle.

Turn.

Yank the door open as I watch steam rise from the letterbox on the video.

"Who is it?" Pearl says.

SMASH. The teen hammers the window on the screen, but the doorstep in front of me is empty.

I watch as gammon lobs eggs at the upstairs window. Thug turns the camera back to him and the teen lighting fireworks.

"Nobody. I'm losing the plot," I say to Pearl. I rush back

upstairs, relieved they're not outside my front door, but the smashed kitchen window they're pushing lit fireworks through is my old house.

That was too close.

I watch as they run off, showing the piss-stained front door, the smashed eggs on all the windows, and small fires in the kitchen.

As they say bye, I catch a glimpse of the *For Sale* sign outside. If it's not been sold yet, it still belongs to Will.

I don't laugh for long.

It takes me hours to calm down. My supplements barely stop me from going under. I go on TikTok to make a start on deleting all the private messages, and notice someone on my *For You Page* has stitched with Will.

The stitcher is laughing, saying how Will can blame queers all he wants, but they've got a screen recording of the live, and have evidence of who did it.

I unblock Will to see his video. He's saying his house has been vandalised by trans radical activists.

He really will blame the trans community for anything.

Why do I feel like all this is going to get worse before it gets any better?

Chapter 34

I'm glad I'm busy today. I've been trying to feel proud since the beginning of June. Halfway through, I'm struggling.

If only I had never started doing those videos, maybe I'd...

Ugh. What's the point in torturing myself? I've got work to do. I shouldn't be thinking about the past.

I think my pitch meeting this morning went well. I still need more testimonials because *MITY*, and a little Greek cafe I did some work for, aren't enough. Hopefully, this new theatre company will say yes. I have a good feeling. Nobody mentioned my content either.

I head to *MITY* to meet up with Lucy and Nick. I've hardly seen Nick since my interview because they're always busy doing the one-to-ones with the kids.

They've shaved off their beard completely, and have a full face of make-up. I don't recognise them at first.

"Thanks again for helping out today," Lucy says.

It was our final session last week, which was sad, but she brought up that *MITY* was partnering with the other groups within the Greater Manchester Trans Youth Support Network, to put on an event, I knew I needed to help out in whatever way I could.

"Here's to the first Fortitude Festival," Nick says. We all toast with our coffees.

Lucy goes over the plan. There are leaders coming from the other charities and support centres. I'm on table duty. If someone needs a table for their stall, I'll get it. It might also apply to chairs, gazebos, and umbrellas. It's not raining so far, but it is Manchester.

Before we leave, Lucy waves someone cool over. Shaved head, jacket decked out in a variety of pin badge flags that state they are non-binary, aromantic, and pansexual. Thanks to the kids at *MITY* I know all the flags now.

"This is Skye, they run *LGBT-Total*."

"The queer sober social group?" I say. Skye's impressed. I contacted them a few months ago about doing free work and heard nothing, not even a no.

"Lucy's been gassing you up. You open to more work?"

OK, maybe I jumped the gun. "Yes."

"Our website's horrendous. We need new energy, if you're interested? Lucy told me you do it for free, but we've actually got a budget."

"Alright Lottery grant show-off," Lucy laughs playfully.

"Our marketing has mostly been Insta, and some rather bad TikToks. I'll show you."

My heart drops. Skye gets on their TikTok, scrolls past a

copy of one of my old videos, being duetted with Will. I have him blocked. I didn't even know he was still doing that.

"What's he saying now?" Lucy peers at Skye's screen.

No. Not today.

Skye shows the video. My skin crawls hearing Will's voice.

"Oh, I've seen this one. I've got it saved."

"Saved?" Skye's confused for a moment. "Ahhh, your case."

"He's going to wish he had never started on us," Nick says.

"Sorry, what's going on?" I'm too curious.

Lucy tells me how Will has been talking a lot of nonsense about *MITY* recently. He's made posts saying the kids are all being groomed, the staff and parents are all child abusers.

"So, I'm suing him," Lucy says, matter-of-fact.

"He picked on the wrong queers," Nick adds.

Is this my fault? I've tried not to mention anything about *MITY* in my videos. Lucy only gave me her testimonial yesterday, so it's not on my website yet. Will can't have worked it out.

I have to come clean.

Lucy continues to talk about the videos Will has done, trying to challenge *MITY*'s charitable status. I can't hold it in any longer.

"I'm so sorry, Lucy. This is my fault." I can't look at them, but they all go quiet, so I have to. They're all confused. "I got Will's attention and made him focus it on

MITY." I tell them about my recent TikToks. "I rewatch every single one, and double check during captioning too. I might have messed up at some point."

Lucy and Nick get eye contact. I want to run away. All these weeks of being better, and I've ruined it.

"I've never intentionally named anyone or anything."

Lucy puts a hand on my shoulder. "It wasn't you. This has been going on for almost two years."

Now, I'm confused.

"If it's anyone's fault," Nick says, "It's mine. When he first started tweeting hate, I was one of the first to call him out. We've argued on Twitter for a long time. I ignore him these days like I do all hate. Don't worry. It wasn't you."

Something flutters in the back of my mind about the first time me and Will went out. Him talking about someone being his enemy. Nick? If only I had been more aware of everything back then, maybe things...

Stop.

Skye breaks the silence, talking about their content and website. I ask if they're sure they want my help. Skye tells me they know who I am. Lucy has told them all about my mission to be better. "You fucked up, owned it, and you're trying to make amends. I know what that's like. Trust. Interested?"

"On the other hand," Lucy grins, "we've got a sponsorship grant decision coming soon. All being well, we'd love you to come back and work with the kids. If you're up for it?"

I wait until I find a quiet corner in The Village to cry. It wasn't easy, it's heaving. There's a mini stage set up in

Sackville Gardens, little stalls being set up all along Canal Street, and trans kids everywhere.

I never thought I'd ever hear anything positive said about me again. I hadn't realised how much it would unknot my stomach. Maybe today I might finally start my diary?

I've got to get through it first. On my table travels, I get greeted by different kids from *MITY*. It feels good.

By 1pm I'm exhausted. It's almost time for the mini-mainstage events. I hurry out of The Village for food. I end up at McDonald's. The quarter pounder tastes good.

As I head back, all the happiness today has brought, comes crashing down.

I see Will down a side-street. He's got a megaphone, a wooden box, and he's not alone.

I cross the road to see if I can hear anything.

He steps out. "Mind where you're... oh, it's you." He looks at me like I'm something he's trodden in.

The chest tightening returns. I don't want to be near him, but I have to know what he's doing.

He leans in close. "Fuck off." He turns back to the side-street to tell his little group, and it is little, there's no more than twenty people, that if anyone challenges them about needing a ticket, they can remind them The Village is a public right of way.

I need to tell someone.

I hurry across the road. Will says something on his megaphone, but I don't listen.

On Canal Street I see a police officer, and tell her about Will. "Look, he's coming."

The police officer meets Will and his gang. They talk for

a moment.

She returns. "If he's protesting peacefully, there's nothing I can do. Unless it gets out of hand."

"Clear off," I tell Will. "You're not welcome."

With a horrible smile, Will stands on his box, puts the megaphone to his mouth. "This man here is a child abuser and groomer."

All his gang chant "Groomer!" at me. Everyone nearby stops to watch.

I put my head down, hurry away around the corner. I hear laughter as I go.

Even from the next street I can hear Will spouting hatred.

He can't get closer to the stalls. The kids don't deserve this.

The stalls don't begin until near the park, but the kids will hear him if they're not watching whoever is singing on the stage.

I should go and find Lucy, or Nick, or someone, but they've got enough to do.

There's not enough time, and what sort of ally am I if I'm not prepared to do what needs to be done?

I hurry back around. They've moved up, but they're only outside The New Union.

"I'm not going to let you get any closer," I shout.

Will puts his box down again, gets up. "You, Ben Cedar, are a groomer and child abuser, and I know it was you who damaged my house."

"You know shit then, because the culprits have been arrested."

It was all over TikTok for a day or two after they were caught. I can't believe Will would lie like this.

Wait, of course I can.

"You are a liar," I shout back, but Will and his gang continue to shout *groomer* at me.

"If anyone is an abuser, it's you, William Gale." I notice a couple of people in his gang I've accidentally come across on TikTok stitches. "And you two, you're not even queer. I've watched some of the hatred you've spouted. Cishets certainly have no say in queer culture."

His gang start shouting, "Cis is a slur." Will joins in on his megaphone.

"Cis is not a slur. Grow up. You're all adults. Leave our trans kids alone."

Will seems happy I've said that, like I've unlocked a secret phrase.

He gets down off his box, passes it to someone, walks towards me. His gang follow, chanting, "leave our gay and lesbian kids alone."

He elbows me out of the way and continues walking. I look at the people drinking nearby. There's quite a few unimpressed faces, but nobody is moving.

He and his gang are getting closer to the first lot of stalls. I look around for someone I recognise to see if they will help. All I find are strangers who aren't interested.

"You're not going any further." I grab hold of Will's jacket.

"Police! Police!" he shouts. "Get this abuser off me."

Some of his gang grab me to pull me off as the policewoman appears.

"This abuser manhandled me," Will says.

The policewoman looks at me, I can't tell if she's on his side or mine.

"Any physical contact and the force will get involved," she says.

Will laughs, continues walking. I put a hand on his chest. He stops. Glances over to the policewoman. I take my hands away as she turns.

They continue towards Sackville Gardens. I can just about see how busy it is up there. So many trans kids and families.

No.

I run in front of Will, stretch my arms out to the sides. The policewoman is still looking. I know he won't touch me, but the street is too wide. He walks around me.

What do I do now?

I look around for inspiration and spot someone I know.

"I need your help," I say to Jacinta. "We have to stop them."

Jacinta's annoyed I've spoken to her, until she sees Will go past. "What can I do?"

I tell her my plan. Within a few seconds she has found friends, and some strangers. We link arms right across the street. From canal wall to McTucky's.

A barrier of queers that Will and his gang will have to touch to get past.

"Leave our gay and lesbian kids alone," Will and his gang chant, but I can see they're annoyed.

Will whispers to a serious woman. It hits me that Michelle and James aren't here. Interesting.

"We did it," someone within our barrier shouts. Will and his gang walk away, but as they turn out of Canal Street, they hurry to the left.

"Wait here in case they come back," I shout, unlinking myself.

I leg it up towards Sackville Gardens. It's full of kids and families, but they've not noticed what's been going on. There's wooden barriers all around the park, with the only entrance over by the bridge.

I spot Lucy there.

"We need a barrier," I say. She's confused, but I don't have time to explain. I have a hunch and it won't leave us much time.

Fortunately, Jacinta has followed. She gestures at me to run towards the main road, then talks seriously to Lucy.

I knew it. They're coming this way to try another entrance.

I meet them before they can turn the corner.

"Go home!" If he gets around this corner, into Sackville Gardens, those kids are going to have their heart's broken.

"Get out of his way you big poof," one of his gang says, as he squares up to me. He backs me against a wall, letting Will and everyone past.

He keeps me blocked until the gang turn the corner.

He leaves to catch up. I run too.

They can't do this.

I almost bump into the back of the gang as I turn the corner. They've stopped.

I side-step them and see why.

Jacinta, Lucy, Nick, Skye, and a load of other queers

have linked arms.

A new barrier.

Will gets on his box again, screams hate into his megaphone.

I'm grateful the barriers around Sackville Gardens are big. Will can't see in, the kids inside can't see out.

They might be able to hear him though.

I go right up to him. "Grow up, Will. What has any of this got to do with you? You're nobody. Nobody cares about you."

I've hit the right nerve. He brings the megaphone down.

"It's got a lot to do with me. I won't let this happen to my community."

"What community? None of this pack of animals you're with are part of the queer community."

"I'm a lesbian thank you very much." says one single woman out of the whole group.

"They're just kids trying to have a good time," I say.

"We're not here to hurt the kids. We're here to protect them and tell their groomers to..." he pulls up the megaphone again, "leave our gay and lesbian kids alone. Groomers. Abusers. Groomers. Abusers." His gang join in the chant.

"You're the abuser, Will. All the things you said to me, and the ways you made me feel. You're the groomer. And a hater. Hater. HATER," I shout back.

I keep shouting it as loud as I can until I feel a hand on my shoulder. It's Lucy. "They can't get past. Let them burn themselves out. I've radioed around The Village. All the entrances have people on look-out."

Lucy pulls me gently back to the barrier of queers.

"Do you know who this transphobe is, you're protecting? Do you know the real Ben Cedar?" Will screams through his megaphone.

I step away from Lucy and the barrier. "You certainly don't know me."

"He said awful things about all of you. About gay men, and about lesbians. You can't have missed what he said about transgenders."

A few people look at me. I'm not sure they knew who I was when they made the barrier, but they certainly do now.

"We don't care," someone behind me shouts. I feel like it was Jacinta but it probably wasn't.

"You should care. He had more videos planned. Videos where he said horrible things."

I hold my breath. I got to those videos in time to remove them, nobody saw them. I want it to stay that way.

"He said trans kids were being harmed. He said elder trans people needed help for their mental health. He said all the alphabetti gays and their gender woo woo was a stain upon our community."

I want to shout back but I daren't speak. I think some of my videos did say stuff like that. Not in those words, but Will had influenced me. We had more planned, but the ones I filmed used words and language I'd never use again.

"Got proof?" Lucy shouts. I glance back. She looks at me seriously. Along the barrier, others are staring at me too.

"I've got written notes."

I forgot he made notes.

"Benny's notes?"

Will goes quiet. I didn't make any notes, it was all him.

Lucy gives me a gentle smile. It helps.

"He hated you all."

"I hate you. Now fuck off, and when you get there, you can fuck off some more."

He calls me groomer and abuser on his megaphone again. I spot some of his gang doing a limp wrist action at me.

"Why don't you fuck off, faggot," one of his gang shouts.

Will stops chanting. His gang chant, "Faggot. Faggot. FAGGOT."

Will tenses up. He looks terrified.

Only for a moment. He's back on his megaphone chanting, "Groomer. Abuser," over the top of their chant.

The gang slowly joins Will's chant, but Will isn't shouting as forcefully now.

I'm not going to get through to these people am I? I could scream and shout for hours. It wouldn't help. I'm making it worse by feeding the flames.

I need to stop.

Will and his gang tell us how we're damaging trans kids and...

I turn my back.

I'm not going to give him any more attention.

I put my hands over my ears and start humming. I don't know what song it is at first, but I quickly realise it's the intro to *Dancing Queen*.

I shout the opening lyrics as loud as I can.

As I get to the next line, Lucy and Nick join in.

By the time we've oohed our way into the first verse, everyone in the barrier is singing. They turn their backs too.

A gap between Lucy and Jacinta opens up. I fit myself in.

We sing as loud as we can. People nearby join in. The chorus echoes all around us. It's so loud I can't hear Will even with his megaphone.

"You OK?" Lucy whispers.

I glance up and down the barrier. Even though everyone sings, some people are glancing at me. I know they're thinking about my videos.

I wish Will hadn't mentioned the new ones I'd done. I'm glad I came to my senses before they ever went live, but I'd rather they weren't brought up today.

I catch Nick looking at me concerned.

"I'm OK," I say, as everyone begins the second verse.

But I'm not.

Chapter 35

Ever since Fortitude Festival, I've avoided The Village as much as I can. Luckily, *MITY* is right on the edge. I do my sessions with the kids, but I don't hang around after.

We managed to keep Will and his gang away, but I know people were wondering what I was doing there after all I'd done. I kept my head down, didn't give anyone eye contact.

I was hoping I'd start my diary after the event. I don't feel like I've done enough. Until I've got something good to start it with, it will remain blank.

It hasn't all been bad. Turning my back on Will made me realise every time I argue on social media, I make things worse. I'm literally giving them the attention they crave, and also allowing the algorithm to boost the hate.

So I removed all my videos. Deactivated TikTok entirely. The app is no longer on my phone. Neither is X nor Insta. I'll be honest, the past month has felt better for it.

My fingers still itch to make a video or check my bio. Luckily the restaurant, *MITY*, *LGET-Total*, and the queer theatre company have kept me busy.

I kept my Facebook though. I wanted access to Mum's profile, and almost two decades worth of posts. It's been interesting reading her diaries, and going to that day on Facebook. Mum is so honest in her diary, but her status updates tell a different story.

Talking of... It's time to read her final entry.

***

Dear Diary. This is Shaun writing while I tell him what to write. I will make sure he writes every word, and nothing more because I have already had to tell him off for writing 'Dear Diary' when I didn't ask him to write that. Show me what you've written. Don't write that.

Okay. Everything I say then. This might be my final entry. Shaun has just said it won't be, but he has to be a bit more realistic. The fact I can't even hold a pen is probably hint enough.

Shaun has just given me a long, hard stare and said he would slap me across the face if I wasn't in hospital right now. That's what friends are for, and I really don't think I've ever had a better friend than Shaun in my entire life.

Five minutes we've had to stop because he started crying, and so did I. I told him he needs to keep going because this is important. If they're my final words, they need to be written. I'm still not giving up. Right now I feel okay. Not quite myself, but the meds they've given me are helping, and although I might be whispering these words very slowly, that's not how they will be read.

My Will has been written. It's not much but in case anyone tries to make problems, it's done. I have spoken for many hours about my death with Shaun. He hasn't liked any of those hours. He's shaking his head now, yes write that. That's what friends do. I give him permission to read these diaries after I'm gone. Whenever that is. He can read them all. So can Benny.

I want him to see that everyone struggles.

My sweet Benny. He will be here. I miss him so much. Don't be sad if you're reading these words and thinking you should have been hearing them. I have been getting these words out one at a time, with many breaks. Shaun told me it's been almost five hours since we started. Maybe I would not even be able to tell you them in person anyway. So don't be sad you're reading them now. Just be happy you are. Because I love you, Benny Cedar. I loved you the moment I found out I was pregnant and I will go on loving you in whatever comes next for me.

I know life hasn't always been easy for you, but you've come so far in such a short time. I am so proud of you, my darling boy. I am always proud of you.

I know you've been struggling. I hear it in your voice. I

see it on your face. I read it in your words. I am so proud that you moved away to find out who you are. I know you've been at odds with the old Benny and the new. It's been a hard few years. Maybe even longer than that.

Benny, I want you to know even if you think I've been angry with you, even if I've shouted or had to put my foot down, I never stopped loving you. Whatever it is you are going through, I hope you can tell me one day. If not me, I hope you find someone else. Shaun maybe. Or perhaps that lovely young person you talk about. I notice your sadness, but I see you light up when you talk about them. Whatever it is, my darling, sweet, lovely, presh-pots, please know, I will forgive you.

You've always been the kind of person who holds on to things too long. Internalises those moments that should be left to fly off you the moment they hit. I'm the same. Don't let it follow you the rest of your life. I was so fortunate to find someone who helped me change my life and my thoughts. Yes of course it's you, Shaun.

If this is the last entry of my diary, then these are the words I'm leaving you with. Whatever you've done, you can change. You can make up for it. You can decide to move on and away and make yourself as proud as I am of you.

Don't hold on to it anymore. I love you so much, Benny. Treat yourself with kindness. Take that pressure off and you will know what to do. I want to see that happy smile again. I want to see the weights lifted off your shoulders, and that brightness you have in your eyes, in your words, in your whole life, return. It won't be easy.

Shaun has told me it's now been over nine hours since we started this. But I had to finish. I wanted you to know I love you, and I'm proud of you.

I won't say goodbye. I know you'll be here, and whenever the time comes to say it for real, we will be together.

You've been my whole life Benny. Now continue to live it for the both of us.

I love you. Forever and ever, and back again. My hand will be forever over my heart and my finger tapping. Sweet, sweet boy. I love you.

Mum xxx

***

I... Take the pressure off? How, Mum? I have so much to do first.

Chapter 36

Cheer up. It's August Bank Holiday weekend which means... It's Manchester Pride again! But I'm nervous. I'll have to face The Village.

"They're here," Pearl calls up the stairs.

Instantly, the constant squeezing evaporates.

I take my uncles, Sid, and Pearl to a great spot on the parade route. As the *MITY* float goes past, all the kids spot me and wave. I'm super proud of them. The applause for their float is immense.

Uncle Shaun's hand rubs my back. "I'm proud of you."

I told my uncles I'd helped *MITY* with the float. What I didn't tell them was Lucy asked if I wanted to be on it. I turned her down. I've not done enough for that.

I get more waves from the *LGBT-Total* float. It's amazing seeing the new marketing I did for them.

"Another one?" Uncle Jeremy says. Have I got a signature style? Or did I tell them in one of the calls we have three times a week?

Pearl and Sid go home afterwards, and I show my uncles around The Village.

It's bustling, but I'm on edge. Waiting for a comment or a filthy look. I instantly lose sight of my uncles in the crowd.

"Benny," someone shouts. I feel like everyone goes quiet and looks at me. It's heaving. I won't be able to escape if someone comes up in my face.

No-one does. Did everyone really look at me or was it just a couple of people? Nobody is looking now, only Lucy, Nick, some of the *MITY* kids, and Skye with a few of the group.

I breathe out to relax, but a little squeeze across my chest appears. Jacinta is here holding-hands with one of the LGBT-Totallers. David and Zoe are with her. I try to keep my focus on the excitement of the *MITY* kids talking about the parade, but I sense my ex-housemate's eyes on me the whole time.

"He replied to my solicitor saying he won't take any of his content down as he is stating biological facts and genuine truths," Lucy says. I'm only pretending to listen.

"So we'll see him in court," Nick adds.

I daren't speak with my old housemates here. Luckily I spot my uncles, make my excuses and leave. I don't want to be ruining anyone's Pride.

David and Zoe glare as I go.

Jacinta though... she smiles.

Uncle Jeremy isn't great in crowds, but with his hand firmly held by Uncle Shaun, he's having a great time. I've never heard him squee as much, or in fact ever, as when he watches his favourite 90s band on the main stage.

He tells us all about the first concert of theirs he went to as we head out towards a bar.

Am I ready to go in one?

I am.

As we make our way to one my uncles will be impressed by, my gaze and breath is caught by someone.

Star.

My uncles and I head in one direction, as Star and his friends pass us by. We both get eye contact, and turn around at the same time.

The Village is rammed. Noisy. But right now it's like it's only me and him.

Screams, laughs and whistles all go silent.

Colourful outfits fade away to nothing.

We're not packed in. It's just me and him and a million miles of nothing but a bated breath.

I daren't smile. He does. I have to look down to check I've not floated away.

"Come on," Kulvinder calls, bringing a packed Pride back to my reality. Star stands still.

"Benny, are we..." Uncle Shaun starts, before Uncle Jeremy shushes him.

I want to run into Star's arms so badly, but I'm hugely aware I've still not apologised properly.

Is now the right time though?

Kulvinder grabs his arm, but Star jerks away.

"The queer stars have aligned," Uncle Shaun whispers in one ear.

"What are you waiting for?" Uncle Jeremy whispers in the other.

I mouth *can we talk?*

Time stops.

He nods.

We meet in the middle, but it's too busy to do it here. He must think the same thing as he lights up with an idea, beckons me into the fairground.

"Will you be OK?" Kulvinder calls, but Star is already getting tickets. With no queue, we're sat on the swings that go up in the air before I know it.

The safety bar comes down. We start our spinning ascent.

I don't know what I'm going to say, but I have to say it now.

"Star." It's barely a whisper.

He frowns instantly. "How'd you know about...?" He smiles, "It's not Star anymore."

"Oh, I didn't mean to—"

"You weren't to know. Settled on Marty."

Marty feels right, and familiar. Ah! "Great Scott!"

"Knew you'd get it. Can't believe I didn't think of it sooner. Of course I told my dad Marty was played by a famous Michael so even though it's a tenuous..." He stops talking, and looks at me like he's remembering all our history. All the mistakes I made.

We slowly spin around and rise up. All of Pride below us. Nothing but sky above.

Now or...

"Marty, I want to start by saying this is an apology. I want you to know, before I start, in case you don't want to hear it, which I'd understand. May I continue?"

I realise he can't go anywhere anyway, but he nods.

"I first want to apologise for my actions. I'm not going to put the blame on anyone else, because I had a choice, and I still did it. I know the things I filmed, the things I said, and the way I behaved, were wrong.

"I also want to apologise to you personally. I hurt you. Not only you, but your friends and your community too, but this is about you today.

"I am so ashamed of my behaviour. You put your trust in me and I abused that. I apologise for everything I did that hurt you. I don't say that lightly. I want you to know I fully understand that my videos where I mocked trans people, my connections with those who seek to disempower trans people, and any unwanted attention you or the trans community got because of my videos, were absolutely vile.

"I thrived on the attention and ignored the hate. I wish I hadn't, but I can't change the past."

We spin further out. Higher. The wind is cold on my face, but it's quiet up here. I feel his body weight move into mine as gravity takes hold. I want to hold his hand, but I have to get the rest of these words out.

"I am trying to make up for everything I've done, but I want to own my mistakes right now. I apologise, not just from the bottom of my heart, but my whole heart, my whole soul, and my whole mind, to you. I did all those things while we were friends and I lied about it.

"I want you to know I'm backing everything up with a change in my behaviour. I am doing things I know won't erase the past, but I hope will prove I won't ever behave like that again.

"You did not deserve to be treated the way I treated you. I hope this apology goes some way towards correcting the past, but I don't expect anything from you at all. I'm still going to put the work in to be better, whatever happens next. I have no expectations from you, I want you to know that. You don't have to accept. You don't even have to say anything at all. I promise you the changes I'm making are going to continue."

I want to keep talking. I want to say how much I've missed him. How my heart has been broken since we went our separate ways. How I wish we could be friends again. More than friends. My heart has never changed. I love him. I'm in love with him. I have been for a long time. I'm not sure I could ever love anyone like this again.

I can't say any of that, it would undermine my whole apology. The apology is all that matters right now. Not my feelings, only his.

I feel strangely calm as we slowly make our way back to the ground.

We get out of the swing. He's not said anything.

We walk down the steps in silence.

I wish he would say something, but I'm thankful he listened.

I best go find my uncles.

"Thank you," Marty says.

I don't know what to do.

Kulvinder rushes over. "Everything OK?" he says to Marty, not giving me eye contact.

Marty nods, turns, flings his arms around me. I'm scared to hug him back for a moment.

His cheek presses against mine.

This is not what you think it is. How could it be? You've not done enough yet, have you?

"I know about the work you've been doing."

I won t lie that makes me happy. "Now what?"

"I don't know."

Is it me that's shaking, or him?

"I forgive you," he says, or did I imagine what I wanted to hear?

We come apart, we both have red eyes and wet cheeks.

"Are you sure?" I barely get the words out.

He nods. This should be the best moment of my life. I should be starting my diary tonight, start on a high.

I won't.

"Thank you. I have to go find my uncles." I put on a small smile.

Marty smiles back. I want to hurry away but I don't want to look stupid.

As I make my way out the fairground, I hear Kulvinder announce, "I kissed him once, you know. Twice actually." I dare a glance back. He's saying it with a smile.

What does that mean?

Marty shakes his head, tells him to shut up.

I can't blink. It's pathetic to cry.

Why am I even crying anyway?

Because something isn't right.

I changed my behaviour. I've made steps to give back to the community. I've apologised to my followers. I've apologised to as much of the community, in real life, as I could. I've even said my apology to the one person who deserves it the most.

Why do I feel like I've missed someone out?

Chapter 37

December 1st.

Hey diary. Today is the day! Ever since Pride, back in August, I've been feeling like something was still off. How Marty forgave me, I don't know. It took us a couple of months to find our groove. It's a slightly different groove now. Having him back in my life has made everything almost perfect.

I was even invited to a party at Kulvinder's last week. I couldn't believe it. He's got a new boyfriend, Darren, who's obsessed with American culture, so he threw a Thanksgiving party. I got told off for being too quiet, but I didn't want to draw attention to myself.

The MITY kids have been inspiring me more and more in the way they talk about themselves and each other. Some of them aren't out at home, but at MITY they understand each other. Nobody has to explain pronouns or sexuality. They get it. They know themselves, and those that don't aren't scared to see what fits.

Marty has always been like that, listening to himself.

My problem is, I listen to others too much.

So a few days ago, when I mentioned to the kids that I wished there was a support group for queer adults, Lucy asked if I'd like to talk to Nick. He's the one-to-one counsellor for the kids.

Today I had my first session. I don't know if you're supposed to feel this good after one session, but I do. I know it's going to take time to work it all out, but I've committed to keep going. I've had new work come in, enough that I've been able to reduce my hours at the restaurant. So I've made a financial commitment to help myself.

We spoke about Mum and Uncle Shaun, but not you-know-who. I specifically said I didn't want to talk about him, but I know he's going to come up eventually. We talked about me and my identity. Nick got me to talk about how I see myself, and what it means to me. I've always considered myself gay. Attracted to other men, but I've let people get in my head about what these men should be like. I've listened to the wrong people, who have made me believe my identity is "wrong" if I'm attracted to the "wrong" person.

But my opinion is all that matters. Nick asked what I think my identity means to me. I said it means I'm attracted to the aesthetic of a man, but mostly I feel my attraction is deeper than that. It's about connection, friendship, laughter, listening, care, time, and hope. When they asked me what sort of future I'd want with another person, I said Marty. I said it's been him for a long time, right back to when we first met. Whoever Marty was back then, I connected with that person and let a friendship blossom, but nothing more. Because I felt I shouldn't. I couldn't. That it was wrong, or bad, or I was somehow going against my identity.

But it felt right, so what does it matter? And Marty is a man.

I felt like I'd finally listened to myself, and yeah, I cried. When Nick asked me how I felt, I said I still felt sad because I knew something was still wrong with me. They helped remind me how Uncle Shaun and Jeremy still support me. That Marty forgave me. Nick asked if I needed to talk to anyone else. I said I did, but I couldn't work out who.

Then they went quiet. Absolutely silent. They didn't write in their little book, they didn't look at me in a weird way, they sat back and let me work it out.

It took me a moment. I was like, OH MY GOD!!!!!

Nick nodded and smiled and told me to go tell them. From the heart.

So that's why I'm starting the diary tonight. Tonight is the night I'm making my final apology to the person who needs to hear it the most.

Dear Benny. It's you. It's me. You have done some awful things, but you don't want them to define you. You've made changes to your behaviour, and to your life, and you've done them without turning them into content. You've taken your mistakes, and been strong enough to make sure you don't make them again. You should be proud of yourself. I am proud of myself. I apologise to myself, and I forgive myself. I won't forget. I can't forget, but I can allow myself to accept I am not that person anymore. I am someone new. I know I'll carry shame for a while, maybe forever, but I know I have listened to others, the right others, and to myself, and have grown.

Benny Cedar, you can let yourself live again. You can't expect everyone to forgive you, but you can accept the forgiveness of those that have given it.

Now you are one of those people.

I love you.

Chapter 38

I walk into the Civic Hall and burst into tears. I'm already emotional due to the stress of being late. I had a last-minute client meeting in Manchester, missed my train, and got the next one, which was delayed. When I got to Uncle Shaun's, I realised I'd forgotten my key.

Now I'm bawling my eyes out. It's my Uncles' fault.

By the Christmas tree, on a table, is a photo of Mum. A tall candle burns inside a hurricane vase. Beside it, a stack of squares of paper, and a note to ask people to write a memory of Eileen. Beside all that, a jar absolutely full of folded squares of paper.

Inside, I can see one piece of paper, slightly opened. It reads, *Eileen always got my pronouns right, even when I was too afraid to use the right ones myself at work. Plus she always gave me extra chips. We've lost a true ally.*

I feel arms wrap around me from behind. A chin gently lands on each shoulder.

"These are for you." Uncle Shaun gestures at the jar.

I can't get any words out.

"You OK?" Uncle Jeremy whispers.

I nod.

She's not here anymore, but I can feel her. Is that stupid?

Everyone cheers as *Come on Eileen* plays. The candle flame flickers too. Maybe she is here? Shaun squeezes me tighter but none of us move. We listen to everyone singing as we stare at Mum's photo.

It's not one she posed for. She hated posing for photos despite insisting we had to take photos at every special occasion. No, this is a candid photo. Taken about five or six years ago at Christmas. Shaun took it, I never take photos.

She's staring at the gift I got her. A *Mamma Mia* stage-show programme, signed by the four members of ABBA. It was something Rahul's mum got for me. She was at an event with them there. I'd asked if she could try get it signed and she did. It lived on our mantlepiece ever since. It's in a box now somewhere. I must find it.

It's a photo Mum never wanted to put up, but Shaun always told her was lovely. She looks happy. Sure, she's only happy because she's staring at the programme behind me on the mantlepiece whilst I play with the iPad she got me. It was second hand but I didn't care.

The more I stare, the more I notice things. The After Eights opened on the coffee table. The multi-print curtains Mum made out of several different pairs she got from the charity shop.

I can see Uncle Shaun, reflected in the front window, grinning. Behind him I can make out Uncle Jeremy's reflection opening a bottle of prosecco. That was a good Christmas.

Wait. What's that? The signed programme is beside her. I can make out the top corner of it on the arm of the sofa. It hadn't made the mantelpiece yet.

She was staring at me.

I hope she would be proud of me. I know she said she always was, but I hope I've done enough to make it true. This year has been a lot, but these last few months my business has taken off enough for me to reduce my shifts at the restaurant. I've put a deposit on a room at a new flat-share closer to the city centre. All my clients are there. My therapist too.

As this year ends, I can finally let all the awful shit stay there, whilst I try to move on.

This is a party. A part Christmas, part memorial party. I can't believe it's been a year since Mum died.

An hour later, I'm a little tipsy. More than a little. I'm even dancing to Mariah and enjoying it. I'm definitely drunk.

Everyone has been super friendly. There's been a lot of tears, not just from me. The place is packed. Not just with queers this time. Loads of people from Ming who knew Mum. They're having a great time. Cishets and queers all celebrating together.

I never thought I'd see it here.

I'm dancing with Rahul and his mum, but I need another drink. Work has been intense. Those kids at *MITY* keep me on my toes.

I back away as I dance. As they raise their arms to scream the lyrics into the ceiling, I turn to make my escape, and trip up over someone's feet.

I skid.

Stumble and...

Oops.

I'm falling into someone's arms.

"Hey," he says.

"Hey." I smile.

In the little bar, Marty and I sit with drinks. We don't stop talking. I go on about my work, he tells me about what he's working on at his new set-design job, even though we both know all this as we text every night.

He looks good in this shirt. I wish he'd fasten those top three buttons. As much as I like to see his chest hair, and his pecs from all the theatre sets he's been moving around, this is a family party.

I watch as a group of boys, two cis, one trans, run and slide along the floor. The cis boys are telling the trans boy how good he is at sliding.

I feel light. Even the sadness for Mum seems to be lifting me tonight.

The Christmas lights above the bar grow brighter. My heart beats like crazy. All I know is, I'm here with Marty and it's Christmas. It could be Christmas now, in the future, or in the past. It could be the Christmas we first met. If only it was, I could change it all.

No bad thoughts. Not tonight. My therapist told me I mustn't push those memories away, they want to be dealt with. I remind them now is not the time.

I smell his usual orange-vanilla scent and the bad memories vanish. Replaced by the time we took refuge from the rain in a queer bookshop and spent hours inside. The picnic we had by the canal where we fed most of our butties to the ducks. The ghost walk we did where I jumped out of my skin because of one of the actors. Marty almost wet himself laughing and we both ended up in hysterics.

"Do you want to get some air?" I ask.

Marty nods.

Ming feels small and quiet. I used to be angry at the boarded up shops, now it makes me feel sorry for the place. There's only my uncles tying me to here, but maybe not for much longer. It seems Uncle Shaun is finally considering leaving. I'm pretty sure Uncle Jeremy is keen on moving somewhere far away. Good for them.

"Hey, I don't really want to bring this up," Marty says as we make our way through the precinct. Oh no. I guess I've gone pale because he adds, "Oh it's nothing bad, it's about, you know, him."

I don't mind talking about him today. I already knew anyway. I'm still off socials but Lucy and Nick have kept me filled in on the whole thing. It seems Will wasn't as bold as he thought he was, as he settled out of court.

"Lost so much, he had to move out of Manchester," I add.

"Has he though?"

I grin, he's going to love this story. "I was looking at house selling sites and saw his apartment listed. After it sold I went round to double check."

"You didn't."

"It gets better. I knocked on and a little kid opened the door, so I asked if their parents were home and, you'll love this, their parents were a trans couple. Feels right doesn't it?"

"What did you say?"

"I told them I wanted to check Will had gone. They told me every last trace had. That's when I noticed they'd changed not only the walls, but the tiles on the floor. Even the light fittings. They knew who he was and said the only thing he was good for, was accepting a very shit offer on his flat for a quick sale."

"I wonder where he's gone?"

"I don't."

We laugh as we continue to walk. It's a nice evening. Cold but dry. We talk about our old Christmases as we walk. Before I know it, we're at the graffiti wall.

I'm nervous to look, but I want the reminder of why saying goodbye to Ming is the thing to do.

I look. "Oh."

Marty follows my gaze. I've told him about this wall. "Oh."

We look at each other with frowns for a moment, then burst out laughing.

William Gale is a transphobic twat it reads.

As we head back, we can't stop talking about it, and how funny it would be if Will had to move to some homophobic small town.

There's a few more people out and about now. Faces I vaguely recognise.

I don't feel that tightening.

In fact, I feel so good, I'm going to do it.

I take Marty's hand. There's people walking past but I don't let go.

He doesn't either.

"This OK?" I ask.

He stops, nods his head, turns to me. His brown eyes meet mine. Ming vanishes around us. The passers-by disappear. The traffic pops out of existence.

I lean forward as he does.

Our lips meet.

They're soft. His beard tickles my chin.

Time stops. Starts. Rewinds. Fast forwards.

We pull away after a hundred years. I don't even want to look around to make sure nobody saw us. People definitely saw us. I don't care.

We go back to the party, hand in hand. Instantly dragged onto the dance floor. I'm surrounded by so much love. The same back in Manchester too.

I feel... good.

ACKNOWLEDGEMENTS

First and foremost my biggest thanks go to my mentor Lucy V Hay (aka Bang2write). She told me for years to write a book, and when I finally did, she gave me all the support I needed. From the very beginning, when it was just an idea, she was there to advise on how to get started. When it was a very over-written second-draft, she read it and helped me contain the story. The Hardest Word has come a long way since that draft, and I'm eternally grateful to Lucy for all her encouragement.

Thank you to my beta readers, Helen Ward, Debbie Moon, Olivia Bagshaw and Ruth Stewart for taking time to read and give feedback.

Huge thanks also to Candy Gent, Christopher Hubbard, and Lucas Leitch for answering my transition questions and being so open.

Thanks also to all the people who have ever answered my questionnaires via Pride Reads. All your personal stories and anecdotes helped me to breathe life into all my queer characters.

Thank you to my partner Darren Adams, for creating my cover. I'm so fortunate to have someone in my life who has such a creative eye.

Thank you to you, the reader, for taking a chance on me and my debut novel. This won't be the last you hear from me, so keep an eye on my socials for what I'm doing next.

ABOUT THE AUTHOR

Drew Hubbard is from Manchester, has loved writing stories from a young age, and though this is their debut novel, has written for children's touring theatre and TV.

Drew is the owner of Pride Reads, a website & newsletter helping all writers write authentic LGBTQ+ characters. He is also a sensitivity reader and has worked with many writers on their manuscripts & screenplays.

Drew's socials:
Tiktok: @pride_reads.
Instagram: @pride_reads
X: @druzif
Bluesky: @pridereads.bsky.social

Drew's author site: DrewHubbard.co.uk

For newsletter & sensitivity reading: PrideReads.co.uk

Printed in Dunstable, United Kingdom